The Optician's Allusion

A Novel

By

Brian Fearn

ISBN 978-1-0685682-0-6

For Maggie

"Everything has beauty, but not everyone sees it"

Confucius c. 551 – c. 479 BCE

1. JOAN

Joan was embarking on a visit to her friend Frederick and she was overpacking her suitcase unsure what the weather ahead in Italy would forebode. Would it be chilly of an evening? Maybe a thicker scarf or a thicker sweater would be sensible, or maybe it would be balmy and the cicadas would rattle under a crescent moon. Weighing the options up, it seemed sensible to take both garments despite the added burden. She was to travel on Dan Air which was new to her. It had a much lower price than B.E.A. and that would possibly mean some diminution in service quality or quality of passengers although her travel agent assured her, in his words, that she would be "chipper" and she did have to take some account of the pennies these days. It was only for three and a half hours after all, but she did so hope she wasn't seated next to someone ghastly who might talk at her for the entire journey or tell her their life story in three hours flat leaving not so much as a fingerspace between their words.

Her cab would arrive early tomorrow to get her to Manchester in plenty of time so that she might have a cup of hot water at the bar into which she could immerse her favourite tea beverage that was now available in a small sachet. She had a little white paper bag saved from a quarter of Everton Mints filled with just enough sachets for the week. That was inside her pink plastic toilet bag, the one with the zip that fitted nicely inside the bigger sponge bag. Hopefully the mints hadn't left a tang that would spoil the tea. Betty, from next door, had brought her the sweets for her birthday. *An odd gift* Joan thought given that she never touched confectionery. But she received the gift with a kindly pursed smile and stood in the cold breeze exchanging small talk with Betty on the doorstep until she went away. Her aunt had always told her never to allow the neighbours into one's home because, as she advised "They only compare with their own circumstances Joan and are never happy about it." So Joan didn't. The gift allowed Joan to give the newspaper boy one Everton Mint each Saturday when he called for his money and that saved her from giving him her usual tuppence tip for eight or nine weeks. Fortunately, the paperboy delivered Betty's paper before Joan's so Betty wouldn't notice his breath. Betty's birthday was a few weeks later but unfortunately Joan missed it, again.

The sponge bag was useful for visiting the Ladies should she need to, without having to undo the entire blessed holdall that she was allowed to take on board. She had taken the Hillman Imp out soon after she booked the flight and made a visit to the leather factory where they had opened a little shop to sell off seconds and rejects. They were still such nice things and unless you scrutinised them avidly you would never know they were less than half price. She had intended to buy a sheepskin coat, but ended up with the bag made of congo leather and a tartan lining that matched her suitcase that had been coated with a tartan pattern paper.

She had thought about driving herself to the airport and leaving the car there but it had a leak around the windscreen and leaving it outside for a week might mean that she would have a footwell of water again, rather as she had when she took it to take an old school friend to the Lake District for a picnic. A complete disaster of a day and not a word of thanks. Anyway, Manchester had started to charge to park and it was almost as much as the taxi fare. Driving the Imp in the dark was not something she cherished, so a taxi it would be.

Joan examined the contents of the two full bags thoroughly again and decided there was enough to meet every possible circumstance. She would need to arise at 5am, thus she wound her new Smiths alarm clock fully and placed it by the bedside. She was irritated by the tick. It was very metallic, but she chose it because the alarm was as loud as her old clock. That one had the twin bells on top which some clumsy guest had knocked off the bedside table. That was the last time she had anyone stay over. They always left a bad taste with some mishap or other. She did wonder whether the clock was thrown at the wall during the night because it did have a very reassuring tick tock sound whereas this new Smiths was just the irritating one tick every second. Anyway, that old clock never did tell the right time after that incident so she put it at the back of the drawer and went and bought a new one from the Jewellers in town. She had considered taking it back to complain, but never got around to it.

Given the taxi was due at six Joan wouldn't have time for her usual morning bath. Every morning she had no more than three inches of warm water for her bath. It was enough to relax on to without the slovenly activity of being fully immersed into the water. One could attend to one's particulars and freshen sufficiently and know that one's hairstyle would not be compromised by accidentally getting wet. So she spontaneously decided upon the unusual act of taking a warm bath before bed. She hoped it would not keep her awake. There was a chill in the air as she pulled the string of the Pifco bar fire up on the wall. It gave a satisfactory long red glow as the bath enamel was somewhat cold. Afterwards she examined herself in the mirror cabinet which the carpenter had put four inches too high for her liking. He was taller than her by that much and she had asked him back on numerous occasions to correct it but he never returned. She had deducted half a crown from his account for the error. Anyway, she could see enough to put her cold creme over her forehead and put her hairnet on before settling in for a sound sleep.

Her main suitcase was, she considered, rather cardboardy. From a distance you wouldn't know that it wasn't an expensive one, what with the printed pattern to make it look like fabric. It was so seldom used that it really wasn't worth buying a new one. Fortunately, it did have expanding metal hinges and she had some thick ribbon from the hem of an old pair of curtains which she wrapped around it with an oversize safety pin for good measure and easy identification at the other end. The cabbie did remark about how heavy it was when he put it in the boot and muttered something about Kitchen Sink. She kept the holdall by her side on the back seat in case she needed anything during the journey.

The tartan case had to be checked-in once the surly girl at the counter had looked her up and down and compared her face to the awful image inside her new British Visitors passport. Her earlier five year passport had been returned with the corner cut off and she didn't want another one of those, not only because of the expense, almost £2, but because she didn't like being described as Miss nor did she like that they did not adopt her description of her 'distinguishing feature' that she had given on her application form. She had distinctly written on the form of her 'Beauty mark to left of top lip' and instead when it came back the authorities had abbreviated her distinguishing feature as a 'Mole over Mouth'.

The process of having to go into the Employment Exchange to get the Visitors passport had been an eye opener in itself. She had swiftly passed the building often when shopping in Manchester but had never been in. She didn't know where to ask amongst the rag tag bunch of men in ill-fitting demob suits and scruffy footwear. A few had this new fashion for long hair beautifully cut and in some cases turned under like Cilla Black but when they turned around they were as ugly as sin. Hoardings inside the big open room were covered with postcards of jobs available for labourers, bricklayers, dustmen, machinists and the like, but eventually she found a bespectacled woman who dealt with the passports. She waited her turn seated where she was told and watched the men waiting to sign-on for their National Assistance at the other desks. Joan paid her seven shillings and sixpence and the woman looked at her intently and wrote under 'distinguishing marks' the word None. The manilla card was folded over to make her simple six page document which would last her a year and thankfully her beauty mark remained as it should, unmentioned.

"Sorry to mither Madam but this suitcase weighs too much. It's nearly three stone and we only allow two stone ten. There might be a charge, but you are my first passenger so I've put Madam in a dead good seat 1A so you are by the front door but mind you get on last if you don't want your feet well trod" she said.

I don't much like the grating accent Joan thought to herself.

Clearly Dan Air didn't know that she always liked to board first so as to get sufficient room, but she gave her the most modest semi-smiling movement of the lips and the slightest nod which neither acknowledged the girl's kindness nor her stupidity, given that she forgot to charge for the heavy case.

Once she was given back her five remaining ticket coupons she left her case with the girl and turned to the bank of phone boxes with one marked for International Calls. She put in half a crown and an operator immediately asked for the Italian number, the connection went smoothly after a few clicks.

"Hello Frederick, I'm at Manchester and my luggage has gone through, so I'm going to have a hot beverage and thus expect I will see you in about five or six hours time."

He sounded surprised by the call when his only response was "Oh, Joan. Hello."

She went on "My room will have a bath won't it Frederick, I cannot abide those continental showers?" but the pips sounded and the operator interrupted asking for more money so Joan remained silent and placed the heavy handset back on the hook ... she certainly wasn't going to use another half-crown for just half a minute to continue talking.

It was daylight robbery she thought clasping her lips. The check in girl who had her suitcase was calling "Madam, Madam!" but Joan ignored her, *She would only want more money* she thought and she walked on.

The uniformed man at a makeshift booth only glanced at the manilla passport.

Another waste of money, the black and white unfocussed photo cost me five shillings she thought as she slipped it back into the holdall side zip compartment and picked up the heavy bag yet again.

She headed on to the Lyons Tea Bar. The same serving girl had obliged her with a cup of hot water last time she travelled through Manchester airport a couple of years ago but now she appeared plump and more a woman than a girl.

Eating the end of day display stock I shouldn't wonder. Those meringues, by the look of her thought Joan.

"Excuse me Miss, could I have a cup of hot water to take my Backache Pills please? It has to be hot" she added pointing at her back. "Such a heavy bag."

Without embarking in conversation the steaming water was provided in a small cup and Joan had to help herself to a saucer and a tray. She picked up a second tray whilst at that end.

"Anything else?"

"No that will be all thank you" replied Joan with one of her lip pursings to indicate approval.

"That will be sixpence please."

"I think you will find that's tapioca stuck to this" as she handed over the second tray. "What did you say?" she continued.

"Sixpence please, t'hot water is now sixpence a cup."

"Really? Even for medical reasons?"

"Aye Duck, owt too many people coming in here with these new fangled sachets and making their own tea right under us noses whilst we pays t'rent." As she spoke to Joan she returned the tapioca tray to the top of the pile, untouched. "Tea is two shillings with milk and a pot."

"How disgraceful" said Joan neither indicating whether she meant the charge of sixpence or the fact that other people follow her intentions with their tea sachets or that the tray was left tapioca'd for the next customer or the extortionate price of a pot of tea. The plump woman was certainly being overly familiar calling her 'My Duck'. She was neither hers nor a waterfowl.

"Very Well" she said as she fussily opened the holdall and then the zipped pocket inside, removed her Lira stuffed leather purse - all in small denomination notes so that she could not be cheated on handing over a twenty thousand note, expecting nineteen thousand change that would inevitably be rolled up as only seventeen. She had been to Italy just once before. Further inside the purse was a little cloth change purse containing a few sixpences and threepenny bits that she kept separate. She removed one and handed it over and then reversed the process of zipping everything up.

She took her bag over to a vacant seat. One by the window so that she didn't have to engage with anyone, not that there was anyone and returned for the tray. By now the cup of water was not hot enough to brew her teabag but she couldn't complain given it was a medical matter. The cups were obviously stone cold and a cold saucer didn't help. At home she kept her bone china teacup near the kettle on her New World cooker with the eye level grill where it could absorb a modicum of warmth. The tea was an unsatisfactory brew but would have to do. Afterwards a trip to the Ladies and then sit and wait somewhere else, away from anyone else, but near enough to the gate to board at the head of the queue.

The Dan Air seats were most uncomfortable, they were upright and did not move and much too hard and there was no window at this position. Apparently it was an Ambassador plane. *Whatever happened to the Diplomat* she wondered to herself. So she would have to look at the side of a door for over three hours - *those oily hinges looked decidedly rusty.* Her new Hush Puppies were scuffed as people passed and a small suitcase with little corner castors toppled when dragged over her foot like a dog on a leash. It had made a mark on the suede which was a nuisance but, thankfully, she had packed the care kit that came as an optional extra with every pair, including the gold colour wire brush. The last passenger on, a hefty fellow who obviously liked his whisky by the smell of him had steel blakeys on his brown brogue heels and she narrowly avoided having her little toe crushed.

On B.E.A. she had not experienced being squashed in like this, so perhaps the extra forty pounds fare would have been worthwhile because the woman in the adjacent seat didn't have the freshest of feet and one of her stockings had a seam that helter-skeltered up her leg like a barber's pole. She didn't spill over the narrow seat, *thank goodness*, but Joan still had her head at a slant because the fuselage was so narrow. *I will have a cricked neck by the time this is all over.* What's more, she thought the ceiling was made of the same pressed cardboard as her suitcase because it moved when her head touched it. *So much for 'Giving Madame a dead good seat'* she thought.

The Lyons tea bar had been stiflingly hot and she had taken off the two layers and the woollen scarf that she had worn in the taxi. The driver was from the Caribbean which was a first for her; she had not been in sole company of a coloured man before. As they were pulling away from the house she saw the silhouette of Betty at her bedroom window waving her off and she had instinctively waved back, but goodness knows why? And how did Betty know she was leaving for Italy anyway? What was going on? First of all the sweets on her birthday and then a wave? It must have been the paperboy who told her because she had suspended her Telegraph delivery for eight days. *No more sweet treats for him if he is going to gossip* she thought to herself, *not unless Betty brings more of her blessed confectionery for me to give away.* The driver was jolly. He had come over from Jamaica on a twenty eight pound ten shilling fare but she didn't understand half of what he said except that it had taken him twenty two days to get to Tilbury, that he was perpetually sick and that he had been a bus conductor in London before moving North where he passed his driving test. But after excusing herself with a dozen 'pardons' and still not getting the gist of his diatribe, she replied with cursory yes and nos at irregular intervals until he finally shut up and drove along the A62. It was an old Riley cab and it smelled of damp carpet and old cigarette smoke and the worn leather seats were covered in a see-through new fangled shiny plastic so her bottom could not get a grip. When going around a corner she was sliding from side to side. She was replaying the taxi journey to herself as the plane taxied out.

Joan was now cold. There was a draught from somewhere and she wanted one of her shawls but it was in the bag and that had been swiftly taken away from where she had placed it on 2A when the smelly-footed woman sat next to her. *She needs to be introduced to the wonders of talcum powder especially wearing open toe shoes like those, a size too small and with those stockings* she thought as she

11

took in more of the woman's apparel without giving any eye contact. Judging by the number of shoes that had passed her new Hush Puppies the plane must be full but Joan didn't look around, it wouldn't be at all seemly, and some of them sounded as if they were singing. *People are strange* she thought. She wasn't at all keen on singing and she was always silent when in church but respectfully stood while those around her created disharmony in their community.

After an announcement they were on their way. The propellers were very noisy, she had brought some earplugs but they were in one of the toilet bags. She could drown out both the singing and the plane if she had them. After a while of being airborne the stench coming from the nearby galley was abhorrent. Like the smell at primary school each morning of those vile lunches she would always refuse to eat.

Joan was first to be served. The food came in an oblong foil dish and it looked as repulsive as it smelled. She asked smelly-feet whether she would like the concoction of mashed potato with a dot of meat and a crush of tomato skin but she passed the parcel on over to whoever the large black clothed article was sitting in 3A. The small wooden cutlery would have given her splinters and the napkin was so small it would not even serve as one sheet of lavatory paper. No wonder this flight was so cheap. She wouldn't do it again, except of course she had to come back on it next week because she had already paid for the return. Her travel agent had waxed on about how good Dan Air was for the money but it wasn't until they were airborne that she realised she was on a Charter, which explained so much. She would advise him of the various drawbacks in due course.

"Finally!" she exclaimed at the hostess. After asking twice, she had her nice new leather holdall bag returned from a compartment. Her first task was to put on a headscarf to stop this blessed draught down her neck and then some hand creme was required. It was in one of the toilet bags, the gold cloth one perhaps, no, that had the Nivea which is too greasy and had that horrid common smell which everyone would recognise. Here it was, in the raspberry colour purse, the Coty Emollient Hand Lotion ... an ideal healing potion, or would have been had her elbow not been knocked and it squirted onto her left shoe. What a waste, fortunately she had kept hold of the napkin and removed her shoe holding it before her so that her clumsy neighbour could not fail so see what damage she had inflicted on the nice new brown suede, that now bore a dark oily stripe across it. She turned away to make a second application to her hands. And she now had her pink wax and cotton wool ear plugs that she could warm and mould to

12

fit her small ears. Although she realised she ought have done this before applying the hand creme and before putting on a headscarf. One plug fell onto her other shoe; so now she had a stripe on one and a spot on the other. At least there need be no further contact with clumsy adjacent, if only she could now find her book. She rummaged. It had somehow worked its way down to the bottom of the bag ... and the blessed bookmark had slipped out and it was such a dull read anyway ... Joan really didn't much like Betty Friedan's voice and as for *Feminine Mystique*? What a title! It was all too American for her liking, but she did agree with Betty that housework and passive sex were not fulfilling activities for any woman, not that Joan had had much experience of either.

In finding her place and re-reading the dull preceding page, she remembered what she had forgotten to pack ... the leather clutch purse that Frederick gave her a few years earlier. It was Canary yellow, a colour she did not favour at the best of times and although exquisitely hand made would be of little use because she didn't go anywhere where such an accessory could be put on show. It was too big for a cocktail party and too small as a handbag and there wasn't much useful space in it as it was all taken by the compartment dividers that were very thick heavy leather. But despite its drawbacks she had wanted to bring it along so that she could take it out to dinner, if they go out to dinner, then Frederick might see that his gift had not been consigned to the back of the wardrobe, where, in fact, it was as she was twenty two thousand feet above Coventry.

She was woken by touch-down and the jolt to her neck and a deafness that might endure for some time. The book wasn't on her lap and her bag had been taken away again by the interfering hostess, probably the one in front of her who stank of too much cheap duty free perfume. It was such a nuisance because she had a tin of those rather effective Simpsons fruit lozenges. Joan disliked any confectionery especially the tinned sort because it was dusted with icing sugar but this ear pressure problem soon went after sucking one of those so they were a medicinal necessity. Unfinished, one could discreetly eject it into a tissue as soon as its work was done, but the tin was in the bag and the bag was elsewhere, no doubt with Feminine Mystique.

She was first off the plane but had to stand in the late sun on the tarmac waiting for her suitcase and was expected to carry it to the terminal and beyond ... *A bit much* she thought, *but it's what happens if you cut corners with a Charter*. She was much too hot in these clothes and thick shoes. Hopefully Frederick would be on the other side waiting for her and hopefully he had used some of that Euthymol mouthwash and dental powder she had kindly given him last time they had met. She found her tin of sweets and removed her earplugs and the pressure deafness disappeared. She didn't have a tissue to hand so she consumed the entire lozenge by sucking on it repeatedly.

2. FREDERICK

Frederick first met Joan twelve years before. He bought a house in the village where she lived and she was on the Parish Hail and Farewell Committee that dealt with hatches, matches, despatches and newcomers. She turned up two days after he moved in and she measured the untidy disarray of boxes and paraphernalia the instant the front door was opened.

Joan launched in "by moving into the village Frederick, if I might call you that, one only needs to know one person and that person is me. I'm Joan, how do you do."

She made an impact on him with that. "I prefer Fred socially" he said and invited her to return a week later for a cup of tea and a chat as he waved at the boxes behind him by way of explanation.

Joan brought along her own special tea in a flask, although she had forgotten the strainer, together with a small packet of Digestives and a few cornered editions of the village magazine which was a folded foolscap sheet with smudged blue offset litho type, all slightly askew. It was mostly filled with Church business like flower arranging duties, service times and the liturgic calendar. He had little interest in this, but politely put them on his utility sideboard. They got along well enough and subsequently over the coming months did a ping-pong round of afternoon teas, although he preferred coffee. Joan never called him Fred. She didn't shorten anyone's name.

In that time they got to know each other, he learned that she had been a nurse during the war and so they had some common interests because he was an Opthalmic Optician. He trained about the same time and was very active during the war attending clinics in Moorfields and he had been asked recently to join the NHS but most of his patients remained private to his clinic.

Frederick had never married, preferring instead the company of his tennis friends with whom he would take tennis holidays and camping trips abroad. His knowledge of Italy was exemplary, he knew it better than many Italians having travelled extensively in the Austin Healey - most often with the soft top down and more latterly in his new Sunbeam. He was fit and handsome for a man of his years. He naturally became amiable with the servicemen who had their eyes examined. He could understand how many of these young fellows could not bear the prospect of war. Many such military chaps befriended him and visited him for years after their National Service, a few had been to visit him in Italy already.

Frederick had invested in the rundown Canonica five years before Joan's visit. He had told Joan about it at one of their village teas and Joan had wondered whether it was near Rome where she had once been and was taken aback by the amount of male statuary about the city. The church to which the little Cononica was once attached was gone, burned out after the war, but the house had survived and was described as derelict when Fred bought it. He saw the potential and set about finding local tradesmen. The local bar and cafe proprietors knew who did what and before too long he had a retinue of young burly chaps who were lithe and fit and able to turn their hand to a wide range of tasks that Frederick would require to be done. He needed a good kitchen and a source of heating and to create the two bedrooms and two showers.

The various smaller spaces downstairs that might once have been used for parishioners confessional, robe storage and other meeting places for the community had lost their relevance and he wanted an open space that could see the fireplace from all angles and take in the view from the french doors that led onto the stone patio and garden, but there were design and cost compromises and eventually the bedrooms, one above the other, ended up with the best views.

He was adept at managing his small team and some of them were so enthusiastic they stayed over to make an early start the next day without the bother of getting home to mother. Fred always ensured he would provide hearty sustenance, plenty of wine and make sure they had something after a hard day's work. Down the garden, beyond what may once have been a graveyard, was a spring-fed pool which was also the source of his drinking and bathing water ... and on the long summer evenings some of the lads who worked over could be heard sploshing and frolicking in their white shorts among the rows of erect cypress.

Now, all that construction work and fun with the workmen had finished and Frederick was in the mode of host, welcoming old friends, neighbours and colleagues from his English life to his modest home in the Italian hills. Week by week for a few days at a time these couples and singles arrived to enjoy some time in the sun and la dolce vita. A visit to the local Osteria or Trattoria saved him from cooking or laying table for the entire duration of their stay and most often his guests would be more than willing to pay so he ordered the sirloin when out.

It had taken Joan about two years to accept his invitation and arrange her visit. He hadn't invited anyone else from the village because he didn't get to know anyone else when living there. She had family responsibilities and other friends in her diary and it just didn't work out until now, but they had corresponded. Given how special her visit was to him he felt he should give her the downstairs bedroom because its shower was adjacent, 'en suite' as they say in France, and the feather bed was so dreamy and warm on the new metal frame made at the local fabbro by a muscled hairy fellow in his leather apron. That bedroom which he had come to use whenever he didn't have guests had the lovely beamed ceiling supporting the wide oak boards of the bedroom directly above. He would have to use the shower halfway up the stairs whilst Joan was in residence. They would need to share the lavatory which was still outside the back door and he was hoping Giuseppe would soon return to integrate it into a porch arrangement so that it became a proper part of the house.

He needed to go into the village ferramenta to get a brush, he must remember that and some scourer to clean the tiles in the shower which were getting a bit grubby. He would take the sheets to the Nonna washerwoman in the village at the same time, so they should come back fresh and clean, if not quite white. And while he was at it, he could send his hankies which were getting shrivelled because he didn't have an iron. He would also try to get in touch with one of the builder lads to come over this evening to help him with the housework to prepare for Joan's visit on Wednesday. Giuseppe was always obliging and good company too.

The house phone rang and it was Joan from a callbox. She was at Manchester airport and on her way. He was sure she had said she would arrive on Wednesday. *Oh goodness* he thought to himself, *it is Wednesday. The days just come and go when you are enjoying retirement this much.*

She would be here in about five hours and he would need to get the Sunbeam to the airport which was another hour or so and he hadn't even made the bed, let alone sent the sheets to the laundry. He consulted his Accurist which was generally inaccurate. It was about mid-day.

Joan had been saying "My room will have ... " when the pips went and she was cut off. He guessed she was saying "My room will have a view won't it?". *Oh yes Joan* he thought *You have an Italian view down through the cypress and toward the pond and the valley. It's a lovely view.* All his guests had said so.

But now, thrown off his expected schedule by an entire day, *What should I do first?* He was mentally questioning and answering himself. His downstairs bedroom was to be Joan's room for the week ... that is where to begin and then the bathroom and then he must smarten himself up to meet her, he can't go to the airport looking like a ragbag.

He considered, *if I take these sheets and turn them top to toe she won't notice that they have been slept in for a week or so, maybe it's a fortnight, but no more.* The feather mattress needed plumping up having formed a Fred shape that he would fit into like a mould, supremely comfortable if you were Fred. He stripped the lot and flung it on the floor and then gave the mattress a hefty whoomph a few times. The dust lingered in the hazy shards of sunlight but it would settle.

He removed his personal toiletries from his nightstand, a half jar of Brylcreme, a pipe and tobacco that he had stopped smoking in bed since one of the lads told him he had bad breath, a pack of gossamer with two remaining which he thought to himself *they must be well perished by now* as ten years had passed since he bought three and used one. He took the crooked drawer outside and tipped it to eject the dust that blew away in the breeze and he was left with a piece of hard chewing gum stuck to the inside ... *who stuck that in there?* The pile of trousers, shorts, grubby underpants, vests, socks and collarless shirts that were scattered over the armchair had to be taken to the bedroom above for a week and that room didn't have a chair so the floor would have to do.

A tabby cat wandered in while he was upstairs and settled into the cosy of sheets and pillows on the floor. It was paw-padding a snug nest for itself, such that Frederick didn't have the heart to fling it out, so he turned his attention to her shower room. The towels were grey and flecked with blood stains from shaving cuts over the past few weeks ... these better go to the laundry too. He would take the whole lot to the Nonna on his way to the airport, it was only a few minutes out of his way and it would get all this dirty stuff out before Joan arrived and would come back in a few days hopefully. He polished off the shower tiles with the pants and vests and tried to buff up the calcified taps. The hot one dripped incessantly even though it was new only two years ago and it had left a green stain in the basin. He gathered his shaving brush and razor and made a mental note to buy a fresh bar of lavender soap when at the laundry. He hadn't been in there since he used it shortly after moving in properly. The beds had been used by lads staying over to get the work done and she had made a lovely job of cleaning everything bright and fresh, but she cost almost as much as buying new sheets.

Whilst gazing at the state of the room he thought it a pity that he hadn't insisted on the builder taking up the brick floor in this space and putting a pipe in for a lavatory while they were at it but the builder had shied away from the idea. *More likely* Fred thought *that he was scared of the idea that there was an old vault or grave below here that contained the bones of past priests and end up digging them up in the process,* so it remained with just the shower and basin and a Lloyd Loom gilt painted wicker laundry basket where the lavatory could have been. Opening the lid he was wafted back. "Oh goodness, mildewy towels. I wonder how long they have been in there" he spoke to himself at the spotty mirror.

The fresh towels upstairs were a bit grey too, but they were clean having been in the sun for several days on the line down by the pond. Swallows took to gathering there of an evening and their droppings baked hard by the following midday and rubbed off hygienically enough. The lavatory was more of a worry. Bleach and the cesspit didn't get along together because it stopped the bacteria doing its work but the last brush had been used to unbung the pipe at the other end and had fallen into the pit. He resorted to the kitchen saucepan scourer but would need to remember to buy another. All these small incidental costs added up when catering for someone.

He busied himself as best he could with some order and discipline. There was so much to do. In the distance the church bell tolled. A funeral perhaps? His Accurist had stopped at ten past twelve. It surely couldn't be the bell for afternoon mass? Could it be a quarter to three already? He hadn't finished the chores but if it was that time he would need to leave now. The car boot was full of the laundry and that would close at 3 so she could go to church. He must drop that off before his long drive to the aerodrome.

He wondered if the place had a bit of a smell to it? The towels from the basket were musty and all the cooking, boiling pasta and the stove spitting fried fish over the place, he reckoned it must do. The best course of action was a liberal wipe of aftershave around the bedroom to give the place a nice scent. He emptied the last of a bottle of Old Spice onto a pair of pants and wiped over the dresser and over the iron bedframe which he hadn't noticed had quite some dust. The cat hopped back on the bed.

He leaned over, "Come on Puss, out you go!" Puss lashed out a claw drawing blood from Fred's purlicue. A glistening red drip fell to the centre of the white cover and the fibres absorbed it in capillary slow motion - a fuzzy red disc that could not be hidden. He used his hanky between his thumb and forefinger. "Joan will understand, especially when she sees this wound."

On the way to the laundry he thought about another Joan he once knew ... his life in practice when he was organised around by smart Miss Joan Prentice. She would sit at the front of his consulting rooms with her thick black rimmed spectacles with sequin pointed sides. Every day she wore a black twin set, matching court shoes with a sensible heel and smelled of 4711. *A sort of female version of Old Spice* he thought. The clients were never kept waiting more than half an hour and ideally less than ten minutes. *I was organised with Miss Prentice, oh Joan, how I miss you*, his thoughts captured into the passing breeze.

The bell rope had obviously been tied aside leaving the last few flat clangs. "It must be three" he repeated to himself as he pulled up at the laundry. He nipped out and tried the glazed doors in the hope that she had left the place unlocked so he could throw the pile in and leave an apologetic note saying he would collect in a day or so, but they were bolted. He went blank. Staring along the village street knowing he couldn't take this lot with him, could he find a place where he might temporarily dump it.

He had that sensation of being watched. Over the road, behind him, an elderly woman dressed in customary widow black, silently watched his antics from her porta. He approached to ask whether she would mind handing over his pile of whites when the place reopened after mass? After her nodding agreement he tied the entire lot into the biggest sheet and knotted it with opposite corners like a giant hankie leaving a small trail of blood over virtually every item within. The scratch was sore and swelling. A wizened hand was thrust forward bending toward him in an impoverished manner and he found a folded 5000 note in his pocket which she took, expressionless, concealing the glee felt within. The Nonna washerwoman didn't realise how much her neighbour opposite profited from this hour over the years. She scribbled 5000 in a small notebook kept especially for the purpose and next to her price put Frederick's name so she might know the expectation next time. It was only the 'straniero' who handed over that much, a local might give her 100 at most, if anything at all.

The afternoon was gentle warmth and he enjoyed the top down in the convertible. The forecast was changeable weather but it hadn't changed much yet. He needed fuel but would get to the Benzinaio once he had collected Joan and they were on the way out of the airport. His arm was aching now. He had forgotten about soap and other essentials because his mental notepad became erased by feline wounds.

3. JOAN

Joan struggled with two heavy bags at the head of the conga-line off the tarmac. Inside the terminal the stench of hundreds of Nationale cigarettes fuming in the arrival space hit Joan as a thick gravy-like fog. She about-turned and pushed her way through the oncoming passengers whilst attempting not to breathe. She hadn't packed her old gas mask. Passengers from the back of the plane were now passing her with their cigarettes alight.

Aware that Frederick would be waiting out on the other side of all those smoking taxi drivers, bus drivers and assembled throng who all seemed to have a red tip glow beneath their nose. She was back near the steps of the plane on the last suck of her lozenge.

"Excuse me, were you the pilot on there?" Joan said pointing up at the plane.

"Second Officer Madam."

"Well you made a very good job of it, flying us here."

"Thank you Madam."

He was carrying the customary oblong Pilot's black bag.

"I need your help if you could," Joan commanded.

"In what way Madam? I could get a colleague to help you with your suitcase if it's too heavy, it looks heavy."

"No, no, it's not that particularly, although some assistance would be appreciated. No, I usually travel BEA you know. It's that I have a health condition and I cannot be exposed to cigarette smoke and that terminal is full of it, it's a veritable fog."

"Ah, I see. Yes come with me and I will get you through with the crew line to the side of the hall."

Joan followed and left her heavy suitcase on the tarmac on the assumption that one of his fellow crew would duly pick it up.

"I didn't realise so many people smoked and those awful Italian cigarettes have a very peculiar air about them" she struck up conversation with the second officer.

"Yes you were fortunate to sit in the front row Madam, I saw you there asleep when I walked through the plane earlier on. Everyone in row sixteen and beyond was smoking."

"So that check-in girl in Manchester did me a favour by being presumptuous that I wanted a no-smoking seat?"

"Obviously gathered that idea from your deportment Madam."

"Yes, I don't much like presumptuous people because they look you up and down and assume things from your demeanour."

"Indeed Madam."

"So that awful draught I suffered down my neck meant I only had the occasional whiff of all the smoking going on back there."

"Life has its compensations Madam" said the second officer.

At that point she was waved through by a lone guard as if she were one of the crew.

"Thank you so much," she said when they were outside.

"My pleasure Madam" as he walked on with his empty bag and gathered together with his colleagues to get a couple of waiting taxis.

She watched as her bag was placed alongside her by some uniformed individual, and thought to herself that they probably had an interesting life flying here and there. Then reconsidered. *Orgies and intercourse wherever they go* she thought to herself. *International travel and low moral turpitude pretty much go together* was her final thought on that matter.

There was a small tobacco kiosk as Frederick had described and a little traffic was all passing one way. Joan stood by the kiosk as instructed and waited but there was no sign of Frederick nor anybody else. A few cars pulled up along the kerbside and collected a couple of air hostesses. A dutiful wife in a headscarf driving a bright pale blue convertible, collected her pilot husband. *Very chi chi* she thought to herself as she watched them go in their very special looking Lancia. Joan wasn't one for turning her neck but there was nobody about looking at her. She now had time to rearrange her bag given Frederick was late. She could now get to the shawl and scarf and wear something more becoming ready for Frederick whenever he might turn up. She had a light jacket that was in a rather nice paper bag that Timothy Whites used for wrapping ladies requisites from their haberdashery counter. There was still some respectability in the world of retailing, although she thought *Woolworths has gone downhill since they had that awful pick and mix counter by the door of every store.* She had visited one a couple of months earlier and they had a record player near the door playing some trollop called Helen Shapiro who she didn't like one bit - 'Woah Woah Woah, You don't know' punctured Joan's tone deaf ears. *Commercial television talent shows have a lot to answer for* she thought.

After twenty minutes or so reorganising the various cosmetics and garments in her bag, she was aware that she had been waiting quite some time. It really was quite unseemly to open one's bag on a public concourse but there was nobody around to see. Her Aunt would have disapproved. She fingered a little eau de cologne behind her ears to freshen a little. She was looking forward to a bath this evening before some supper. The woman in the kiosk had locked up and disappeared down the corridor Joan had exited by and that's the last she saw of anyone. It was becoming deserted. She gathered her bags and walked a little way toward the wire fence at the corner. There was a locked gate. She peered around as best she could see with the wire mesh blocking her vision. There were a few people lingering but most taxis and cars had gone and she could see another larger tobacconist kiosk still open, the light was on and the woman who had just left her kiosk appeared to be gathering the newspapers there. Joan realised that in avoiding the smog she had exited the building at the side and she must retrace her steps because Frederick had obviously meant they should meet at that bigger tobacco kiosk. This blessed suitcase was getting heavier, she was quite sure. *How much did it weigh? Three stone? That's the weight of a fat child. Almost half her weight. No, it's not that heavy, she hadn't that many clothes. The scales were obviously faulty.* Joan's thoughts were always elsewhere, wherever she was, she was recounting past steps.

There was nobody guarding the corridor but the door was locked and although she was going a bit deaf she was certain she could hear her name being called out in an Italian accent, more like Joanne, on an echoing Tannoy system.

She needed to attract attention. Someone had foolishly locked her out so she could not return to the smoky hall. While she had a moment of peace in this corridor she put her bags down to find a suitable object to make herself heard. She hated harsh sounds so she would need to first insert her earplugs which she had put into one of the toilet bags in the side compartment.

4. FREDERICK

Frederick was aware he was at least half an hour late. He guessed that the plane he saw earlier at about 4000 feet overhead was her aircraft and due to land five minutes later. There weren't that many planes into Verona and that was forty minutes ago. The usual herd of black Fiat 1100 taxis at the terminal doors had all but gone and two tour charabang buses were departing in a cloud of exhaust fumes so there was space for him to pull up by the Tabacchi without any bother. There was nobody around and Joan was not to be seen. *Surely she should be here by now* he thought to himself as he parked and went inside where maybe she had already been out once and was sitting waiting inside.

Fortunately there was someone at the information desk. Using his well practised Italian he asked if the flight from Manchester was in. The response was given in a cut glass English accent worthy of the BBC Home Service.

"Yes, it arrived forty minutes ago and the passengers all appear to have gone on by bus or taxi to their destination."

"I was supposed to meet a friend and she hasn't turned up."

"She may have been taken unwell and might be in Del Donne; give it five minutes and I will put a Tannoy call out for her if she hasn't appeared by then."

He walked back to the kiosk outside but they were gathering unsold newspapers to send to pulp. He walked the length of the terminal in both directions. There was another smaller kiosk around the corner but that was shut and probably for staff. He returned to the Information desk.

"Would Joan Badger recently arrived from Manchester please go to the Information desk where your driver is waiting to meet you" and she repeated it. There was a delay of a second or two between each of the loudhailers around the terminal and while waiting he struck up conversation with her. She had a badge entitled Information but he couldn't call her that.

"Do people go missing very often Miss Err?" Frederick asked expecting Err to fill in the name but none was forthcoming.

"Usually they have forgotten they are being collected and they walk out and get into a cab, maybe it is the effect of a few hours flying, maybe they are tired or dizzy ... but it does happen from time to time. Often their driver is late and they think they have been forgotten."

"I am late" he admitted. "I didn't know this new Dan Air airline flew into this airport? Nor that you could get here directly from Manchester."

"They don't usually and you can't," she responded. "That was a charter flight for a group of opera types who are going to Verona for the week. The flight crew will be back in a couple of hours after having a meal and fly the plane back empty tonight." She paused. "Well almost empty, maybe with a few cases of Barolo."

"Do you think my friend Joan was herded onto the bus to Verona? I've just spent almost two hours coming from that direction."

"She may have done, I've no way of knowing really, but normally they have a tour guide who counts the number of heads and might ask to see a ticket or have some booking sheet. I will call for her again. If she is in the Ladies she will know to come this time."

They waited. The huge ceiling fans twenty feet above them had brown dusty edges from swirling nicotine that escaped from the jalousie windows running parallel to the runway. Enormous light bulbs cast a yellowing glow.

Maybe she couldn't understand the announcements, that was probably the issue thought Frederick. The sunset was close and a cooler breeze rushed through the terminal clearing the earlier smog. It was otherwise quiet apart from a cleaner pushing a wide mop gathering dead cigarette butts.

"I will give her one last Tannoy call and then I'm finishing my shift so I'm afraid you will have to go home and wait for a phone call. As you say she could be well on the way to Verona by now in that old bus."

It was at that silent moment they both heard a distant rat tat tat on glass and their eyes met in recognition. Somewhere in this vast space Joan was stuck behind glass. Click click click. Rap rap rap. Chink chink chink. They followed the sound which echoed a little, difficult to source. Perhaps she was clinking on pipes? They moved back toward

27

the doors that went out onto the tarmac but they were closed. The rapping, clearer now, came from a side alley along which they could see Joan clacking at the glass.

"She's gone through the crew exit somehow. Wait here" Information said.

Fred waited while she went to find the tobacconist woman who had a key. That's if they hadn't cashed-up and gone home for the night. Having found Joan, Frederick could give his hand attention. It was swelling from that blessed cat scratch.

5. JOAN

Joan had upset herself after all that banging and now Frederick was talking at the thick glass attempting to discuss how she had managed to get there - but Joan wasn't in the mood for it, so she kept her earplugs in and feigned deafness. She sat on her suitcase which buckled a little along the expanding hinge side. She was further dismayed when she noticed that she had damaged the edge and cracked the mother of pearl face of her lovely Stratton powder compact. Her mother, Florence, had bought her that shortly before she died. "Oh, what a fine start this is," she muttered.

"The kiosk couple were just locking up but this was on the hook just inside the door" said Information proudly holding the key aloft and with aplomb she turned the lock.

Joan did not acknowledge her, nor the effort she had gone to to solve the dilemma.

"Oh Frederick, at last. I'm so sorry, silly me. I exited through this alleyway and have been standing by the wrong kiosk for the past hour waiting for you. I then became stuck in this corridor after someone locked me outside" she effused.

"Never mind Joan, you are here safely" he gave her a spongy hug such that she felt like a brittle twig stuck in a marshmallow. "Why didn't you just walk around the fence and follow the cars on the road?" Joan metaphorically collapsed inside with her own stupidity but simply pursed her lips and shrivelled the eyes at him in her best "What a silly remark" fashion. And Frederick didn't pursue the matter.

Information had overheard this exchange and exasperatedly wished them both well as Frederick exclaimed profusely "I really cannot thank you enough." The door was locked behind them and she hoped perhaps for a few hundred Lira for her trouble but no Lira were forthcoming. Rather than hang around to the point of embarrassment, she wished them well again ... another family crisis safely sorted out ... and made a retreat to close her desk.

They stood at the boot of the car and once he unlocked it with the fiddly little key that fitted inside the handle. Joan noticed a pile of what appeared to be less-than-white soiled undergarments. *Surely not,* she thought to herself, *maybe just oily rags that he uses to maintain this tatty old car.* Frederick shoved them aside and the boot was then full to capacity with the cardboard suitcase. He thought to himself *How long is she staying for? Feels like she has brought the kitchen sink with her.*

"There's nothing for it Joan, I'm afraid you will have to have the holdall on your lap" he said as he held the door open for her.

"What have you done to your hand Frederick? I have Iodine tincture and some old Distaval sedative tablets in my bag somewhere, I will find them when I'm seated. Hold my leather bag would you please while I get comfortable."

Having struggled to bend her backside into the seat Joan thought it appropriate to remark

"I didn't know a Sunbeam sports car was so close to the ground Frederick. I have an Imp at home you know, probably made in the same factory as this and I thought that was a small car." *My knees are virtually touching my chin* she thought.

Frederick manoeuvred the bag across her front through the roof space, it just avoided her nose. It pinned her in place, however she could see through the screen if she looked through the stiff handles.

Frederick secured the cloth roof over their heads and clipped down her side and then swung himself into his seat to clip down his side. The pop-studs didn't all function so there were gaps here and there but it seldom rained so they would be fine.He started up and took to the thin steering wheel to get them toward the fuel station before it closed for the night.

"A woman in the village bought one of these convertibles. She's a blousy type as you would imagine. Anyway, it fell to pieces what with the rust. So shoddily made at that Rootes factory in the Midlands somewhere. I suppose that's what will happen to my little Imp in due course" said Joan

"We don't get the weather here for rust Joan" was all he was allowed to respond before she interjected.

"I feel a little claustrophobic in here Frederick" Joan advised realising there wasn't much that could be done about it. Frederick wound down his window. Joan could not reach the handle on her door.

As they pulled into the nearest Benzinaio she said

"Do let me pay for this Frederick, it's the least I can do for coming all this way to fetch me."

She had no idea how far they would travel to get back to his home.

"It's difficult to reach one's purse in this position, it's buried rather deep I think, and I will find the iodine and pills while you fill up."

Frederick chatted with the proprietor knowing from earlier times that Joan and her purse had difficulty coming together.

"Tell me how much and I will reimburse you when we get there, which I must say I am looking forward to seeing after all the descriptive letters you have written to me." She paused. "Tell me Frederick who was the swarthy young fellow in the little polaroid photo you sent me recently? Was he one of your workmen?" But without waiting for an answer she went on "Sit still a moment and let me put this on your cut because it's swelling nastily."

The tincture made him flinch and his hand went slightly numb and a yellow purplish.

"Goodness Frederick, that fresh petrol certainly put the Tiger in your Tank didn't it! What a roar we are going along with."

The din was unbearable for her, but she knew the earplugs were near the top of the holdall as she hadn't long taken them out. Frederick remained silent about his blown exhaust. Getting a new one out here for an English sports car was prohibitively expensive. Besides, it announced his arrival in the village and his young fellows in the village who had helped out at the Canonica would magically appear.

The bag shielded Joan from the oncoming headlights and she had a glimpse from time to time of the fading pink and purple twilight. For some distance they followed a slow open truck filled with ripe grapes on the vine that were to be pressed.

"Frederick, would you mind closing your window? That truck is giving out a lot of fumes which make me somewhat heady and little nauseous."

Frederick wound the handle as far as it would go but there was still a gap which you could slide a hand through between the glass and the roof.

"I didn't think about the fact that I would be sitting on the wrong side of the car Frederick and with this bag on my lap I cannot see over it to see if it is safe for you to overtake." she advised

Frederick had pulled out a good few feet into the path of an oncoming car in order to pass the stinking truck. Joan thought she would meet her maker. She had almost 'gone to the ladies' in her seat when the horn was blasting at her, although it was a good deep tone and not harsh or tinny so *obviously from a quality car that missed her by inches* she thought.

"Thank goodness they don't bother with those new fangled seatbelt things here" she added, noticing the Sunbeam had none. "I saw an advertisement for some as an accessory, you know, for my Imp. Have you thought of having them? They were only thirty nine and eleven plus post and packing of ten shillings more. Just for the front seats. In the Imp I mean. They were in an advert from Shopportunities in the News of the World, not that I have the News of the World of course, it's full of salacious gossip and tittle tattle. Not my sort of broadsheet at all. No. My neighbour Betty insists on putting it through my letterbox every Tuesday when she has finished reading it. There are some bargains to be had. Of course I would need my garage man to fit them which would be an extra expense. What do you read now you are here Frederick?"

Frederick listened to all this thinking to himself *I didn't realise Joan could be so chatty.* He turned to answer her for once but she was asleep face-forward on the holdall. Frederick wondered *Have the carbon monoxide fumes poisoned or just silenced her? There are reports of people passing out behind these old Fiat trucks spewing smokey gunk.* He realised that he hadn't actually said much on this journey, it had been a succession of unanswered questions and statements. That was fine. *It was her excitement although she wouldn't admit to it.* He let her sleep as he drove on the familiar road up through the hills. The village was unusually quiet. The little cafe near the laundry had its lights on but there was nobody on the terrace. He thought of stopping off here for a snack or nightcap before getting home, but that was best forgotten given the sleeping beauty by his side. He had not known it so quiet before, he had spent many an evening joking with the lads over a beer during the period of house refurbishments.

The cool air hit her as he opened the doors and the breeze blew through the car across her neck. She felt the handle marks imprinted into her face as she lifted her head and the few unsprayed hairs near her forehead blew toward the driver's door. Frederick lowered the soft top to get the bag off her lap without pulling it across her flat breasts.

"My goodness Frederick, I think I must have dozed off after that car beeped at us when you were on my side of the road. That's getting older for you" she said.

As he lifted the bag, unsure whether the remark about age was about him or her, she felt pins and needles start in her toes and feet. She remained in situ. She could do nothing else. Frederick took the holdall indoors, turning on the lights. She saw him place it in a downstairs room. He returned for the suitcase from the boot because his injured hand could not bear the strain. Joan remained seated watching him drawing the thin cotton curtains that did not quite meet. *I have some safety pins in one of the toilet bags to deal with that if that's my room* she thought.

The cicadas were rattling and the moon was bright, but there was a slight chill. So many stars to see from this seat and the longer she looked the more she saw. It was wondrous.

"Are you glued to that seat?" he said as he rummaged in the boot and gathered all the undergarments that had failed to get into the earlier laundry drop.

"I'm a bit stuck Frederick I'm afraid. My legs have gone to sleep with having the bag on my lap for such a long time." She was squinting at the little Smiths dial on the dashboard and thought it read ten to ten.

"Is it really twenty one fifty Frederick?"

"It is. It's taken a little over two hours to get here Joan, we were stuck behind some very slow vineyard lorries." He held out a hand to help her up.

The pins and needles were agonising and it felt like her 150 denier stockings were rolling off down her legs with the suspenders imbedded into her thighs. Her plaid woollen skirt was hot and itchy and much too thick for the climate despite the occasional breeze of relief wafting up into it around her.

"Whoops a Daisy" he said whilst she gripped his arm.

Joan stumbled a little on the old brick path that would break her ankle if she wasn't careful.

I will have to watch that and these hush puppies are all wrong for here she thought. He supported her into the house.

"Welcome to my humble abode."

The yellowing bulb glowed over the table and she was touched that he had bothered to assemble a small vase of wildflowers, although they had been there a week and were somewhat faded.

"How enchanting Frederick that you should find such a place is admirable." She looked about her.

Quite a bit of dust and a few cobwebs she noted to herself. She had sensibly packed some of those new Dunlop household rubber gloves as she thought she might have to set to work a little. Her mind was considering *Frederick is bound to be a little rough around the edges.*

"What was this place did you say Frederick? An ecclesiastical building of some sort wasn't it?"

"It was a Canonica Joan, so it was attached to a church but that was ruined in the war. They say that some men were making munitions in the church and the whole place blew sky high and the roof collapsed and the place was abandoned. It was a wreck when I bought it. There were several little rooms in this space downstairs here, I guess where they stored vestments and other church paraphernalia. There is another church we passed in the village, you will see it when we go for a walk."

She gazed at the open space he was waving at.

"What is that funny smell Frederick? It's like a mix of cooking fat and aftershave" she blurted, but before he could answer she carried on.

"And where does that door go to up there, halfway up the stairs?"

"That's the second bathroom Joan."

So Frederick didn't have to explain the unusual odour which was a relief to him. He thought the place may have had a pong earlier on and he was obviously right.

"Would you like a cup of coffee Joan or something a little stronger?"

"I could do with using my bathroom please Frederick if you would like to show me my room and then perhaps we could have a little nightcap under the stars ... I will find a headscarf to avoid that chill breeze."

"Ah yes of course, let me show you right now. Would you prefer red or white wine or something stronger? A G&T perhaps?"

"Yes a Gin would be lovely Frederick, No ice thank you but lemon if you have it."

He led her into the bedroom and fortunately the bulb was dim so the muted tidiness was quite becoming, or so he thought. Joan had other ideas. *That iron bed will obviously creak every time I move and the mattress looks decidedly unsupportive but that remains to be seen. I will certainly need more than one G&T to get off to sleep on that.* The wooden ceiling was just old boards the joins of which you could see straight through to the room above which was dark. *Maybe it was a loft.* There was a large reddish brown blotch on the white counterpane to which she said

"Oh dear."

"My hand I'm afraid Joan, a cat scratched it as I was making the bed earlier on. The iodine has helped a little. And, here is your bathroom Joan. I usually have this room because it is, as the French say *en suite,* but I've moved upstairs during your stay so my bathroom is on the half landing. And allow me to show you to the lavatory. It's just outside the back door."

Joan's lips pursed to resemble a Medlar fruit, but she remained composed as she was shown the facility. It had a heart shape cut into the wooden door that opened outwards.

"I don't know why Joan but sometimes the light out here doesn't come on, but the chain will always flush well. Shall we have a code that we will whistle when we want to enter and we will leave the door slightly ajar when unoccupied?" They both stared into the dim water closet and Joan could see it had a painted floor and that is all, she felt, that could be said for it.

The air remained silent and the medlar remained present whilst Frederick said

"Well I will leave you here then shall I, whilst I go make us a nice strong G&T. Rendezvous on the terrace in fifteen minutes or so I suggest. It's just outside your bedroom doors."

Joan sat on the comfortable wooden seat, the slice of new moon was visible through the heart in the door. She had not used an outside lavatory since she was ten when they went to visit her other Aunty. She heard Frederick preparing the drinks. She stood to adjust her heavy skirt and peered through the heart and saw him lighting church candles and cover them with an open glass cloche. She waited for him to go inside before flushing with an almighty clank followed by hissing. *No sleeping through that din* she thought to herself. She would just have to get used to this. After all, it was only for a week.

"What brand of gin is this Frederick, it has an unusual tang, or maybe it's the tonic. I don't suppose you can get Gordons or Schwepps out here?" asked Joan.

"No it's the import duties that make such a difference in price. My friend Lionel brought me this when he visited a few weeks ago as a special treat."

"These are delicious olives Frederick. So here we are at last after all your hard work you have made a home in the sun. Chin Chin. Congratulations."

Joan raised her glass.

"I'm certain of something Frederick and that is that I couldn't do it, I wouldn't know where to start, let alone in a foreign country miles from home. Although this is now your home of course. Do you speak Italian well Frederick? You seemed to get on at the garage well enough, a bit stilted perhaps but you get by don't you?"

"Would you like another Joan and a few more olives perhaps?" asked Frederick.

"Oh my, I seem to have been going a bit heavy on both those but after a while the flavour grows on you doesn't it. I can't quite put my finger on that flavour, there is something like a hint of parma violets, do you know what I mean? Perhaps you don't taste it because you often have it."

Frederick went inside and prepared another in double measure so as to help Joan sleep and drained the tin of olives and took them out to the terrace.

"Here we go."

"Thank you Frederick, I'm suddenly feeling rather exhausted and aware that I'm firing off questions to you without so much as a breath."

Frederick could detect that her neck was sagging under her chin and there was a fold of skin that must have developed in that couple of years since he last saw her. Her hair was still in a tight perm but the moonlight didn't do favours for her complexion. It showed the ample powder she had applied and the unevenness of it with thicker patches on the cheeks and chin and a light patchy dusting on the forehead. He could never quite understand women and makeup because he rarely thought it beautified. In his working days he had to get close to the patients face to see the eye with his lenses and all too often be close to flesh covered in powdered hair, just those small light invisible hairs but when powdered would stiffen and stand on end in their fake blush. Joan was using too much makeup but it was late in the day.

"I will sleep well Frederick" said Joan as she popped in another olive, twisting it around her mouth before ejecting the stone into the bowl.

"I sat next to a woman whose feet absolutely stank Frederick and further back in the plane people were singing. It was a charter plane you know, where a group of people going to some event buy up all the seats and my agent managed to get a spare. Heaven forbid but I have to travel back next week with the same lot. Fortunately I had a seat right at the front and I must make sure of that on the way home."

"I have never flown here Joan because I didn't know you could and what would I do about getting here, a taxi would cost a fortune. I have always driven down on the ferry from Dover and it only takes three or four days across France going through Chamonix and skiing country. I love tennis and there are several nice pensions I have found en route that have a tennis court and a proprietor or son who love to beat an Englishman. I became a regular for them, before I finished the house that is." As he was concluding he noticed Joan's eyes were shut and her lower lip had dropped open so that a small pool of saliva was gathering around her lower teeth. He touched her cold thin hand and said

"Would you like another or a nightcap perhaps?"

She scraped her chair back.

"No no Frederick, I must go to bed, I'm being bad company and starting to doze. Perhaps you can show me to my room so that I don't stumble on these uneven cobbles in the dark out here."

Joan fell face down onto the bed fully dressed and passed out.

At around 4am a barking dog woke her, she had been dreaming about a dog. Her mouth was dry and she needed to go to the ladies. The light was on and she exercised her jaw to salivate, conscious of being virtually unconscious. Her head felt hot and there was slight movement behind her. She lay still looking toward the wall wondering if Frederick was in her bed behind her. *Has he taken advantage of my unseemly state? Surely not s*he thought. She never became drunk and yet clearly that tangy violet flavour gin had knocked her out. There was another small movement and then a purr. A cat. There was a cat on the bed snuggling next to her neck. She hated cats. She hadn't moved and now felt incapable of moving at all. She was still dressed and had her lace up hush puppies on. The distant dog barked with continual monotony. She lay still. Above her the ceiling creaked and she heard a deep trumpet sound. *Frederick must be in the room above me, asleep and he has broken wind. Surely not. Surely he wouldn't be so unseemly.* Was she in some sort of nightmare and yet to wake from it. She would have to get up and use the lavatory. *Oh Dear God* she thought to herself as she brought together just where she was. She lay still, terrified the cat would claw at her. She had a sudden thought *My book! where's my book? I think I've left it on the plane. It wasn't very good, rubbish really, but I never will know about Feminine Mystique.* Within seconds unmoved she was again asleep under the influence of Italian gin and a warm pussy.

6. FREDERICK

A cock crowed on the hillside as dawn broke and the distant dog stopped its incessant bark having finished its nightshift of protection. Fred woke to the sound of the bird most mornings because he kept his windows open and the outer shutters closed ... the air was pine scented as the trees absorbed the morning dew.

Looking at his trusty Elgin clamshell clock he saw light coming up through his floorboards around the rug. This significant disadvantage of having a guest in the room below, especially one as proper as Joan, was the trapped wind would cause him some discomfort until he was outside. He shuffled into his slippers and descended for his morning constitutional.

The rising sun projected a heart shape onto his vest whilst on the wooden seat as he considered the breakfast table he would prepare for Joan if he had enough to feed himself, let alone her as well. He had somehow lost a day and she was here as planned but earlier than his body-diary had expected. He was done and pulled the hissing chain, taking a quick look into the meagre pantry on the way to get dressed. He would have to nip into the village for some fresh provisions and be back in twenty minutes to rustle up something respectable for when she emerged.

The village was already busy, country people believed in living in the light. He bought eggs, oranges, tomatoes, olives and a bar of expensive lavender scented soap at the grocers and a fabulous large fresh loaf at the bakers. Treats like this were only available to the local early birds. On the way back he stopped at the laundry to see when his sheets would be ready, but oddly it was still shut. Like an icon the elderly woman opposite was on her doorstep. She beckoned him over.

"She's dead." He looked quizzically, so she dispassionately repeated "She is dead, collapsed in the church apparently, found by Father Leo, there's a remembrance tonight and a cortege in a couple of days."

He felt it heartless to say what was on his mind but she sensed his question and she beckoned him in to her porta and pointed to the tied linen bundle just as he had given it to her yesterday. He picked it up silenced by the news. He didn't really know the 'Nonna', the lavandaie, the washerwoman. He couldn't describe her features but she was perfectly pleasant and a helpful lady who worked hard and made a good job of his linen a while back when it was utterly filthy. He realised he hadn't actually seen her for almost two years. An honest hard working woman and presumably the hard work killed her. He shifted the groceries to the front seat and bundled the washing back into the boot of the Sunbeam. What a shock. Just like that. Gone.

It wasn't until he was halfway back to the Canonica that he realised the old woman hadn't given him his money back. He had paid her five thousand Lira to hand it over to the Nonna and she had kept the fee. It was too late to turn around. Joan might be up and wondering where he was, but at some point he would have to track her down to get his money back ... *what a nerve*. And he would have to get through this entire pile of laundry somehow. *Oh Lord.*

He could hear the shower dribbling as he entered the house. Joan had obviously fathomed how to work it which was a blessing. She was probably unaware that he had been to the village. He unpacked the groceries and filled the kettle. He had to bring a kettle over from England, a chrome one with a huge red button on the side because he couldn't find an electric kettle anywhere around here. As he was filling it, he saw a pair of Dunlop rubber gloves beside the sink. Perplexed he touched them, he even said aloud "Rubber Gloves?".

Joan was in the shower room adjacent to the kitchen sink ... a brick vent at ceiling height allowed a little steam through. He guessed she had been slightly scalded because as he switched on the kettle he heard "Oh bugger" and he knew that before long all the hot water would be gone. She would learn the hard way of the limitations of life in the Italian countryside.

There was a clatter like the shower rail and curtain falling. "Oh Bugger" again so he assumed his suspicions were correct. She would need to be more careful.

His Mokapot pop-popped on the stove and the electric kettle was ready if she preferred tea. The fresh loaf rose on the board among dishes of marmalade and butter. A few old oranges made a little juice for the jug. He took the lot out to the terrace with some fresh napkins. He knew Joan was very particular about her napkin so hers was rolled into his only decorated wooden ring.

The coffee smelled so delicious that he took a cup for himself awaiting her arrival. *She won't be long*, now that she was out of the shower.

He tuned the radio to RAI and settled back to chat interspersed with the music he had come to like. He hummed along a little to Nini Rosso, it was a nice tone on his Murphy wireless he had brought over with him. The sun warmed his swollen hand and the bread smelled delicious. The music was jolly orchestral and vibrating, he turned it up a little ... life was worthwhile. It was all set to be a good day.

Joan was being a little longer than he anticipated and he was peckish. That loaf looked so tasty, *maybe a treat of the crust with lashings of that nice fresh butter would suffice with another cup of coffee,* the loaf would still look good and maybe Joan didn't like the crust, what with her delicate lips coated with that pale lipstick and powder. Yes, it wasn't impolite to have that, just to keep going while he waited. The coffee was really delicious and the sun was up and warming through the lemon tree. He noticed that she had fastened her bedroom curtains together with safety pins *presumably to preclude the many peeping toms in the village* he smirked, *so she won't be making a grand entrance through the french doors onto the terrace* he thought.

He considered that after the arduous journey yesterday she would probably appreciate a day of peace and quiet, maybe relaxing in the garden, such as it was, or a short walk around the lanes out of the village. He would suggest she try the nice wooden steamer chair down by the cypresses although he better remember to go down there with a brush and cloth to wipe off all the swallow muck. There were not too many mosquitos by the pond this time of year thanks to the swallows gobbling them. And perhaps they could go to the trattoria in the village tonight and have the good pasta al funghi or the one with the squid ink. She would like that and it wasn't too expensive. He might have a steak later in the week after she had enjoyed her stay.

He savoured the buttered noggin with a crunch on his crust coloured teeth, butter oozing between them. *Maybe one slice more whilst waiting.*

They were playing some Dean Martin on the wireless, maybe because it sounded Italian. *Amori.*

He sang along a bit and then thought of his two sisters Doris and Viola, both dead, killed together by an unexploded bomb that was buried in the garden of a house they moved into about ten years ago. They were apparently pegging out the washing at the time. They both

41

loved that song and were probably singing it as they went heavenwards. He could remember the moment he was told. He was in Moorfields and had been removing an eye of a patient with macular atrophy. A nurse had advised him to sit down as she read the telegram.

Peculiar how music can trigger the most random of memories he thought.

Perhaps he should put on an egg for himself if Joan was going to be much longer. *No wonder I never married* he thought. He called out to her pinned thinly curtained doors.

"Joan dear, breakfast is on the terrace." Should he have called her 'dear' he wondered?

7. JOAN

No bath. She always had her morning bath and never stayed anywhere without a bath. This shower had lived up to her expectations of a shower, it dribbled hot and cold intermittently so she both scorched and froze. Her hair had become a huge frizz, it was standing on end with the consistency of fuse wire that she would have to put into curlers later on, fortunately she had brought a dozen along in one of the toilet bags. The shampoo Frederick had left for her in a glass bottle resembled the liquid soap that her aunt used to boil down with soda crystals and water combined with bits of carbolic left over from her Monday laundry day. It reeked of lavender which she detested and had ruined her freshly permed hair. She knew as soon as she tried to get a lather to remove the awful stench of cigarette smoke absorbed at the airport, that it was reacting with the setting lotions and soda they had put on to get the colour right. *What a mess.*

She opened her damaged compact to find the mirror was also broken into three pieces. One crack went directly across her lips turning her mouth into a bolt of lightning and the other went up the bridge of her nose creating Fagin's broken cartilage. It entirely altered the shape of her face. She looked all boss-eyed and a chinless wonder. It upset her equilibrium - already askew from the vile circumstances in which she found herself. She made a mental inventory. *Flea ridden cat, barking dog, outside lavatory, cheap gin, filthy bedding, grey towels, no bath, unreliable shower, insufficient hot water, horrid shampoo, broken compact, hair like an american Troll doll.* If she were at a hotel she would be at the front desk by now banging on the front counter bell. She was almost tearful.

The bathroom mirror was too high to see anything except a steamy image of her soapy frizz and now she had to see her deformed face in this broken compact. She had had that for years and replaced the powder cartridge a few times. *So stupid of me for using it as an implement to rap on that glazed door.* The door survived intact, but her lovely powder compact was ruined. Fortunately she had brought along a ghastly cheap Rimmel one that her friend had bought for her birthday as a standby and would need to find that, she could replace the powder in it with the finer Elizabeth Arden.

Looking around this room that was to be her space for the coming week was a sight of complete disarray. She had unpacked a few things, not found her book and placed the remainder on the bed but where was it all to go? The nice new Dunlop gloves were out by the kitchen sink, placed when scurrying outside to the ghastly outdoor lavatory but where could her clothes go? The wardrobe that reeked of mothballs and cheap aftershave was stuffed with thick trousers that he obviously wore in England but not here and dressy shirts with grubby collars or no collars at all. She stood still in the thin greyish towel and could smell coffee, she hated that smell, so Frederick was evidently up and about. And that cat. How had that cat entered her room and how had it exited and when did it go? She looked under the bed but saw only dust, large wads of fluff, some dirty underwear and white socks one of which was inside out.

And now to top it all, the wireless was on outside her window playing some awful Italian music ... sentimental stuff like Ave Maria. She detested music at the best of times. What did people see in it, or rather hear in it? Such a cacophony. She would make sure she tripped over the wire and pulled it from the plug. It would stay off if she had anything to do with it.

However, on a positive note, what she had done was to find the safety pins to put across those thin cotton curtains that didn't meet. She had found a few near the hair curlers. They were in a little folded paper bag that smelled of mints to which she admitted she was partial to just a half one now and again for medicinal purposes for the tummy. Not confectionery. One had to be careful not to choke on those whole mints.

While pinning the curtains she could see the back of Frederick's head, he looked like he was consuming a slice of bread and butter without a plate or napkin. He could do with a haircut or at least a visit to the barber to shave off all those grey hairs down his neck. It took three pins to make a good job of the fastening, but now the edges of the window showed up. *Oh well, nobody could see anything but the wall through there* she considered.

How can one look presentable and respectable in these circumstances? she muttered. And to top it off, she had a rotten headache from drinking too much cheap gin. *Oh dear God, six more days of this* she thought to herself.

In the event, she left most of the stuff on the bed and put on a lemon crimplene frock that she had recently bought in Hoopers of Torquay whilst on a trip to Babbacombe. That was a classy shop in what was becoming a low rate resort. She had transferred to The Grand because she didn't like the company of those on the coach trip. She wouldn't do that again. *That was a charter* she considered, seeing the parallels with her flight. *I'm not a charter sort of person.*

Now she had better put on a smile and get out there and have some breakfast such as it will be. *The lemon colour is very Italian and stylish* she thought. She gathered her mascara set as she liked to apply this between breakfast courses. Oh, she nearly forgot, her special lemon teabags, she took one from her weeks supply of fourteen. Hopefully Frederick had a small pot in which to brew the tea, it never tasted the same if made in the cup like she had at the airport yesterday and it made such a ghastly mess to fetch a bag out of the cup. She didn't think to bring her small Spode teapot. *Drat.*

Frederick was calling from the terrace to serve Breakfast. She hoped he had some bananas. She was partial to a half banana for breakfast.

"Good morning Frederick."

8. FREDERICK & JOAN

"Good morning Joan, I trust you slept well after your nightcap."

"Yes, thank you Frederick, I don't really remember much after such an arduous day. I went out like a lantern."

He thought *why can't she just say 'Light' like everybody else.*

"I've prepared some coffee and orange juice and went to the Bakers to get a fresh loaf."

"How pleasant, may I have my tea made in a pot if you have one, I have brought my own sachet."

"Of course, the kettle has boiled, I will switch it on again. Do you prefer a mug or a cup?"

"Oh, a cup, with a saucer and a teaspoon please."

Frederick went in search of a teapot, he had one somewhere, maybe at the back of the pantry but finding a cup with a matching saucer might be an even more complex task. *What does she want a spoon for?* he thought.

"Here we go Joan, I found the teapot, this nice big brown one was my mother's I believe. Pop the sachet in and I will fill up with boiling water."

"I had better do it Frederick, I know just the right amount of water so as to not dilute it too much nor have it too strong."

With which she went to the kitchen 'accidentally' tripping on the cable to the wireless and pulling it from the plug, creating a little flash at the socket and silence. *That's the end of Amori, whatever that means* she thought.

"Oh dear, so sorry Frederick, how clumsy of me. Don't worry about fixing it for me, I am tone deaf."

In the kitchen she faced a disarray of paraphernalia surrounding the kettle and considered she would tackle this lot a little later with her functional new gloves. She returned to find him cutting another slice from the loaf.

"Do you have any bananas Frederick?"

"Afraid not Joan, but I will put that on my village list for tomorrow. I did get you a fresh bar of soap for your shower. It's lavender and it's by the kitchen sink in case I forget."

"Yes, I did notice that the bar which is in the shower has the consistency of a hedgehog. Perhaps you would like to take that one to your shower room on the stairs."

"Shall I cut you a slice of this delicious bread Joan and do try these preserves that are made in the village, the lemon marmalade is particularly good from a tree just like this one here" as he pointed behind him.

"I think that the flavour might clash with my tea which is very delicate, but a half slice of bread would be very pleasant thank you. Is there a butter knife or should I use this?"

She held aloft a bone handled knife which had been glued together at some stage, clearly worse for wear.

"I will show you later where all the crockery and cutlery is, so you can choose a knife you like."

"That would be most satisfactory Frederick, I can help you get some order into your kitchen later if you like?"

Frederick thought *that is more of a statement than a question* and that he wouldn't have much choice about it. Joan was about to put him and his home in alphabetical order, thus the rubber gloves. He surmised that she meant well. He passed her half a slice and put the other half on his plate.

"Can I offer you some freshly squeezed Orange juice Joan?"

"Just a little please, I need to care for the enamel on my teeth. Did you ever use that Euthymol powder I gave you?"

"Oh yes Joan, a pink scouring powder wasn't it?"

"Did you ever buy any more?"

"No, I went back to SR in a tube and over here you get Chlorodont which has a pleasant bleach flavour that you might like."

That figures she thought *competing with the lavatorial breath.*

"I find Euthymol excellent to prevent discolouration and staining."

"What do you think of the jam Joan?"

"Yes quite pleasant especially given it's made in a rudimentary continental kitchen, but I've never been one of sweet tooth."

"Well, let's think about today. I imagine you would like to rest here. There are some wooden steamer chairs down the path by the pond. We could have a sandwich for lunch and a glass of wine and maybe have a walk up the lane to see the view of the valley. If you like we could eat out tonight at the trattoria in the village."

She started her mascara routine using the broken compact. She had heard that Princess Margaret used the same brand of mascara so it would give a good result ... *but as for the frizz.*

"That sounds a good plan Frederick, I need to finish my unpacking though." She was done with one eye and moved over to the other. "I would like to know where to hang my things as I've laid them out on the unmade bed to save them creasing. They are not all crimplene like this super new frock."

"It's very fetching Joan and it goes with your new modern hairstyle this morning" he said folding the jammy half-slice into his mouth. "Would you like some more to eat? You haven't had very much. I have some nice eggs from the village."

"No, no thank you Frederick, one has had quite ample sufficiency thank you." She didn't feel inclined to mention the awful lavender detergent stuff that had ruined her perm. She touched in her eyebrows a little with the brush.

"Well, let's leave the table for now and let me show you around the garden."

She finished her tea that had a tang of Tetley from the old brown pot, dabbed each side of her mouth and rolled the napkin into its ring to allow Frederick to escort her. The distant bell rang from the village church.

"That bell reminds me Joan. I had rather a shock this morning when I went into the village. I took in a big pile of bedding, towels and personal garments to the laundry lady yesterday and this morning I found out that the Nonna, that's what we call the laundry lady, died while she was in the little village church. The one that is tolling the bell just now."

"Oh Goodness, that must have been a shock Frederick, did you know her well? It's flat by the way."

"No, not so well that I would attend the memorial service but I have all the washing in the boot of the car and will need to find a way of dealing with it, it's quite a bundle." He continued "What is flat?"

"That explains the soiled undergarments I noticed in the boot yesterday. Is there a laundrette nearby where you can put a few Lira in and use a machine or two to do the hard work? The bell, the bell is flat, its cheaply made, I might be tone deaf but I can tell that bell clanks doesn't it, it doesn't ring like an English village church bell that is cast and tuned, it's flat and clanks."

"I've used a laundrette that is on the way to the Lakes for the past year or so but that closed and moved somewhere else and I don't know where it's gone. I will ask tomorrow morning in the village, maybe someone will know." *Yes that bell is flat,* he thought as he had never noticed before but now every time it rang he would think of Joan. *She is rather flat too.*

"That's a good idea Frederick as we do require clean bedding and towels this week."

They continued down the brick path between the cypress. The grey towels put out a week ago were stiff on the line. A layer of weed had developed over the pond and the only delineation between that and the surrounding grass was an edging of rushes and dead Iris. He led her to the steamer chairs and brushed off fallen petals and bird droppings indicating they might sit. Joan was reluctant to get her new frock soiled or caught on a splinter because it had cost her £6 at Hoopers so she, like Frederick, remained standing as he recognised the tone of an approaching motorbike. Moments later the cypress parted and a swarthy tanned young Italian man dressed in white

49

approached them. He had brilliant white teeth ... thirty of them seemingly gleamed all at once.

"Ah, Giuseppe, How lovely of you to call by, what brings you here? Let me introduce my friend Joan who has flown over to visit us for a week."

Joan held forward a hand which Giuseppe clasped as he pulled Joan toward him and embraced her on each cheek. His masculine strength and his hirsute handsomeness quite flustered her.

"Go get yourself some coffee and juice from the breakfast table up there and bring it down to join us at the pond," suggested Frederick and the younger man bounded up the brick path, Joan watching the muscular thighs encased in snug white shorts. She practically fell into the steamer chair as she considered those teeth completely ignoring her new crimplene frock.

Joan hadn't seen teeth like that since she was ravished by her first proper boyfriend over twenty five years ago. She always called him ravishing to her friends because that's how she saw him. She gave herself up to him, put herself on a plate to be devoured, swooned under the influence of his pheromones, laid back and thought of England or anywhere. The ravishing was total and extreme. She had succumbed to hours and hours of endless lust and animal instinct. She had never before encountered such feelings which she engrossed herself in mercilessly for what were just a few short weeks before he was conscripted into the War effort. Her last letter to him was when he was finally billeted off to BFPO 61 Milan to serve his time. He never came back.

She was aware that Frederick was talking to her while she had gone on a voyage of past time, conscious that parts of her were igniting like lighting an old stove that needed fanning. Frederick was explaining the role that Giuseppe had played with him in the conversion and restoration of the house and garden but he could see Joan had been thrown off kilter by this younger man and that she was not listening.

Giuseppe joined them with a mug of coffee, having gulped the remains of the juice from the jug.

"Giuseppe, come sit down with us, pull up a chair. Now, listen, before I forget, I need to ask you what to do about my laundry. I have a heap of washing to get done from the beds and bathrooms and I took it to the village to the Nonna and I've been told she died at the church. I need to find a laundrette with machines to help get it done ... I can dry it here but it's much too heavy to wash by hand, even if Joan were to help me."

Joan raised a mascaraed eyebrow but continued to visually absorb the new guest who was sitting with his hairy legs spread out before her.

"I heard about that, I hadn't seen her in a while but nearly everyone in the village knew her" said Giuseppe. "Such a hard working woman. Lost her husband in the war and then had to take in washing to survive so my Mum told me and never married again, but had a fair few gentleman callers of an evening apparently."

"I didn't know that about her, I only used her laundry service a few times."

That's evident thought Joan.

"Have you considered buying a washing machine Frederick? A friend of mine Pedro works with his father in an Electrical shop and he showed me a new machine called a Candy with a glass door at the front. It's made here in Italy and is selling so fast they just cannot make enough of them. Shall I ask him to set up a demonstration for you? It's fully automatic, a new idea, you put the laundry in, add special washing powder and come back after an hour or two when it's ready to dry."

"Well, I hadn't thought of that. What a good idea. What do you think Joan? Does that sound a sensible idea? I expect they are pricey."

Joan was fixated on the brilliant white incisors. They were identical to her first love. Could this fellow be his son? His handsome features morphed in her mind so that the unforgotten features of her lover became this man's face before her.

"It sounds eminently sensible to me Frederick. It will get you into the habit of keeping clean white linen always ready for eventualities like me or other guests turning up. Your guests won't have to sleep in soiled sheets, nor use greying towels." She smiled at Giuseppe knowingly, she hadn't taken her eyes off him.

"But where will I put it Giuseppe? It will need water and electricity and a drain."

"Oh don't worry about that Frederick, I will soon be able to put those services in for you. I think outside next to the lavatory would be a good place. The machine won't come to harm in this climate. A little lean-to roof perhaps to protect it from the rain. I will fix it with Pedro now if you like and see what can be done ... can I use the phone to ring him at his shop?"

"Certainly, go ahead, no time like the present." Giuseppe went up to the house to make the call.

"Such a helpful young man isn't he Joan? He has been a godsend in getting this place done. A real now person. I am very fond of him."

"He reminds me of someone I used to know very well. He is ... she searched for a word that wasn't too forward nor revealing ... delightful and very handsome." She looked less drawn and tired, enlivened. "He seems to like you too Frederick."

Giuseppe returned and sat.

"That's all arranged Fred. In Verona tonight at 6 and they will take your washing in and demonstrate the machine and then you fetch it back all washed later on and if you buy a machine that service is complimentary and if you dont you owe them 10,000 Lira for the laundry. How does that sound?"

Frederick went over and kissed Giuseppe on each cheek. Joan felt she needed a reason to do the same.

"Perfect. That's our evening fixed then Joan, or rather rearranged from what I was suggesting earlier, unless of course you would rather stay home here? A bag or two of laundry and an evening meal out near the electrical store in Verona? I said he was a now person didn't I" he laughed.

"Delightful" she said again observing not only the wonderful smile from Giuseppe but thinking *He knows that I hate changing arrangements at short notice.* "And, even if you decide it's too much money to invest you will at least get that bundle of grubby items in the car washed and get it pegged on the line tomorrow, I think you should take those stiff grey towels that are on the line too?" she volunteered.

Although her speech was in autopilot disapproving of the circumstance in which she had been placed, Joan was in her own past-lover world as the men conversed in Italian. The sound was musical and she was the one who detested music, but this sound was verbal opera for her. She smiled at Giuseppe as often as possible so as to see the teeth gleam back. She did the same to Frederick so as to not show favour, but the brown tombstones that grinned back had a deadening effect on her mood. Her mind was in a very different place, writhing, squirming, panting with the pleasures of the flesh she had once experienced. She felt thirty years younger inside her old semi-emoliated crust. Giuseppe had ignited feelings that she had put in cold storage for the past quarter century. It was unsettling. After a while she arose

"I will just clear the table and wash-up the things. You chaps catch up on whatever it is you need to discuss."

After a quick visit to the clanking lavatory she gathered the dishes, put on her gloves and started on the sink. Everything was removed and put on the big kitchen table, the sink itself received the first thorough scour, then one by one, piece by piece she set about reorganising his cabinets and their contents to bring some logic and ergonomic sense to the space. He had stuff all over the place. It was as though each moving-in box was emptied into any available cupboard in the order that the boxes were opened. From now on plates would be near bowls and serving dishes and cups near saucers and glasses near jugs. She would make sense of it all. But first, the cupboard interiors needed a thorough wipe and virtually everything within needed degreasing. The morning dissolved, like the grease.

9. FREDERICK

"We ought leave at about four Joan, to give me time to find this place. I don't have a map of Verona and Giuseppe gave me some basic directions but I am not that familiar with it. I've been to the Arena before of course." He looked around the kitchen.

"My goodness this all looks clean and tidy Joan. Only yesterday did I give it a good tidy but it looks like you have taken it to another level altogether."

"I just hope you will be able to find things now that I've put them back in some sensible order and you even have some space in the dresser drawers. Let me show you what I've done this past couple of hours. Where is your young friend?"

"Giuseppe will be in to say goodbye in a mo."

She heard the hiss and clank and understood.

"Goodbye Joan, It was very nice to meet you. I see you have brought a good woman's touch to this kitchen already" he grinned.

Joan removed her rubber gloves and held his biceps expecting a kiss on each cheek but instead he leaned over and tenderly kissed her forehead, despite a facefull of frizz. She melted. Such tenderness from such strength of frame.

"Perhaps I will see you again this week" she said meekly looking toward the floor but inadvertently looking into his groin.

"You will."

The motorbike left with a throb and Joan was surprised by her own thoughts which moderated around *I wonder how many cubic centimetres he has there between those strong thighs?* And she reprimanded herself internally for such lewd thoughts, never before had she thought such smut. She was both disgusted and elated within herself.

Frederick was opening and closing cabinet doors which brought her back to her present.

"Joan, you have performed a miracle and found a place for everything. I shall treat you to a good supper later this evening. Meanwhile I had better help you sort out your bedroom and find room for your clothes." She smiled but was elsewhere.

The remainder of the day turned into one of sorting out his upstairs bedroom before she could find space to sort out her room below. By three o clock all the preparations that he should have done before she arrived were now complete and Joan had made a shopping list of household necessities for him to get this evening or at least soon.

"Joan, did you ever meet my assistant Miss Prentice? I don't think you did. Coincidentally, her name was Joan as well and she used to organise me at work. Marvellous woman with a remarkable resemblance to Dick Emery. You seem to have done her job here today, I can't thank you enough."

"Who is Dick Emery?"

"He's a TV personality, very popular at the moment with his own show. He dresses up as a sex-starved spinster called Hettie. It's quite hilarious. For me especially, because it's the spitting image of Joan Prentice. But Joan was a wonderful organiser, like you are here. I really do miss the English humour on the TV. Here the TV is just voluptuous women pouting on second rate game shows."

"I don't have a television Frederick, it's not something I subscribe to, popular entertainment seems to revolve around smut. My friend has a television and she is forever watching that abominable Charlie Drake. I hope you don't see me as a sex starved spinster" she withered within. *Clearly I am.*

"Oh no Joan, you told me you haven't been married, so you can't be a spinster, can you?" but the remark was lost on her. "Now would you like a sandwich before we head off to Verona? It's an hour's drive and I want an hour to find the place. We can't be late because that laundry will soon get the mildew in this heat."

"No Frederick, you have something, I'm not hungry. I want to get ready if you are taking me to dinner this evening. Will we be going with top up or top down on the car? Will I need a headscarf and neck wrap? And what sort of place this evening, formal or informal?"

"How about top down on the way there and top up on the way home tonight, and informal dining Joan, we will find a trattoria nearby. The district this shop is in is on the main road into town and from what I remember is quite a smart area so there will be somewhere nice I'm sure. We will find somewhere with tables outside, it should be warm, there's no wind."

Frederick eventually found the frying pan and the eggs and butter and made himself an egg sandwich but breaking the egg was an action that still hurt his purlicue which appeared to be healing after the scratch. Joan meanwhile had found a box to stand on to look in the mirror. Her hair was still standing on end but she thought it made her look a little younger and more modern and Giuseppe seemed to like it like that, more natural than her usual tight perm. She touched her forehead where he had kissed her and stood looking at herself daydreaming for a good five minutes. *Teeth so white and a perfect smile and luscious glossy Italian lips.* Her mind was awash, like being fifteen. She resolved to leave her hair in this natural state for this holiday at least and just put a brush through it. The hairbrush was packed next to the shoe brush so after doing her hair she groomed her hush puppies and was able to remove most of the marks that the travel had wrought upon them. She held them aloft, pleased with her investment in them, the assistant had said they will brush up well if she invested in the care kit and for once it seemed to be true. Only the hand creme had left an oily stain. She hung her crimplene frock that she had forgotten she had on whilst doing all the household chores. Normally at home she would wear her housecoat. She had packed that so it was very remiss of her to undertake housework without so much as a pinnie. However, it didn't show any signs of being worn for the purpose. She had brought three headscarves along, a sheer pinkish brown one, a sateen one and a thicker woven one with some silvery threads. She considered the climatic conditions for the forthcoming journey and decided to take all three. The woven one for the top down journey tied under the chin, the sateen around her neck and the sheer for the cafe if they sat outside and there was a draught or breeze. She chose a sensible skirt, not wool and smart heels and then laid out some fresh underwear. It was time to give the shower another go although she wouldn't use the new lavender Castile soap but instead the Camay beauty bar that she had brought along. Somehow, the shower didn't seem so bad this time.

Frederick couldn't remember where he should put the pan and butter and eggs after he had washed them so he left them on the side to ask Joan later. He felt much better for a sandwich and knowing he had a plan for all this laundry. He went upstairs and gathered another pile of shirts and clothes that Joan had set aside for the wash during the tidying. He thought he would have no choice but to buy a washing machine now that he had at least three loads. He also better go fetch those grey towels off the line. *This new machine will certainly earn its keep.*

10. JOAN

It was a lovely afternoon for the drive. The headscarf with the additional satin scarf holding the corners snug around the nape made for a comfy drive and with just a handbag on her lap she had a more comfortable ride than last night.

Frederick had had the courage earlier to get the bundle from the boot and shake it out and fold it neatly into piles of bedding, towels and clothes whites and coloured to make the whole experience less embarrassing at the shop. He folded his underpants in such a way to hide the embarrassing marks from the shop assistant. The lot was however starting to pong.

By fiveish they were on the outskirts of Verona and the sky was turning orange.

"Could we stop somewhere Frederick and put the top on now because we are getting blasted by fumes from the trucks and cars?" asked Joan.

"Certainly, as soon as I see a spot to pull over. There's no wind and the natural basin of the surrounding mountains keeps the smog over the city sometimes. It looks like it is such a day today."

"I didn't realise they had such pollution here Frederick. It really is making me feel quite sick."

He pulled into a bus stop, hopped out and pulled up the cloth roof and then wound up his window. Joan did the same, but both windows had a half inch gap.

It's not far now Joan, here are some directions from Giuseppe. Sinistra and Destra means left and right. We are on Via Luganano just now and must make a left soon when we cross a railway line. Keep your eyes peeled for me. Again she was on the wrong side and facing the oncoming traffic.

They found the shop at the intersection of half a dozen roads, all of which were busy with cars and there were no traffic lights so drivers were sticking their hands out of their windows to indicate where they intended to go. It was an improbable convergence of cars and trucks and although they had half an hour to spare, it was just a contest of who could squeeze into the spaces drivers allowed for each other. A few tempers were drawn but it kept moving. He was able to park within a few metres of the shop.

"I will just nip inside and find out where they want me to take this laundry Joan. You wait there will you in case the car is in someone's way."

Outside, the pavement was broken from heavy delivery trucks breaking the marble and granite laid centuries ago. In the window there was an electric mangle next to a cardboard cutout of a voluptuous model looking delighted into a non-existent modern appliance that had been sold, taken away and instead she was admiring a tin bath that had been put in its place. Inside the shop was the Alladin's cave of any Italian shop. This was not Rumbelow's, they wouldn't win awards for display. Fridges, cookers and washers stood this way and that, interspersed with other modern and old electrical goods like radios and mixers piled above. Cardboard boxes lined the walls and a man sat at a desk in the rear corner surrounded by metal spikes with papers speared onto them.

"Hello, I'm looking for Pedro? I've been sent by Giuseppe about a washing machine."

"He will be back at 6. He is out delivering one just now. Soon we shall have a waiting list for them." said the older man and left it at that so Frederick went back out to the car until 6. Joan had a handkerchief over her mouth and nose.

"I won't be able to sit at a street cafe Frederick in amongst all these fumes I'm afraid. I had no idea there would be smog like this. And everyone passing by is making more smog by smoking in the street as if it's the height of fashion to do so. I haven't seen anyone yet who isn't smoking. They are smoking in their cars, on the buses, even on bicycles. Don't they realise they are killing themselves?" She covered her face with the hanky and a scarf.

"Well I'm sorry to say that Pedro won't be back until six and we have to wait for this demonstration but the shop isn't very interesting Joan so I doubt you would want to go in. I have just come back for my pipe so as to have a smoke out here while we wait. I'm sure it won't be long. If you can't beat 'em and all that" and he lit up and stood under a tree observing commerce at work along this street of merchants. An hour later Pedro parked the open flatbed truck in the space in front of the Sunbeam.

"Ah Signori, I forgot about you coming. Come, come inside. Bring your laundry and your wife too, she will be interested to see the workings of the machine."

"She is not my wife and she isn't interested in washing machines" said Fred as he gathered his smalls and damp towels for the first most urgent smelly load.

Pedro was an enthusiastic salesman. He had set up a demonstration area in the yard behind the shop.

"So Mr Frederick, this is the machine. Put your dirty items in the porthole making sure to leave some space at the top, do not stuff it full to the brim" indicated Pedro.

"Now I show you the program dial which you turn like this and press down like so and then wind it back. The program we want here is for hot whites and this table shows you what to choose" he indicated the printed choices. "And then we add a cup of suitable powder that does not foam like ordinary powders into this compartment here and then finally we press this grey button and the machine will start."

The machine took on water and Frederick lit his pipe watching the garments go around getting gradually soaked for four or five minutes.

"So if you come back here at say 8pm just before we close your washing will be done and afterwards I will explain the prices and and you can take it away all clean and decide."

"Oh, well I have a little more laundry in the car actually Pedro, I didn't know how long each wash would take but I have sheets that are too big and heavy for me to wash by hand and they rather need doing now."

"Well Mr Frederick, if you can commit to buying the machine now then I will ask my mother to attend your other laundry in the morning in this machine and let's say it will be all ready by tomorrow afternoon. May I explain the delivered price to you now and then you can bring in your other items once we are agreed."

Frederick knew he was in a cleft stick and liked the young man enough to see that he was as honest as Giuseppe had indicated, so they went to the father's desk and worked on the numbers. *Maybe paying a few Lira more than a comparable department store but this little business deserved to earn a living and they were being very obliging with my laundry* he thought.

Joan was pale and distressed when he returned to the car, her delicate lace edged hanky was over her mouth and nose. He gathered the big bundles of sheets and grey towels from the boot and marched back into the shop, pipe on its last puffs of ash.

How much longer must I be here in this dire fug of traffic thought Joan just as Frederick bounced into his seat forgetting he had put his pipe in his back pocket and heard the familiar crack as the stem broke from the bowl under his weight.

"I'll return tomorrow morning Joan and collect the washing, they will deliver a machine later this week but it's costing a quarter million Lira for this new fully automatic machine. You just shove the washing in with powder and it does the entire job in under two hours. Quite amazing Joan. How are you feeling?"

"I'm feeling very sick Frederick, there is no escape from the fumes. Where is it all coming from? The sky is brown with it." She turned to look into her lap as he extracted the bowl of his pipe from his back pocket and popped it out of the window, he couldn't reach the stem.

"I understand Joan, let's turn around and get out into the fresh air in the countryside and find a trattoria on the way home so that I can treat you to some supper. I'm sorry it took so long."

He was thinking to himself, *this is turning out to be a very expensive week of entertainment. I have to pay Giuseppe for the new water and power supply and drive back all this way to fetch the laundry and now more expense on yet another pipe, that was a nice briar, that one.*

Just five kilometres up out of town the air was clear, skies golden and Joan remained still. Frederick pulled up outside a quiet Trattoria just off a village road and stepped out to open Joan's door, his hand was again giving him some pain. There is no way he would have been able to manage the laundry by hand. They took a table by the door with only half a dozen other customers and a couple of old fellows at the bar putting the world to right. By her demeanour Joan was presenting herself to Frederick as a delicate female, one unable to withstand the rigours, sights and smells of modernity. When unfamiliar with an environment she clearly had limits of endurance that constrained her and those around her. The line between acceptable and unacceptable was tight and clearly drawn in her mind. Others had the task to navigate and discover this line. Frederick determined he would steer the evening once they had ordered an acceptable fish dish.

11. FREDERICK

"The eyes are the window to the soul or so they say," said Frederick observing Joan's rheumy eyes.

He was comparing hers subconsciously to the clarity and brightness of the North Star that had appeared in the clear evening sky.

Joan was sipping a white whine as she pronounced it, frequently adding aitches into words beginning with a W.

"This is a very dry whine Frederick, I've not had a white Valpolicella before from a regional vineyard. It makes one's teeth dry and almost powdery and I think the teeth say a lot about a person. I do hope this doesn't remove my enamel."

"It's what they grow all around here Joan and it's not sold elsewhere as they mainly make red wines. Some of the lads who worked on the Canonica go treading grapes at the wineries of a weekend with bare feet and sometimes virtually completely bare. This bottle will be from the last batch of it. From next year onwards it will be called Soave and only reds will be called Valpolicella."

Joan pursed her lips. "Should I be drinking it if it could be unsanitary, one never knows what could be on the feet of those young men. Although I will say it improves with the second and subsequent sips. What were you saying about the windows of the soul?"

"Your eyes look tired tonight Joan and I was just thinking about my past career. A lifetime looking through lenses into so many souls."

"Yes I am tired Frederick, I was sitting in the car a long time in that traffic. I watched the pandemonium at that junction. Six roads all converging and yet there wasn't a single accident. Quite bizarre. You would never see that in England." Having made her mark, she continued "do you really think you have seen their souls?"

"Yes Joan, I do. Nearly every eye I have looked into almost begs to tell me a story. Did you know that the retina is really a part of the brain? It's the only part of the brain that isn't inside the brain or rather not encapsulated by the skull."

"Well Frederick, when in nursing we did have it explained that what the retina sees is directly processed there and then sending cues and reaction at the speed of light directly into autonomic systems of the body. If you see a number nine bus coming toward you, about to mow you down, you don't stand about thinking I better move from here, it just happens, you shift, sharpish, taking in the surroundings around you" she said.

"I think that old expression is true about the soul because we are really just our brain carried around by a skeleton with muscles and limbs, so we feed ourselves to keep our body alive which is really about keeping our brain, our soul, alive isn't it?"

"I suppose it is Frederick."

"And, Joan, when I looked into someone's eyes with my various trial lenses I was also looking through their lens as well, the one that sits between the cornea on the outside and the retina, being the brain - their soul, on the inside. Occasionally they have their spectacles on so I am then looking through three lenses, but you get my point."

"Ok I am following you" she said as the waiter brought the first course and refilled her glass.

"So I get a magnified image on my retina of their retina. Do you get what I mean that I am seeing their soul magnified?"

"So what does their soul look like Frederick?" She asked as she shoved all the lettuce to one side of the plate.

"At a physical level I am looking at lots of veins and arteries, thin lines branching all over, bringing blood and oxygen to their retina to keep it alive and functioning for all those cones and rods, the light sensitive nerve endings to be able to do their seeing, to send messages at the speed of light into their responsive bit of brain for processing."

He continued as Joan fiddled with the crudites and a small piece of tomato, the waiter topped her up.

"But at a different level, at a spiritual level, beyond the physical, I can see or feel the person's soul. My face is inches from theirs. Maybe they never get as close to another human being ever. Our faces almost touch. My eye is looking at theirs with a bright light shining at them but they cannot see me or my retina through that eye. It's all one way.

Their soul is revealed to me, but not vice versa. It's a very odd position to be in Joan. It's highly personal and intimate in a way. Of course there are professional boundaries to be adhered to. Yet sometimes I think my patients are going to kiss me. In fact once when I was examining a young RAF recruit he did just that. It really was quite a surprise."

"Do you think he was one of those hommersexuels?" she asked with the peculiar intonation that came from a middle class background ... a sort of 'us and them' attitude wrapped in a confection of both disgust and intrigue.

"Without doubt Joan, but his sexual predilections weren't the point, it was that I had seen his soul. This young chap was just an example of hundreds, maybe thousands of men and women I have seen at close quarters over the years. He was lonely, lost, frightened of his future, befuddled by a domineering mother and an obsequious father - I met the whole family one by one. But his soul, Joan. spoke these emotions and more. This chap who was, say, twenty seven and in the prime of life was about to be sent up in a plane to foreign parts to possibly lose his life before it had really begun. He had faced odd strictures in his upbringing and he didn't know himself. He wanted to be himself but he didn't know how. He felt he was a misfit. He wanted to be happy but he had had no joy. He had no reference points, no cardinals. And his soul cried out for help Joan, it really did. I think that is why he kissed me, to see if he could find some love by an instant reaction. Clearly, I could have been outraged and grossly offended or reported him for misconduct and made a terrible fuss. But I didn't, because this was not an eye examination for him, but a personal healing. And he was but one of thousands of clients where I have looked into their brains and felt their unhappiness, their aloneness, their inner kindness, their upset, their basic lack of understanding of where they fit. You know, I think that is it. A soul needs a place it can fit. Like getting a suit or a smart dress ... if it doesn't fit, it doesn't feel right, doesn't look right and is a waste of effort and money and can't be shown to the world. If you know where you fit and you feel comfortable then that is the basis for showing yourself to the world. You need to fit and feel comfortable in your own skin."

"You would have been in terrible trouble with your professional body Frederick had that business of kissing a client ever got out. You could have been struck off. Weren't you worried about that?"

"Not at all Joan. The chap kissed me. I was close to his face and he suddenly could not control his own soul and needed to kiss someone close. It could have been you or Miss Prentice or whoever was nearest. He was at his boiling point and immediately afterwards was dramatically apologetic saying such things as 'Oh dear God, I don't know what came over me, I am so very sorry and would you like me to leave now' and things such as that. I settled him."

"What did you do about it Frederick?" asked Joan

"I told him to wait in the chair a moment. I turned on the light and opened the blind and called Miss Prentice in to sit as a chaperone in a chair reserved for parents when I am examining a child. Miss Prentice sat down in the corner and the chap was as red as a beetroot. I took to my consulting chair and then reached out my hand to hold his hand firmly like a father to a son. I suspect that neither his father, nor his mother had held his hand since he was a baby, if even then. He needed human touch, nothing more. And I said something like ... 'I have examined your eyes very carefully today and can see that you have a number of issues which will preclude you from National Service on front line duties. This means I will be prescribing you some spectacles and that you will be confined to desk duties only within the RAF and probably be posted to Lansdown in Bath for the duration. That will be my recommendation to your superiors who sent you to me today. I've asked Miss Prentice here, waving my hand toward her, to come into the room to act as the witness to my examination. I can see that you are a sensitive young man and doubtless highly intelligent so I will also be adding to my report that you may be a suitable candidate for the Special Operations Executive at Bletchley Park'. And with that Joan, I think I gave that young man a place in which his soul would fit like a tailor making a good suit. I had done what was right for the boy."

"But Frederick, it's common knowledge that Bletchley Park and the SOE was rife with hommersexuals."

She had said it again in that Home Service ministry manner and it grated on him.

"Exactly Joan. By putting reference to that in my report I was alluding to his commanding officers that this young fellow needed to be around like minded men so that the war effort would get the best out of him. The Romans and the Greeks did the same with their armies. The Sacred Band of Thebes from the fourth century before Christ comprised just male couples who would fight to the death for each other, such was their love and loyalty."

"Really?" the waiter exchanged their plates for the main course and refilled her glass. "Have you seen him since?"

"I've heard from him. He worked in intelligence until the end of the war and then became a lawyer in Chambers. He wrote me a very charming letter alluding to his life with a friend without saying anything specific."

She adjusted her shawl and was about to speak but then reconsidered and refrained, inserting her fork in the fish so as to roll the skin away from the flesh. They remained silent a while as they ate. Frederick poured the last of the bottle into Joan's dry glass.

"Tell me Frederick, what do you see in my eyes, where is my soul?"

"One should never mix business with pleasure Joan. But I can see you are tired and sensitive to the environment around you. Your eyes look clouded and sore this evening after the journey and the tribulation of being in that dreadful smog in Verona. I think I should look more properly toward the end of your week. But I could say you have mislaid something and haven't yet found it, but hope to."

They exchanged small talk and then Frederick settled up.

12. JOAN

Frederick was up at 7am, cool showered and had been to the village and back by 8.45 for groceries, another loaf, a pipe at the tabbachi and then on the way through went to advise Giuseppe that he had bought a machine from Pedro and needed the wiring and water pipework done. As it happened Giuseppe wasn't awake, but his mother took the message, pleased to know her son would be out from under her feet. As he drove off he heard her alarming call up to Giuseppe that would have woken the village.

Back at the house Joan was snug in the feather bed but awake. If that cat had been in she wasn't aware of it and she had slept well. She heard the Sunbeam and guessed Frederick had been to the village. He called through from the kitchen.

"Joan dear, I need to go back to get the laundry this morning and settle up for the new machine, so I'm going to lay the breakfast table for you and have a cup of coffee and will be leaving shortly." He was still calling toward her bedroom door as she emerged in a full length pink satin embroidered dressing gown. "Oh, well I guess you heard that" he said as she nodded.

"Good Morning Frederick, I didn't hear you rise. You must have been early. I was dead to the world until ten minutes ago."

He was filling the kettle and unloading the shopping.

"I have some bananas for you and another fresh loaf like yesterday's, there's plenty to eat. I will have a coffee and slice of toast and leave you to get yourself some breakfast. You know where everything is, which is more than I do. Where does this frying pan go?"

"Give it to me" she said, "I've been meaning to say about a cat that comes into my bedroom during the night. Is it your cat or just a stray? Is it the one that cut your hand?" She reached out to see his hand which was slowly healing. "How does it get in?" She put the pan in a drawer under some bowls.

"It adopted me when I moved here. Foolishly I fed it when it was a scrawny little thing and now look at it. Vicious though, when it doesn't want to be disturbed. I was making the bed before you arrived and it lashed out. It must come in through that missing window pane in the door in the bedroom."

"Let me get my tea sachet and I will sit with you, whilst you have your toast."

They sat at the outside table and she then noticed the missing window pane. She had noticed a draught around her ankles and now knew the source and why the curtains fluttered.

"Couldn't your young chap Giuseppe attend to that and replace it?"

"It's one of those jobs I keep forgetting to ask him about Joan. But I will. Maybe you will remind me because he will come back this week and get the pipes and wires done ready for the new washer."

"How exciting Frederick and how modern you will be. I don't know anyone with an Automatic Washing Machine. What is it called again?"

"What do you mean, what is it called? Shall I call it Doris?"

"No, I meant what brand is it? I want to tell my friends when I get back."

"It is a Candy Superautomatic 5."

'Then call it Candy! The American word for confectionery."

"I think Candy is a Jazz trumpet number by Lee Morgan. Do you know it?"

"Music is not one's scene Frederick, I'm tone deaf to it. It annoys me."

"That reminds me I must get some flex to mend the wireless, The old flex partially caught fire Joan, the copper wire was covered in cloth. Lucky you didn't get an electric shock when you tripped. They will have some at the washing machine shop won't they."

"It's a pity you have to drive all that way again today."

"Would you like to come with me this morning?"

Not bloody likely thought Joan but she made one of her many available negative faces which was enough.

"I understand. I don't mind going again, we do need those clean sheets. We will be pegging out all afternoon. Meanwhile you can get some rest and settle down on the recliners where we were going to be yesterday before things took a turn. I better head off now and see you in a few hours with a car full of clean wet linens."

"And a length of flex Frederick, don't forget for your wireless" she called after him.

He gathered his keys, cheque book and wallet and left her to it. Joan swished about the space that she had to herself for a while. Her sachet was still brewing and possibly going cold. She laid up a plate with a proper breakfast for one. Her usual when she was at home and nobody else to please. Then took her tea into the bedroom and was choosing some clothes for the day ahead. She could wear a swimsuit perhaps if it was going to be warm enough. Standing on the box she felt her hair was pretty good in this new informal style although the roots were going rather white. Her eyes certainly looked better than last evening. She could pass for ten years younger if anyone were interested.

It would be good to strip this bed she considered, but if she did and the fresh sheets were not dry by tonight, the dirty linen would have to go on again. So instead she plumped it all and made it look respectable despite the bloodstain on the counterpane.

It had been months since she wore the bathing suit. It was a nice Contessa one, by the same makers as her girdle which she had recently abandoned, and had the plunging back to it which went down to the panties, which she need not wear today. *I have a nice back* she thought *might as well get a tan.* She decided to wear that and the dressing gown on top for the day. She could dress for dinner tonight. She found her mascara and took it with the breakfast tray down the brick path to the pond. It was already nearly 10 and gloriously warm.

She was just peeling the banana when she heard a familiar sound of a motorbike. *Could it be his motorbike?* She fluttered to its sound as it came closer. Sure enough it was Giuseppe. He called out as he approached the house but there was no response. He returned to his bike and had a bag of tools and materials which she watched him carry back toward the outside lavatory.

70

Leaving her tray a while she meandered up to the house and stood quietly behind him. His white khaki shorts were grubby around the edges and a little threadbare and very short in the modern style so that his massive thighs went from his knees all the way to firm buttocks encased within. His strength oozed out of his torso. He was a little over six feet tall whereas she was five feet one. He crouched down to look at where he was going to set up the washing machine space, calculating how he could get cold water and electricity to the spot and how the machine would drain away. She could look down the back of his shorts. His hairy back and legs met and formed a wave down to his backside. She was being unseemly in her vulgar consumption of this lothario and it was making her heady. She felt heat.

He stood and turned and jumped back.

"Oh, you surprised me, I didn't know you were there."

She blushed profusely and felt more heat and realised she was clutching the part peeled banana. It could not have appeared more inappropriate. Her pose was not lost on him.

"Good morning Giuseppe.' She held out a hand to defuse the situation and simmer down but in doing so handed him the banana which he took.

He held it in front of his massive chest, silently and slowly he continued where she left off and peeled the skin down for her, one length at a time, slowly revealing the circumcised inner fruit. He held it toward her mouth. Her heart was pumping blood at such a pace that it made her ears go bang bang bang. She opened her mouth and he inserted the tip of the banana and then withdrew it before she could bite, then did the same again, and then again. The suggestiveness was palpable. The moment magical.

What would Betty Friedland say to this situation? Am I revealing Feminine Mystique?

Quiet. She pursed her lips so that he had to push the banana in and then withdraw it and then again and leaving a few moments, again. She did not bite. Instead she gave out a little moan. And he did the entire routine again. She felt she might orgasm right there in her swimsuit and dressing gown.

71

This time he peeled the banana completely and inserted the base into his own mouth and bent forward to offer the other end to her. She complied and sucked it in and blew it out. He smiled and she saw those wonderful teeth again holding onto a banana that she wanted deep inside her mouth.

Housework and Passive sex are not fulfilling.

He bent forward further so that the fruit pushed back into her throat and his lips just touched hers ... and then he withdrew so that she did not gag. His hands were now on her shoulders, slowly pushing the dressing gown apart revealing the swimsuit below. He sucked at the fruit and ate it, grinning widely. His eyes engaged with hers unwavering and unmoving. The gown was on the floor behind her. He moved the straps of the costume over her shoulders and pulled them down her arms as he crouched down before her. Right here on the patio by the back door, adjacent to the outside lavatory. But for Joan, she was in heaven. She had not been seduced like this for a quarter century. Her brain was saying over and over the same line

If not now, then when?

Her breasts were before him and he tenderly kissed them, using his tongue and lips with exquisite expertise to thrill her senses so that they perked and enlarged and as she looked down her knees trembled as she saw that he had pushed his trousers down to his knees and his erection was curved upward toward her, thick and long. She had never seen such largess. It was a colossus. A single eye that she hoped would penetrate her very fabric within a short while. He pulled the swimsuit further down and held her hand firmly and carefully as she stepped out of it to stand before him outside the back door completely naked. He bent forward and licked her belly button and then down to her pubic hair that she had not trimmed and then a little further until she squealed again and again. And only then did she slide her fingers into his glossy mane of hair and hold his head moving her fingers around his earlobes discovering his manliness and his strength being gently caressed by his tongue and lips kissing her most intimate place.

As he stood, he gathered her up so that her legs parted and naturally wrapped around his strong torso and only then did he speak.

"Shall we go to your bedroom?"

And she whispered "yes please." *Yes. Please.*

As he carried her, his member pressed her from underneath and behind. He would take her soon to a place of elation. But first he sat her on the edge of the pine table, the first station on this journey, in the kitchen. *I want this ride, full fare, the entire journey.* She touched and held on to the train. At the tunnel he recognised her discomfort, she was unused to this journey. He started as a slow train before becoming a steady goods train, only later would he develop into an express. One after the other. Each stopping at stations on the way and every one with a valid ticket to ride.

Passive sex is not fulfilling.

They remained joined as he carried her to the bed and he sat on the edge, her astride. She pushed him back and he revealed his delicious grin, closing his eyes facing the ceiling.

Thus Active sex must be fulfilling. If not now, then when. Active not passive.

This engine was big enough to ride sidesaddle, in reverse and facing forward into the delicious grin of it. *This is Heavenly* crying out in the delight of orgasm after orgasm. This man had technique, veracity, strength and stamina whether above or below. It was relentless and Joan brought the journey to its conclusion on Frederick's soft feather bed, creaking, clanking, banging against the wall they shouted and cried out to each other in the final explosion, the tank blew its whistle again and again in the final bursts of steam. The journey was done.

13. FREDERICK

"Oh goodness Giuseppe, you are getting on well. The wire ready and the pipes in place to connect. I didn't know you would come here today. Well done" said Frederick.

"Ah, Frederick, you know me, how you say, the early bird catches the worm. I will need to get some wood to make a little roof for the machine but otherwise I had these small materials."

"Look here, Giuseppe, I have a little length of flex too and wonder whether you will repair my radio. Joan tripped on the wires a couple of days ago. Where is she by the way?"

"Joan is down near the pond, sleeping I think in the sun, she seemed exhausted earlier. I will do the flex another day if it is OK? I like to finish this job first."

"Yes of course, do you need my help? If not, I will bring the laundry. Pedro's mother finished all the bedding and towels and I need to peg it out down by the pond."

"I'm pleased you met Pedro and his mother, they are a good family and very fair with their customers. Be quiet down there Frederick, Joan is very fragile and needs to rest after her morning."

Giuseppe turned to concentrate on getting the pipes in place, amazed he could put on the facade with Frederick. He had been thinking about Joan, the older woman, slow to get going then tempestuous. Just a couple of hours ago and so unexpected. He was stirring again. Perhaps he could get a banana to snack upon and just eat it this time.

Once Joan had returned to earth, she had showered using Lavender soap, gathered her costume, gown and another banana and wobbled back to where she had been a hundred minutes earlier. For the first time in a quarter century she ate an entire banana in one sitting, a late breakfast. *From now on I will always have a full portion.* Giuseppe had showered after her, he was drenched in sweat, the bed was wet and he turned it back to air.

Frederick had settled his account with Pedro and had been given a bonus laundry basket. He obeyed Pedro's mother's instructions when she accompanied him to the hardware store where she told him to buy the boxes of Persil and Dixan. It certainly was an expensive day. He had never pegged out so much washing and it was all notably clean, fresh and white. Peering through the cypress Joan was sound asleep in just a bathing costume. She looked a lot better than he had seen her in years. The sun and rest were obviously doing her good. He gave Giuseppe a smack on his muscular bum when passing into the kitchen to prepare a supper for later. He assumed that Giuseppe would stay for supper, he generally did if he worked late. Frederick started peeling the carrots and thought to himself ... *I wonder if Giuseppe will stay the night but maybe he will be embarrassed to do that with Joan present. Let's wait until Joan is gone next week.*

"Something smells delicious" said Joan as she sidled alongside Frederick at the sink and she held his forearm as he was now peeling some potatoes. "Thank you for inviting me to stay this week Frederick, I think I shall be having a nice relaxing time."

Frederick thought it strange that she was tactile, she was generally so brittle and now seemed soft.

"Did you have a nice sleep Joan? You must have needed it after the stress of the past couple of days. Would you like a cup of tea - your special tea bags?"

"I will have whatever you are having Fred. Shall I make it? Would you like to have something together out on the terrace? Giuseppe has gone I think. I thought I heard a vehicle."

"Oh he will be back, he has gone to fetch some wood and things for the little roof to protect the machine. He took the Sunbeam, he moved his motorbike into the shade. He is coming back to have some supper with us this evening. I've made a chicken casserole type of dish, would that be alright?"

"I haven't eaten any chicken in years, but it sounds lovely. I'm pleased Giuseppe will be back, he is such a nice strong man isn't he Frederick. How did you meet him?"

Frederick put the kettle on and fetched the teapot down onto the tray.

"We met at the local osteria in the village. The owner, Pepe, a jovial fellow, great fun, always telling jokes, has a regular coterie of young guys who drink there and it's almost like an informal labour exchange. The local builders and anyone needing some job doing, like this washing machine, just tells Pepe and next thing you know you are hooked up with the right man. Giuseppe has been my right hand these past few years since I started this refurbishment, an angel."

He is certainly that, in spades she thought.

As he said it, he realised the unintended double entendre was more fact than fantasy. But Joan heard the remark from her perspective considering with some relish what Giuseppe's right hand had been doing with her a few hours ago. She blushed up a little but Frederick was pouring hot water. They took the tea and mugs out to the terrace.

"I've been in this dressing gown all day Frederick. I'll change for dinner, don't worry I haven't lost all respectability" she said smiling and thought to herself *not only have I done just that, lost my respectability, but I've become a complete slut and a liar and a pretty good one of both.*

"Oh, I have days like that Joan and mooch about the house in my underpants all day ... looking a sight for sore eyes. Sometimes the lads working here would catch me at the end of a hard day's work and pour wet cement into my underpants, as a protest I think. They thought it funny that an older man would mooch about like that. But you know around here they have a very relaxed and casual attitude about all manner of things that we in England are all buttoned up about. In comparison we are so Victorian in our attitudes. Not that I am suggesting that we should lower the moral tone, but we could be more relaxed about sex and age and sexuality. It's starting in England and I heard the expression the Swinging Sixties with Carnaby Street being shoved up as the epitome of fashion with mini skirts and flowery shirts but it goes deeper than that."

"I think I am coming to agree with your Frederick, It is quite a stress on the system to be utterly proper and seemly all the time. I should know. I've spent the past quarter century being the perfect old maid. And for what?"

Frederick was quite astonished at this admission by Joan. What had come over her? She was notoriously spinsterish in her manners and behaviours and frightfully brittle with correctness.

"Exactly Joan, Let it all hang out as they are saying." He poured the brown tea.

'This is a rather nice cuppa Frederick. You know I haven't had a cup of Breakfast tea for years. I lost the taste for it and then turned on to those Lemon flavour sachet bags. Perhaps it is those that have made me so sour?"

Sour. Old Maid? What is going on with this self flagellation suddenly? he thought.

"Someone said to me that people can either be a glass half full or glass half empty. But you know after the second world war there had been so much suffering and so much unhappiness around that it is only natural that there had to be some loosening of the corsets of life about now. We had it too bad for too long and people want to be themselves. I'm fortunate to have come here. It is a Catholic country with high church values but it has young people who intend to change many of those strictures and although they still respect family they seem to respect individual values too, becoming almost Buddhist in their views. Sex is sex and all that." said Frederick

"I think a lot comes from our parent's values Frederick. My aunt taught me alot about moral values and what was right and proper when I was a child and teenager. I spent a lot of time with my Aunt. She was a spinster, she had never married. She went to chapel at least once a week and generally more often. She read the bible over and over again, often referring to John Knox. But she had habits that she passed to me. How to lay a table, how to use a knife and fork correctly, how to choose one's napkins, how to pass the cruet ... what we might call table manners. How to resist discussing sex with anyone. How to steer a conversation onto what she called proper topics, how the weather could often be used in that way. You know she said it is always a useful phrase to say 'There may be fog by teatime I understand.' That sort of thing."

"Did you ever have a regular boyfriend Joan?"

"I did. He was lovely. The nicest man I ever wanted to meet. He made me feel so special. We had discussed marriage which we would arrange after he returned from the war, but sadly, he never returned, well not alive he didn't. He was a casualty of war and so I became one too. That was about twenty five years ago."

"And nobody since?"

"No one Frederick."

Up until now. She chose her words carefully because she realised she had just lost her second virginity, completely lost it, in complete fulfilment. And yet whilst asleep afterwards she also understood this was probably a transitory event. For her it was a passing chance to indulge in a handsome younger virile man who had the loveliest smile and maybe for him it was a bit of fun with an older woman. Although highly passionate, it was unexpected and all the more thrilling for that. Who would have thought that a bunch of bananas could have set off that wonderful chain of events.

"Love is but a Dream." sang Frederick

"Oh really?" asked Joan

"It's a song by The Harptones. It was on the other morning when you tripped over the wire."

"How does it go?"

"Something like;
Love is but a dream
It's what you make it
Always try to give
Don't ever take it.
But I can't remember any more."

"I hope they play it again."

"Not until Giuseppe replaces the wire, they won't."

At that point they heard the Sunbeam return. It had a few timbers poking up above the passenger seat through the open roof.

14. GIUSEPPE

Giuseppe had changed out of his working shorts and vest. He had washed his hair and been to a barbers near the woodyard. His smartest cream linen jeans and brogue shoes set off against a silk shirt made him look the part of eligible bachelor. He carefully unloaded the few timbers so as to not spoil the car or his clothes and then he was ready to socialise.

Joan had excused herself from the tea table and disappeared to her room to change out of her bathing costume and dressing gown which she had been in for nine hours - *apart from an engaging interlude.* Frederick helped stack the wood up against the wall of the lavatory ready for the next part of the project.

"You are looking very dashing young man. That colour suits you and your lovely olive complexion."
Frederick touched Giuseppe's cheek and felt decidedly old and scruffy. He imagined the young fellow had dressed up to impress Joan.

"I need to fetch in the laundry. Do you want to make yourself a drink or want to help me?"

"I will help you my friend. I will always help you Frederick. You know that. You have been good to me these past few years since you moved here."

Giuseppe held one end of the sheets that were fabulously white and now crisp whilst Frederick was at the other end and they folded in rhythm as a duo. Younger and older man. When they met in the middle Giuseppe leaned forward and kissed Frederick on the cheek. They did the same routine half a dozen times and when they had finished the sheets they folded the towels the same way. Their friendship was mutually pleasing like an uncle and nephew and oddly the kisses were an exchange of care rather than sexual or passionate. A form of bonding that suited them both as it was and who was to say they should not do that, they did not need to ask nor explain. It was just as it was.

Giuseppe being the stronger of the two carried the huge pile of laundry up to the house whilst Frederick gathered the basket and the tea tray that Joan had forgotten earlier.

"Shall I help you make the bed Frederick?"

"That would be kind. Let's leave one set of linens down here for Joan's room and take these up to where I'm sleeping this week."

Frederick checked and stirred the casserole and they ascended to the second bedroom. Giuseppe didn't mention that Joan's sheets would need to be changed tonight.

"This lot will be going in the new machine in a day or two Frederick and you can try that out. Hopefully my pipes won't leak." *I've drained those thoroughly enough this morning* he thought. "Shall we fold them again to keep them neat ready for the wash?"

And as they folded and paced across the wooden bedroom boards they grinned and met lip to lip. Joan was below and could see up through the floorboards and hear them clearly doing the house chores. She was comforted by their camaraderie and friendship and occasional laughs. The rug under his bed saved Joan watching Giuseppe belt Frederick across the bottom with a pillow or any of their intimate behaviour. As they descended they put the fresh towels in the shower on the landing and Joan emerged from her bedroom, her hair saturated waiting to frizz in her new informal style.

"Do you have a hairdryer Frederick?"

Frederick pointed toward his shaven head and raised an eyebrow.

"Don't worry Joan, we have nice clean towels and sheets here. I will dry your hair and then make your bed for you" said Giuseppe as he grabbed her hand, gathered the linen and pulled her back into her bedroom, shutting the door saying to Frederick "you need to put the potatoes on!"

"Oh Giuseppe, you are so forward and bold in front of Frederick like that. He will think we are lovers."

"Aren't we?" He put the linen on the dresser, turned around, picked her up, laid her on the unmade bed and climbed atop of her on his elbows keeping his weight off her tiny frame. They remained respectably fully clothed. "Kiss me and tell me we are not lovers." She didn't need telling twice.

After tongues writhed together for a few moments he hopped off.

"Now let's dry your hair. A bone dry towel and vigorous massage as if towelling a dog after a rainy walk." He put her hair into a state of fright but Joan went with it.

"I love it. It's the new you. A statement to the world. Joan the free" with which he planted another kiss with those luscious lips firmly onto her softening mouth. Withdrawing again and catching the corner of the ruffled sheets he said ...

"Let's strip this, instead of each other. Go over the other side and let's fold these. I just did this upstairs." He pointed to the ceiling. "With Frederick. Let's fold like this and then meet in the middle."

And as they met her bent forward and he kissed her. And so they went on repeating the actions from the room above. He even thrashed her lightly across the buttocks with a pillowcase.

"These will all get cleaned up in the new machine this week and now let's put on the fresh and clean so you get a good night's sleep tonight."

"Don't worry about that Giuseppe. After today I will sleep like a baby. I've been wondering about your age. Do you want to tell me how old you are?"

"I'm thirty one Joan, just last week."

"A wonderful age. At the peak of fitness. You are old enough to know what you like, where to get it and how to ask nicely. You are half my age Giuseppe."

"You are a wise woman Joan and a good lover too if I may say, just laying there and offering yourself and then taking control. Age is only a number. You are only as old as the person you feel."

"Oh really, well I really felt you Giuseppe."

He grinned at her with those lovely teeth as they returned to the kitchen to help Frederick with laying the patio table for supper.

"I've prepared a hearty chicken casserole with mash and veg, as fuel for Giuseppe and all his hard graft today drilling and joining and

81

getting us ready for the machine. The breasts looked so good this morning that I couldn't resist them when at the market and just look at the size of this nourishing carrot."

He held it aloft and it was thick and about nine inches long with a tight bunch of green fronds at one end. Joan caught Giuseppe's eye as he was grinning. They carried the dishes out to the table.

"That's very thoughtful of you Frederick" said Giuseppe.

"It's been a hard day but one of the most enjoyable days I have had for months. How about you Joan? Have you had a nice day? You slept a lot, you must have been exhausted."

"A lovely day thank you Giuseppe. Really relaxing and I feel I have unwound years of tension in a matter of hours. The rest has done me good and I'm looking forward to this meal because I'm ravished."

"I think you mean famished Joan. Ravished would, in your words, be most unseemly."

"*Oh I don't know*" whispered Joan. "Shall I serve?"

"Yes do please. Give Giuseppe a big portion. He is a growing lad."

"Hardly a lad Frederick, he told me he is thirty one."

"Well he needs feeding up to keep him going apace."

Joan thought this was getting a bit close to the mark so she diverted the conversation as the Queen Mother might have done.

"I think there is some mist coming up from the valley, I will go in and fetch a scarf in a moment."

"Is that something your aunt might have said Joan?"

"Most probably, in order to steer a conversation."

"Did you live with your Aunt?" enquired Giuseppe.

"Yes I did for a while when I was about ten to age twelve. It's quite an impressionable age about then. My mother had been very ill after having my younger brother. She never spoke about it, but I assume now that it was something gynaecological. My father worked at the mine and he wasn't able to look after me so my Aunty took the reins for those couple of years."

"That was kind of her. Was she a kind woman would you say?"

"She was a spinster and had not married. She was very different from her sister, that's my mother. She had strict values and proper behaviour was paramount. She had taken herself off to a London training school for Nannies and Ladies Maids when she inherited a little money from a relative. They taught her deportment, received pronunciation, formal housekeeping and the rules of social etiquette. And whilst I was with her she taught me what she knew."

"Did she work in a country house or in a fancy town house for some titled people then?" asked Frederick adding "please pass the salt."

"She did get a letter of appointment and then the War began and the household was disbanded because the mansion she was destined to work at was given over to a Ministry to become a hospital for wounded soldiers. So I think she was very disappointed that she had invested her inheritance in all that fine training to then find that the world had become a different place on day one."

"And what about after the War?" asked Giuseppe. "Wasn't she asked back then or couldn't she get another job like the one she had been offered?"

"No, it had all changed in England by then. People seldom had staff and maids after the war. Spare rooms had been given over to billeted children who were evacuated to the country from London to avoid the bombs or to those called Land Girls who picked crops or tended animals. Many big houses were just demolished as uneconomic, some were bomb damaged, some had lost their owners who were killed in service and thus there was no head of household to work for. Some wealthy families faced financial ruin. If you consider that she had no actual experience of service and there were plenty of experienced servants coming back from war, she had no chance. And by then she had settled in her cottage away from the devastation in the cities of Manchester, Newcastle and Leeds so she became a private teacher." Joan paused to eat the chicken on her fork and then continued.

"She was very popular with middle class families who wanted their children to grow up with respect and manners and be apart from the general ruffians that were coming from state education such as it was during the latter part of the war and they paid her fees without question so she led a reasonable life."

"Do you think she was overly fussy with her manners and ways Joan?" asked Frederick.

Giuseppe helped himself to seconds and topped up everyone's wine.

'Well, it's funny you should use those very words Frederick because only a short while ago I had a holiday with a girlfriend who I've known since my career days and she became very irritated with me part way through the holiday saying to me "Oh Joan, for goodness sake you are being overly fussy." I was taken aback because we had never exchanged words before, so I asked her to explain what she meant and she had been making up a list because I had irritated her that much. When she went through the list I was seeing my Aunt and how she had instilled the behaviours into me. So by default I think the answer to your question Frederick is Yes, she was overly fussy."

"Are you going to share with us what was on the list?" grinned Giuseppe.

"I suppose that is only fair. I can't remember everything as it was quite lengthy but included items such as; Having too many different clothes and forever changing from one garment to another, as I'm about to do because I will put on a shawl when I've finished this delicious chicken; Eating only half a banana or half a slice of toast or halving anything that I should really consume entirely. She got very cross about that and one day in the holiday she cut a banana lengthways to illustrate the absurdity; She also complained about me having only the special tea sachets and only ever two cups a day one morning and one afternoon; Doing my mascara at the breakfast table; Keeping my tea sachets in a paper bag inside a plastic bag inside a tea tin inside a special cupboard; Wearing stockings instead of more modern tights; Having purses inside bags, inside bigger bags like a Russian Doll; Saying One instead of I; Insisting on cloth napkins at dinner - you will both note I do not have a napkin this evening and in consequence have spilled some of this luscious gravy onto my nice evening frock which I shall expect Frederick's new machine to clean spotlessly in the next day or so; And finally I remember she was cross that I put an aitch in words starting with a W that should not have an aitch, like saying white whine. Her list was filled with things like that.

But if you excuse me a moment before we have our dessert I would like to get a shawl because I really am a bit chilly."

She left the two men at the table. The casserole and other dishes were empty. Giuseppe put a hand out to Frederick's and held it a while.

"Thank you for a delicious supper Frederick. You are good to me and I appreciate it. I think we can both help Joan this week to avoid her fussy old maid status."

Joan clanked and hissed and returned to the table wearing her woven shawl.

Dessert was served. Joan went to bed. Giuseppe helped Frederick clear up and then they went up to bed.

15. FREDERICK, JOAN & GIUSEPPE

Frederick needed a visit to the Bank. He had paid for Candy and all the associated works and drawn a fair bit of cash of late and he needed to get the car exhaust seen to on the Sunbeam as it was becoming embarrassing announcing his arrival wherever he went and it seemed that some of the fumes that Joan was complaining about emanated from that source and seeped up into the cabin. That's OK when the top is down but soon the winter rains would start and the roof would be up and the workshop needs to make the windows to wind up to the top and maybe then an oil service. It all adds up.

The Italian Bank was always a half day job and an appointment might as well just say the day and not the time. Sat on uncomfortable wooden chairs, if there are any, for over an hour whilst waiting was arduous for just fifteen minutes with the manager or clerk. He still had some investments in England, War bonds and Gilts but to encash those was such a rigmarole and then to exchange them for Lira took well over two weeks from instructing his London broker. Everything went at the speed of paper and the final step was the speed of the Italian Bank clerk which was dead slow or stop. However, he would have to do it otherwise he would be technically broke. Whilst moving the money and given that Candy would soon be in place spurred him on to finishing the job of integrating the lavatory into the house so once the money was moved he would be able to discuss that with Giuseppe.

"I need to leave you alone today Joan to go to the bank and do some other chores out and about. Will you be able to entertain yourself alright? I will be back well before supper time and will get some fresh fish and vegetables whilst out."

"That's perfect Frederick. I feel the need for a long walk to get my system moving. I have done too much sitting and laying about these past couple of days. Do you have some recommendations as to where I can go and see some views?"

"In that drawer over there was a little notebook, did you see it when you tidied through? Inside I have drawn some simple maps which various guests have used for a few walks over time."

"The manilla covered one like a school book?"

"Yes that's the one."

"Here it is, I've put it in the bookcase." She flicked through a few pages and found the relevant hand drawn maps. "That's perfect. I will do this one with the village as the starting point."

"You will see the little church and the closed up laundry house. I bet you will also see the old woman in black opposite watching all the comings and goings in the street. You will be a novelty for her today."

Joan went and changed into some comfortable black slacks, a yellow blouse and, given the conditions were dry, thought that the Hush Puppies might be a good choice to break them in properly.

She left at the same time as Frederick was ready with his briefcase of meeting papers and he showed her where he hid the key under a stone by the lavatory, but he didn't lock the door explaining that Giuseppe would be working on the little roof so would need to come and go. She excused herself to have one last clank with a sunshine heart on her bosom and followed the dusty trail left by the sunbeam down the lane.

Once it was apparent everyone had left the house, Giuseppe flung back the clean sheets and walked over to the upstairs window, quite naked and showing the sunny world his semi-proud manhood.

He mulled that Joan clearly hadn't realised that he was still in the house. He had heard their conversation after breakfast about her walk and the bank visit. And when, twenty minutes after they quietly got into Frederick's bed together and when he had silently passed him the tub of brylcreem from the bedside cabinet, Giuseppe untied Frederick's pyjamas and pulled them down just far enough keeping him on his left side facing the wall. Slowly and quietly he made love to the older man which Giuseppe found immensely thrilling especially knowing Joan was in bed possibly asleep directly below them. He reached around to bring them both to a conclusion and only the pyjamas would require to go into the new machine. They slept well.

He now admired the view of the erect cypress and thought to himself *I love the naughtiness of all this between both of these adults, both seeming so proper to each other and both tempestuous in bed. How different the skin of each, Frederick with such a hairy torso and Joan with her smooth breasts.* He had an erection from these thoughts and knew what that would lead to, so shook himself down and put on his shorts ready for the day's work ahead, he needed to concentrate.

Measure twice and cut once was what he remembered from being taught his carpentry skills.

In the event, by early afternoon he had finished the new structure and left provision for the integration of the lavatory into the house should Frederick ever get around to doing that. He had figured how it could nicely integrate into this new lean-to. Pleased with his day's work he locked the door and hid the key under the stone and used Frederick's bicycle to go home to Mum.

16. JOAN

The little truck had three machines on the flatbed. Frederick's Candy was at the back - last on, first off. Pedro tooted his arrival having created a dust cloud behind him. Joan was down by the pond with a little watercolour set she had packed and was attempting to capture the scene of the tall cypress on the hillside with the green pond in the foreground and the rolling hills beyond. She covered her work with a scarf when the dust approached. Frederick was in the village shopping for fresh bread and groceries. Pedro let the back of the truck down, put up some metal sliders and headed off to the house to find help.

The door was open and he called "Ciao" several times, going from room to room. He knocked and then entered a closed door. Feminine clothes were on the bed and cosmetics around the bathroom. "Ciao". She had rinsed some underwear earlier and it was on the pull out line that she had brought along fastened to the shower tiles. He checked his surroundings, looked closely and gently stroked the satin knickers. He heard footsteps and called "'Ciao" again on his way out to the kitchen.

Joan had heard him calling and set aside her painting to attend. He was emerging from her room.

"What are you doing?" she commanded.

"I was looking for Mr Frederick. I bring his machine."

"Well he is not in my bedroom is he?" making clear her displeasure. "You don't just walk into a Ladies bedroom."

"I knocked. I didn't know whose room is whose" as he closed the door behind him. "I need help with machine so I go sit in my truck and read the newspaper until a man comes to help."

"One of them will be back soon to help, they are in the village."

Joan went into her bedroom and closed the door. She checked her belongings. There was nothing to worry about. His words were honest and she was being over-reactive. She put away a few articles she had rinsed and left on a little line and made her way past his truck down to the pond and her waiting easel. The scarf had kept the paper protected but it was now dry in the arid atmosphere.

Yesterday's walk had inspired her to paint this morning and as she did so she thought of how she was unwinding in this gentle atmosphere. She had no idea what day it was and how many days she had left. *However many days it is, it's not enough.*

The paints dried quickly here unlike in England where a watercolour was perpetually running down the paper and you spent half the time recovering rogue drips and bringing paint up to where you wanted it to settle. Here you didn't have to lay the paper flat where it might puddle but could use the easel easily. *Hmmm easy easel. Perhaps they were invented somewhere dry and hot? I must go to the library and look that up in the Oxford Reference when I get home* she thought.

As she attempted to capture the depth of colour and magnitude of the cypress in the foreground and the dappled light over the blanket weed on the pond with a few lilies making their space to a gentle landscape beyond, she turned her thoughts to her walk yesterday. The village had been quiet apart from the clank of the church bell *that is really a flat toneless clang* and the occasional cockerel crowing. And as Frederick had suggested she did see the woman in black on her doorstep whose beady eyes followed her progress through the village. She took a turning opposite, in part to avoid this lingering gaze and in part fascinated by the myriad of washing lines criss-crossing the courtyard and garden of the former lavanderia. *So many little outbuildings behind the house. How did this woman - God rest her soul - manage the big sheets and heavy towels all by herself,* she had thought.

The lane behind the laundry only seemed to serve the back of that house and it became a dead end which turned into a footpath leading through a meadow of dry grass and wildflowers. It was at this point that she consulted the manila notebook that had become a guests guide booklet. She was facing the sun and it was in her eyes so she turned to create shade to be able to see the faint map that had been drawn with a pencil. As she looked up she could see over the stone wall of the lavanderia and all the washing lines. She noticed a man emerge from one of the outhouses at the back, she was too far to see his features but he looked swarthy from a distance and then a moment later another person dressed in black, a woman in a long black gown she thought although with quite short hair. She paid no heed and returned to examine the map. This locality was not shown but she thought if she crossed the meadow she might pick up the route as if she had emerged from the other end of the main road through the village. So she turned and decided to do this and her walk had progressed very nicely and she had seen some beautiful views and encountered some very steep hills. The vineyards were just turning red.

It wasn't until she was here today painting this scene from the pond that she thought any more about that walk. *Maybe that second person wasn't a woman in a long black dress, maybe it was a church minister? I suppose the washer did the vestments.*

Up at the house she heard Pedro's truck being manoeuvred.

17. GIUSEPPE

"Hi Pedro."

"Oh Giuseppe, you made me jump. I didn't hear you turn up."

"I cycled here, so as to be quiet. Joan needs to rest."

"I haven't really met her before. She was in the car when Mr Frederick came with his laundry but she did not come in the shop. Anyway, she just told me off for being in her bedroom, so I said I will wait for you or Mr Frederick. I think she is down by the tall trees."

"She is OK when you know her. I see you have the Candy on board, shall we get her into her rightful place?"

Pedro came down from the cab and had to adjust himself, an action not lost on Giuseppe. And then he jumped up onto the flat bed and prepared the sack truck.

"I was just reading the paper Giuseppe. It's not often your village makes the National News."

"Oh, what's that then?" as he took the weight of the machine.

"A woman died leaving the local church over a million Lira."

'That's a good sum, who was she? I didn't know anyone wealthy around here had died."

"That's just it Giuseppe, she was the Nonna of the village, with her own little laundry."

"Oh Her! My mother knew her. She never told me she was worth that much money. How did she have that much stashed away when she was still taking in laundry."

"The newspaper doesn't ask that, it says she died suddenly after taking communion wine and left her fortune to the church ... it's very strange."

They shifted the machine to its new home under the little roof that had been constructed. Pedro attached the pipes whilst Giuseppe fitted the plug.

"I will ask my mother about all that when I get home, she will have heard I suspect. I tell you what Ped, put the bike up on the truck and we will go home together now and have coffee and you can show my Mum the newspaper yourself. Leave the washer instruction book on top there for Frederick, he won't be back a while and Joan seems preoccupied today. Let's go."

-o-

"Hey Mama, Mama, Pedro is with me and wants to show you something. Mama?" he called again.

"Ciao 'Sep, I am coming" she kissed her son on either cheek and then the same with Pedro as she wiped her hands down on her housecoat. "Come, I have coffee in the kitchen."

The young men followed and sat at the small table. Pedro folded the newspaper and placed it where she would sit.

"What's this then?" She pulled her spectacles up from the string around her neck. Pedro pointed to the article."

"My my ... who would have thought ... the Nonna ... phew ... over a million Lira?" she exclaimed and looked up, pulled off her specs and then replaced them to continue reading. 'The Church, her entire fortune ... died after communion wine." She gave the paper back to Pedro and held her coffee cup in both hands. The men looked on waiting for a reaction, but all she said was "Well!"

She stood, removed her housecoat, took a black coat and an even blacker headscarf from the hook and walked over to the door.

"Where are you going?" asked Giuseppe.

"Church" she replied and was gone.

Pedro gathered his paper, gulped the last of the coffee and followed her.

"Where are you going?" asked Giuseppe.

"Two more deliveries to get done before I can get back to the shop. Ciao" and he was gone.

Given he was alone in the house for a while, Giuseppe went to his room and pulled a magazine from under his bed.

18. JOAN

She was the only one home. Her paintings were not terribly satisfactory. Her mind had been on other things. The walk the day before and then thinking of the passing years. All those hours, days, weeks, months without intercourse. Her unspoken assumption that she would remain untouched until she died. Then this sudden unexpected surge of memory and innate lust that had taken over her during the past forty eight hours or so. The way she had yielded without being asked any questions, without any formalities, without any verbal communication as to whether this happening was what she desired. It had just all fallen into place.

And now, not only had she willingly opened herself to this momentous and enjoyable intrusion but moreover she had also opened the most cavernous thing - her own mind. She had, over supper the night before last, willingly volunteered a personal confessional and had told both men about her irritations. They were witness to her self immolation of the very behaviours that made her Joan, the Joan that everyone knew. Joan the fussy. Joan the awkward. Joan the difficult. Joan the abrasive. Joan the tricky. All the adjectives that she had overheard in the past spoken about her during or after some event or meeting. Maybe they were even pronouns and those who knew her might say amongst themselves 'Oh yes dear, we had Miss Tricky over last night for drinks' and they would know who they meant and smile amongst themselves in mutual empathy and maybe sympathy.

How would she go on from here? Nothing seemed of any import whilst here. No need to stand on ceremony, no need for a napkin, no need to worry about making an unseemly noise in the outside lavatory and wasting paper as a silencer. How could she be just ordinary and drink ordinary tea and say ordinary things like wine rather than whine. All these odd jumble of thoughts and self analysis had come to her from the act of being thoroughly, hugely, repeatedly and ecstatically penetrated.

It was at that very moment, standing in front of Candy, that she somehow connected her past career in nursing to her present state of mind and oddly felt by doing so that she had never before seen herself as a patient to whom she could offer help. She had always been the nurse, the efficient nurse, the dispenser of medicaments, the organiser of other people's lives, but never her own and now she connected the two. She was a human being. She had the same underlying drives and juices. The same hormones and same reactions to physical events. And only through this self recognition did she consider that her very chemistry had turned from acid to alkaline when he had ejaculated into her, creating both a changed body and mind chemistry. A change for the good she felt.

But would it change back? Would it last? Would she become sour and acidic again? Would people be able to cope if she were pleasant to them? Would they think she had gone mad? She would seem like someone else entirely. Joan the reformed. Would she need a regular top up? She couldn't travel to Italy for it. And, anyway, this was a passing fling surely, a holiday romance as they were called. Giuseppe was half her age. Should she find herself a lover nearer home? How would she do that? Would she place an ad in the lonely hearts column of a newspaper? She couldn't hang around in pubs as a woman of sixty. She would be laughed at and besides what would her friends think of her becoming a haggard. There was so much that was now clear and so much else had become unclear.

She picked up Candy's instruction booklet. It was entirely in Italian but had a few hand drawn illustrations. There was a small lid on the top of the machine which she opened and it had two white metal cavities with numbers imprinted into the metal l and ll. There was the big dial to the right that somehow one could turn and press. And there were four buttons, a white one on the left then the ten numbers with the types of laundry under each number and then three more buttons white, red and black. She had never seen such a machine before but thought she might give it a go. She went and gathered the pile of dirty linen that had come from her bed a couple of days ago and shoved it through the porthole. This was all programme 1 for white cottons. That much made sense. But how to turn this dial?

Joan heard the Sunbeam arrive.

'Hello Joan, I see Pedro has brought the new machine. Have you got it going already? Quite the domestic goddess.'

'I can't understand the instructions Frederick. Can you help?' She handed them over.

19. FREDERICK

"OK we put the powder in here and here, choose our programme, click twist and set to Go and turn on the black button. There it goes. Our very first wash. What did you put in it?"

"It's the dirty sheets from my room. So when shall we come back to put them on the line?"

"In about ninety minutes. Let's go in the kitchen and I will make us a cup of tea and I will tell you about my morning. When did Candy arrive?"

"I'm not certain Frederick, the last time I saw it was on the truck and I found that young Pedro coming out of my bedroom."

"Probably looking for me I would guess. Did Giuseppe come and help?"

"I don't know, I've been doing a watercolour down by the pond. When I finished a little while ago I came back up to the house and here was Candy ready to use. Did you get on OK in the village?"

"I went to the doctor to look at my hand which isn't really healing very quickly and he gave me a jab and some linament. Then I went to see the woman opposite the laundry because she owed me some money and I've been with her for over an hour."

"That's nice to make good neighbours. I expect she is in shock at losing her friend opposite."

"Well that's just it Joan, it's the talk of the village. It's all rather intriguing. Let's take this out to the terrace and I will tell you."

They took another look at the fascinating new machine, the laundry was all wet turning this way and that and they left it to its job.

"I suppose one day all washers will have a door at the front although it seems counter intuitive to me" said Joan.

They took seats on the terrace.

"Well Joan, it all concerns the Nonna, the laundry woman who died. She was apparently quite well off and nobody can make out how. And this has all come to light because she left her entire estate to the Church and its worth over a million Lira. Yet, she died in the church immediately after taking her communion wine on the afternoon you arrived. The old lady opposite took in laundry while she was shut and made a little on the side but they weren't friends particularly."

"Did you get your money back Frederick?"

"In fact I didn't. She argued that she did the transaction with me in good faith and that it wasn't her fault that the Nonna had died. And she said she had spent the money on food that evening. Enough for the trattoria I shouldn't wonder, but I wasn't going to labour the point. She had some fascinating insight into the unknown source of her neighbour's wealth."

"Shall I top up your cup? Tell me more while I do." offered Joan

"I am unsure how much of this is tittle tattle and how close to the truth it could be Joan. But apparently there is a newish priest at the Church who has only been here a year or so. He is apparently a much younger man than the last who went off to retire in the priestly way, at some seminary to teach younger priests. This one comes from Palermo in Sicily. He was very friendly with the Nonna, she being one of the most faithful of his congregation. The church is only footsteps away from the laundry, maybe ten houses between them and the backyard of the laundry has a gate that leads onto a back footpath."

"Yes, I know because I saw it on my walk around and went along the back and saw all the washing lines and the garden. But what has this got to do with you Frederick? It's not unusual for a rich widow to leave her fortune to the church" said Joan.

"Well it's none of my business really although it sounds as though there is more to this than meets the eye. Why was an ordinary working woman known locally as impoverished able to leave a million Lira? And why does the old woman opposite smell a rat and tell me things which perhaps nobody else knows? It's all very intriguing Joan. I am intrigued, aren't you intrigued? I thought nothing much happened around here. That's why the lads took such an interest in building the Canonica because it was something out of the ordinary with an unusually friendly old foreign man paying the bills."

"It is strange admittedly Frederick and I think the timing is odd because it's all a bit fast isn't it? Normally bequests and probate and such like in England take ages to sort out and you don't find out who the beneficiaries are for weeks after a death. Perhaps it's different here in Italy, I don't know, but if anything I would have thought their processes and red tape would take longer. How come it is so fast to reach the national papers? It's as though they are trying to alert someone of something."

"Yes, Joan you are right. I hadn't considered that part. I tell you what, how about we go and have supper in the local trattoria tonight and we can have a walk around the village and I will show you the old laundry and the church. We should be able to get a table outside being mid-week, it won't be busy."

"OK Frederick, but it's my treat for your hospitality."

"I was hoping you would say that" he grinned his brown tombstone best and went to fetch his new pipe and tobacco. "Shall we say be ready for 7?" he called.

"Perfect. I will go have a rest a while, all this excitement is too much for me and then I'll get changed." said Joan

As they passed the machine it was doing a spin, vibrating and walking itself away from the lavatory.

I shall get Giuseppe back to make a level base for that machine. More expense! thought Frederick.

At 6.30 they were both ready. Joan had put on her lemon crimplene again with a simple shawl and her Hush Puppies that were proving quite comfortable now that she had acclimatised. Frederick had on his brogues. They noticed Candy had moved a fair way from her position.

"I'd quite forgotten about this laundry Joan. Let me fetch the basket and we'll put it on the line before we go. It will be dry by morning. I have some sheets and a pair of pyjamas to wash which I'll bring down."

"I'll peg out Frederick while you try to move the machine back to its rightful place and get the next load going. We can peg that lot out tomorrow."

Joan gathered her purse containing the Lira, absent-mindedly she was about to leave without it and yet it was to be her treat. They had a relaxing walk into the village and linked arms which gave them both some comfort of an enhancing friendship and gave the appearance that they were a couple as they entered the trattoria. Frederick thought *this will put pay to any rumours going around the village.*

Pepe gave them a nice table with a red gingham chequered cloth and he brought out a candle in an old wine bottle covered in wicker and old wax and lit it.

"That is called a Fiasco Joan. It means flask in Italian and it's an old empty bottle of Chianti. They say they put the basket on to sell the stuff because it tastes so awful."

She laughed and said "well we won't order a bottle of that then, let's just treat it as a candle holder" and she laughed again chuckling to his small remark.

"Have something you really like Frederick. They appear to do a sirloin steak. Would you like that? It would go well with the Red Valpolicella. I'm going to have the Orata I think, it's years since I have had that, I think it's dorade or bream." *It's years since I've had several things* she reflected *but it won't be years before I have them again.*

Pepe looked after them well. Frederick had his usual sirloin medium rare and Joan's fish and vegetables were cooked to perfection or so she complimented Pepe and left a good tip. They enjoyed a bottle of red and white respectively. The meal was a success and Joan was terribly pleased. They strolled back in the bright moonlight naturally arm in arm, slightly tipsy. They chatted about the Nonna.

"When I was on my village walk Frederick, taken from the manilla book, which I put back on the bookshelf by the way, I detoured slightly to go through a lovely meadow. It took me down the side of the Lavanderia and around the back. I could see all her washing lines and while I was looking at the map I saw some people come out of the outhouses at the back."

"It's just along here Joan, can you show me what you mean? It's a bit dark but I brought along the torch."

"Why dont we come back tomorrow Frederick and I show you in the daylight. We could do the walk that I did together and I can show you a delightful derelict mill that I found beside a stream."

"That sounds a nice idea Joan. And thank you again for the delicious supper, Pepe really did us proud. We don't need to travel miles to find a good restaurant around here."

"I've thoroughly enjoyed the past few days Frederick. At first when I arrived I thought I wouldn't settle but young Giuseppe soon saw to that *saw to me more like* and I feel so relaxed and content. Better than I have for years. It's difficult for me to describe to you."

"Yes that young man does a lot of good to a lot of people, but I have concerns for him a little because he cannot be a butterfly all his life and as far as I am aware he is surrounded by older people rather than his own age. In the next ten years he will need to settle with somebody and fall in love. At the moment he is sowing his oats I think you might say."

"Indeed, he is young enough to do that with vigour and handsome enough to find fertile soil. Would you say that your Windows of the soul theory perhaps applies. You ought look into his eyes?"

They remained silent on the remainder of the walk home, each in their own world of experience of Giuseppe's gliding intrusion accepted into their very life and soul.

20. JOAN

There's quite a lot to be said for an outside lavatory in this climate Joan contemplated as she adjusted her position so that the sunrise created a heart-shaped burst of gold upon her nightdress. She went back to bed after a hefty clank and hiss. *I'm just so relaxed, I could sleep all week.* She had a second sleep for another couple of hours. The air was gentle and warm with the sounds of nature and the village.

Although they had dinner out last night with the idea of talking about the laundry scandal they hadn't mentioned it and had instead become absorbed in a discussion about the village where Joan was from and the neighbours that Frederick knew whilst he was there. A few had died and others had been through their own life changes and he was intrigued to catch up. Joan, being now the Chair of the village committee, pretty much knew all the gossip and was quite entertaining with it.

Joan prepared the breakfast table because Frederick was also having a lay in. The injection for his hand was having some peculiar side effects and mixing it with a bottle of wine didn't seem the best idea. It was still giving him discomfort and he had dropped his steak knife at one point during the previous evening meal. Joan knew the whereabouts of everything in the house now and given there weren't many oranges left she added some lemon juice and sugar to the jug to make a St Clements. She then went back in to face the mirror. Her hair had calmed down a little and was starting to fall into a natural parting. She decided to take scissors to the fringe to keep it from her eyes. She had brought some small scissors with her and when searching through her holdall bag found a sheet of paper that wasn't hers. It was a program of Opera events and must have belonged to the woman who sat next to her on the plane. Maybe she dozed off too and dropped it and it fell into Joan's bag whilst on the floor. She sat on the edge of the bed and read through it. It sounded quite a full program and concluded with a piece, that given she didn't previously listen to music, was completely foreign to her but sounded intriguing. It gave her an idea. She completely forgot about her hair and changed into some practical day clothes and could hear Frederick above. He obviously didn't know she was down below as he let out a bellowing fart. *Better out than in* she thought. She went to the kitchen to prepare some toast as the loaf was getting a little stale. She heard a clank and hiss.

"Good Morning Joan. Did you sleep well?"

"Wonderfully thank you. I woke at sunrise and then went back for another couple of hours. I must say this environment does instil the most wonderful sense of relaxation doesn't it?"

"It does Joan. And let me thank you again for the superb meal and wine last night. That too was superb and such scintillating company."

I haven't been called scintillating for a quarter century. "How charming of you Frederick. Thank you. I've some toast just coming out and I think everything is here for us. Would you like coffee as usual? I'm having some." *Rather than those sour sachets* she thought.

Frederick sat and waited and then arose and looked at the watercolours laying on the sideboard. There were just three held down by a stone on the corners which had stuck them together slightly.

"These are rather good Joan" he called as she emerged with the Mokapot and toast wrapped in a clean tea towel.

"They are for you if you would like them. A couple of others weren't much good and I burned them."

"How lovely, thank you. I think I will ask Giuseppe if he could frame them."

"You could give him one if you think he would like it."

You have no idea how much I would like to do that he thought to himself as he replied "I think I will."

"Shall we go for a little walk after breakfast and see around the back of the laundry, the way I went the other day?"

"Yes let's do that. Phew, this juice is sharp Joan" he said as he took a gulp, eyes opening wide.

"And then I would like you to show me where the bus goes from for me to get to Verona. I would like to explore myself because there is a breeze today and it won't be all polluted like the other day" *And most of the fumes were coming from the Sunbeam anyway* she thought to herself.

"There is one bus a day that is called the Express which is a complete misnomer, but it doesn't make so many stops so is half the time taken of the other buses. That goes about eleven I think and takes about ninety minutes. It might be full as lots of the local ladies use it to get to the department stores in the city."

"Well let's aim for me to be on that shall we, and if I miss it I will go tomorrow."

Her Hush Puppies were so they were ready to leave but upon passing Candy he said "Oh, we forgot about the washing again Joan, that lot we put out yesterday and now this lot waiting."

"Perhaps you can do it all when you get back, otherwise I will probably miss the bus." explained Joan

He opened Candy's door as a reminder and off they went.

"You will need some reminder method about the washing Frederick otherwise it will be on the line for days on end getting covered in bird poo or going stagnant inside Candy. We will devise a system for you, part of your new life routine."

They linked arms and Frederick slowed his pace to keep in step with Joan.

"She doesn't miss much" said Joan as Frederick waved his loose hand toward Francesca, the woman in black opposite who was doing her usual street surveillance. Francesca lifted a wizened finger in acknowledgement but no other part of her moved, save the eyes. They turned down the side alley to the rear path.

"When I met her the other day her biggest revelation to me, quite indiscreetly I thought, was that the Nonna was accustomed to having gentleman callers of an evening. Seemingly customers with a bag of laundry, they would stay half an hour and leave with a similar bag. Francesca implied she was a laundry woman and a part time prostitute and that the money she was leaving to the church was, in her words, Immortal Earnings."

Joan laughed. "Who would think it, in a little village like this. Presumably it was all local men who knew her. So they will all be more than just worried about how to wash their smalls from now on."

Frederick chuckled. "A million Lira is a lot of money Joan. She would have either had to charge a good deal for the pleasure or been at it night and day."

"Or both" added Joan.

"Look at this lovely meadow Frederick, have you been here before?"

"No this is new to me Joan, it's very beautiful and what a stunning view. I didn't realise the back of the shops had this outlook. You don't see it from the village street."

"Well if you cross the meadow and go over to that corner you come out on the walk in the manilla booklet. If you look in that you will see I've drawn a new map for future visitors so they get to see this rather than a Butchers and Bakers shop. And this is where I turned around and saw people coming from the outhouse of the laundry, just look behind us."

"Oh yes, there are a couple of doors open and there is a light on. Do you see it Joan? I think there might be someone in there now. I wonder who and why that is? Who would be poking around the laundry less than a week after she died. I wonder if Francesca saw them or knows anything."

"She presumably is too infirm to get around the back here to be the watchdog here as well as at the front" said Joan.

"I think we need a bloodhound rather than a watchdog Joan."

"Well it's a quarter to eleven Fred, would you escort me to the bus stop and then maybe meet me here again on the express that returns please."

"It will be a long day for you Joan, will you be alright? You won't be back until about seven."

"I will be fine thanks."

"You don't have many scarves or shawls or anything if it gets chilly."

"I'm sure they sell scarves and shawls in Verona if I need one."

Within five minutes they were at the stop and Joan joined the queue.

"Don't wait here, go and tell Francesca what we have seen."

She had a window seat near the back and a nice young fellow in shorts sat next to her after asking politely. *What would they say in Carnaby Street ... I must be getting my mojo back.*

21. FREDERICK

Francesca was still on her doorstep watching the comings and goings of the street. He approached.

"Was that your wife on your arm? I thought you were a bachelor, so everyone said."

Oh, so they do talk about me in the village he thought. "No just a girlfriend from a place I used to live."

"She went around the back of the laundry a day or so ago when she had a walk about the village."

Joan's right, she doesn't miss much at all. "Yes she did."

"So did she show you just now what she saw then."

Good lord, this woman is a veritable Agatha Christie or her character Miss Marple. "Yes she did as a matter of fact."

"Do you want to come in and talk to me about it?" volunteered Francesca.

"I think I do, but you seem to know what I'm going to say already."

"I might, but it's good to get a second opinion" and she turned and led the way into the adjacent small parlour that was quite gloomy with the shutters closed. A fly hovered around the vermillion cloth lampshade but she didn't turn on the light, instead she was able to open the top half of the shutter so that nobody on the street could see in.

"Well" said Frederick matter of factly "I took away from our discussion the other day that you thought she was a prostitute in the village and that she had accumulated substantial immoral earnings that she decided to leave to the church to repay for her sins. Or words to that effect."

"I said no such thing. I presented only that she had numerous visits from men at all hours. For all I know they were single men needing their laundry done by a competent laundry woman."

107

"So how do we explain over a million Lira? That is a lot of money Francesca."

"I know. What did you see behind the laundry? My legs won't carry me there and there are dozens of washing lines usually covered in sheets and towels. Are all those still pegged out?"

"Well no, the lines are barren. There's no washing at all to be seen."

"So who took all that in? Where has it all gone? Whose washing was it anyway? It wasn't your laundry because I gave that back to you. Have you washed it?"

"Goodness me, I hadn't considered any of that. Where is the laundry she would have done that morning? I've washed all mine already. I am the proud owner of a Candy which reminds me I have to get back soon and bring some in and peg more out."

"What's a Candy when it's at home? That does sound like a prostitute."

"It's an Automatic Washing machine made in Italy and so far it's worth the expense. I was going to say that my friend Joan who you saw me with earlier" ... Francesca interrupted "and you took to the Trattoria last evening" ... he continued thinking *Dear God this woman is a minefield of nosiness* "well as I was saying Joan saw some people coming out of the outhouses around the back when she was on her walk the other day."

"So who was that?"

"Well Joan doesn't know anyone here, she is only here a week. This really doesn't add up does it Francesca. The woman dies suddenly drinking her communion wine, she leaves a fortune to the church, the church announce it in the National press within days albeit a very small article almost like a personal column advertisement, the following day all the laundry is gone, then two people are seen mooching about the outhouses - but nobody saw them go in? Did you see them go in Francesca?" "No" she interrupted and he continued "and then today we saw the light on in one or two of the outhouses."

And she added "yet from the street it all looks the same with the doors locked and all services at the church are back to normal times and attendances."

"So" Frederick said "what are we going to do about it?"

"What can we do about it? It's none of our business and nobody has made any complaints and nobody seems to be concerned about any of it except you and me, and maybe your friend Joan. But there is something very odd, very odd indeed."

"But we don't know why" said Frederick.

"I suggest you go home to your washing. There's not enough pegging-out these days!" she said.

He smiled and rose to leave. The old woman tapped him on the shoulder.

"You are smart cookie. You and your friend will make sense of it. Come see me when you do and we will compare notes. Meanwhile I am going back to my sentry post. I find out a lot there. Bye bye Frederick. Call in any time, I might have an update. I don't have a phone."

Frederick made his way home and unpegged his fresh smelling sheets and then loaded his basket and pegged out his nice clean pyjamas *hmmm* he thought *Brylcreme doesn't leave a greasy residue like Vaseline* and another batch of sheets. *This laundry all takes time but it's a good occupation to enable one to think how this mystery all fits together. Five hundred metres of washing line would take hours to peg out and bring back in let alone fold and iron.*

He needed to have a sandwich and a beer and rest down by the pond before walking back to the village for the seven o'clock express.

22. JOAN

"Hello Frederick, thank you for coming to meet me. What a lovely day I have had. Will you hold these a minute while I put on this shawl please?" She handed him several paper carrier bags.

"Looks like you have been doing a bit of shopping."

"Yes, a little and some discovery of the delights of that city. What history it has Frederick. The Roman Amphitheatre is just marvellous. And all the lovely Piazzas, not that I saw more than a handful. There were several tourists about."

"Have you had anything to eat? I've put together a little cold chicken salad that is in the pantry should you like?"

"Oh Frederick, you are spoiling me. Sounds delicious. Listen to the birdsong, isn't it magical this evening?"

"That's a Mistle Thrush chatting with another. If you listen carefully you can hear the replies coming from near home" he said as they walked steadily and he carried the bags.

"Frederick," she paused, "would it be alright if I stayed a little longer, perhaps another week?"

"Of course it would be OK. There's nobody else arriving and your help about the house with the chores is very welcome as is your company. But what about your charter flight home? You can't easily get back to England from Verona. You would need to travel from Milan or Roma to get back to London, maybe Manchester, I don't know."

"They advised I would have to scrap my return ticket, they don't give refunds on charters and I just wouldn't turn up. I went into a travel agency whilst in the city and they were frightfully helpful. There is a weekly service on Alitalia from Rome to Manchester but Rome is a long way from here. Or there is an alternate day Alitalia service from Milan to London airport."

"Either way it will be a rigmarole of a journey compared to me taking you to the Dan Air plane in a couple of days time. But it's entirely up to you Joan." They were almost at the house, passing the Cypress.

"Let's get that washing gathered off the line there Frederick and talk about travel arrangements over supper." These sheets smell so fresh. And your pyjamas here are so dry they are stiff enough to stand up by themselves" she laughed at the thought. They folded the sheets together in their routine, both thinking the same thing *I wonder where Giuseppe is at this moment and what he is doing?*

"I will carry this heavy linen in Joan, you bring up your bags."

Joan set the table and chose a bottle of wine whilst Frederick put away the crisp linens and plated the supper.

"Shall I pour?" she asked

"Please" as he stood behind his chair surveying the table to ensure everything was present and correct.

"I bought you a little something Frederick whilst I was at the shops. I hope you like it as a little Thank You for looking after me so nicely so far." She passed over one of the three bags.

"Oh Joan, how kind. How did you know my size? How very smart. Thank you."

He walked around the table and gave her a hug and a kiss on the cheek and he considered *how soft and fragile you feel compared to the brittle stick of rock I met at the airport just a few days ago.* She held his arms in the way she had held Giuseppe and she thought *the arms of an older man don't have the firmness and muscular strength of the young virile one, they are slightly flabby feeling, but very kind. Shocking breath though.*

"I helped you move your clothes if you recall and there were many shirts there with worn collars so I thought you could use some smart new shirts. And I bought a white for formal and the pink for more informal evening wear. The man in the outfitters said pink was all the rage this year for men's shirts." Joan explained

"And they have collars attached instead of those separate things with the studs." admired Frederick

"Well, with Candy over there, you will be easily able to keep them clean and bright." Joan sounded like an advertisement

111

"I was thinking I will have to buy an electric iron and ironing board as well. When will all this expense end?"

"It won't end Frederick, this is progress. You have seen it at the cinema haven't you, all those American films showing the huge fancy cars they drive and their homes filled with gadgets and appliances for every conceivable need. They say we will have robots one day doing all this for us. But for the meantime you will have to buy an iron."

"Here's to our first robot, Joan. It can iron my new shirts. Chin chin." and he held his glass aloft and they chinked before sitting down to the salad.

"I'm pleased you will allow me to stay a little longer Frederick. I have a hidden agenda now in asking and I must reveal. Whilst out I bought three tickets for You, me and Giuseppe to see something." She pulled over another of the bags and took out her purse of Lira. She handed him the three tickets. He turned to reach the sideboard and put on his reading spectacles.

Antonietta Stella; Carlo Bergonzi; Ettore Bastianini; Fiorenza Cossotto; "IL TROVATORE"; G. Verdi.

"Good Lord Joan, these must have cost a fortune." It's this weekend. But you don't like music?"

"There's a lot of things I thought I didn't like and a little voice in my head has been saying to me 'try everything once Joan and if you don't like it then you don't have to do it again'. But what I've been trying whilst I've been here I've found I do like and I do want to do again. So, in for a penny, in for a pound, I decided I would like to try opera. This is the grand finale of what those other charter passengers on the plane have come to see and I want to see what they were singing about."

"Well, well you are turning out to be a dark horse. This should be lovely. But we will have to contact Giuseppe and let him know he is invited too."

"I expect he will turn up soon enough" and she topped up their glasses.

23. GIUSEPPE

"Are you going to be under my feet all day? What have you been doing in here, this room absolutely stinks, let's fling open these shutters."

"Oh Mama, give a man some peace. I've been up all night with a mosquito in the room, it's driven me doolally. It was trying to drill into my ear every half hour just as I was dropping off. I finally killed it at two. Oh Lord, I have to go to work today. What time is it?"

"It's eight thirty, where are you working today?"

"I'm helping Pedro today, they are going to clear the shop of everything, put it all outside and then have a good clean and redecorate the shop. At the end of today we should be able to put it all back in some order so that it is on proper display. You should see the place now, it's such a jumble because they keep selling things off the shop floor and filling the space with something else. It will be hard work but fun." He jumped out of bed in his old underpants. Mother was tidying around him, piling the girly magazines.

"Where did you disappear to when Pedro was last here Mama?"

"I went to the Church to see Father Leo. I told you I was going there. I needed to find out what to do about my work there."

"What work there? I didn't know you worked for the Church. I thought you went there to pray."
He was sitting on the edge of the bed, pulling on odd socks.

"Since your father died I have had to work just to manage. I can't survive on the small amount you give me whenever you work, that barely pays for the food we eat. There are other expenses like electricity and water and how do you think I afford clothes for us?"

"Oh Mama, you should have said. I have a little savings you can have, we will sort it out when I get home. What have you been doing at the church?" He was getting a quick shave at his hand basin, the one he was able to use for a pee in the night. Fortunately Mama would put the scouring powder around that for her usual weekly clean of his space.

113

"I do laundry, the Church vestments and the excess stuff that the Nonna cannot, or rather, couldn't manage as she is, I mean was, so busy. I needed to know what will happen now that she has gone Giuseppe, I need the little extra money."

"What has laundry got to do with the Church Mama? Why didn't you work with the Nonna in her laundry house?"

"That is a good question Giuseppe. It is just how it began and it carried on like that. I've only been doing it since Father Leo arrived and he was the one that suggested it to me. The Nonna would send over a big blue bag of the laundry that she couldn't manage and I tackled that. It was mainly all the smalls from her regular customers. I saw the same pants and knickers, week in, week out." It paid well.

"So where did you do that? Where did you dry it?"

"There is a room at the back of the church and a small courtyard where everything can dry out in the sun." She was stripping his bed. "Do you think you could take these sheets with you Giuseppe to Pedro and ask him if we can use his demonstration machine just this once? It would be a great help."
"Sure, let's fold them tight and I will be able to bag them into my bike panniers. There will be room for yours as well. Go strip your bed while I make myself and you a nice pot of coffee."

"You are a good boy to your Mama Giuseppe" and she kissed him affectionately on the neck as they folded the sheets. His mind was over at the Canonica and the sheet folding there a few days ago. He went down to the kitchen with the bundle.

"So what did Father Leo say about more work for you?" he asked as he poured the coffee.

"He was in a strange state, I think the shock from finding her dead in the pews only days before. He was a bit distant and didn't really know how things would proceed and he hasn't made contact, so I will have to go see him again. The only thing was he asked me to go to the Laundry and remove all the sheets and towels from the lines at the back and to fold them and put them on wooden drying racks in the biggest out-house. He had the keys."

They sat in silence a while and pondered this nonsense situation. What had Father Leo got to do with the Nonna?

Giuseppe volunteered what they were both thinking.

"Do you think Father Leo is true to his vows Mama? Was he perhaps having an affair with the Nonna? Why did he have her keys ? Did he help you with the sheets and towels?"

He stopped his questions when he realised the time.

"I must go. I promised I would be with Pedro before they open the shop, I might not be home tonight if the work goes on late, so don't worry about me."

"I will go see Father Leo again today and see if I can get any sense out of him. He knows I need the pay."

"Don't worry about money Mama, we will sort that out in the next day or two." He kissed her on the head and took the sheets to stuff into the panniers and with a throb he was gone.

Mama spread her arms on the kitchen table and cried into her housecoat. *Oh, how hard life is since being alone. God rest your soul.* This was not the first time she had sobbed in self pity.

Pedro and his father had already shifted some of the smaller objects outside when Giuseppe arrived and father withdrew to his desk at the back of the store leaving the younger men to get on with it. There were no deliveries today because this place had to be rearranged.

"Hi Pedro, so sorry I'm late. A pesky mosquito buzzing in my ear all night. Before we get going Mum has asked a big favour. Can we wash our sheets in your machine and I take them back when we finish?"

"Sure, let's do it now and then we can crack on with shifting this lot. I bought some distemper so as to give the place a whitewash inside before we have to put it all back this evening. It's not going to rain so all this will be OK on the street. The neighbours will grumble but they understand the mess we are in." They were in the rear demonstration courtyard. "So why are we doing this? Is Mum not well?"

"She is upset Pedro, she isn't going to be earning any money now because the Nonna died and my Mum had been doing the washing that Nonna couldn't manage. I suppose sub contracting really but it was all a bit peculiar because it involved the church too. I couldn't understand it to tell the truth."

The lads had soon cleared the shop and had put the bigger appliances facing out to the road on the edge of the pavement and made a gangway for people to get through with smaller stuff against the shop windows. The distemper was virtually solid chalk and they had to split the canister into two metal buckets and add water to get a consistency so that they each had one bucket and large horsehair brush. They started in the corner behind Dad's desk. The desk was the only object left and was too heavy and loaded with paper so they sent father out for a coffee and a haircut and started there, one going clockwise and the other anti with an objective to meet at the opposite corner some time later in the day. It was tough work, up and down the ladders and wiping up the splashes but gradually they worked around. Giuseppe had the window and a couple of girls made a significant fuss outside as they watched his shorts going up and down the ladder. He made sure they had an eyeful of what they wanted to see after a moderate amount of teasing. Pedro did the same when he was over the door but his audience was a man in a coat feigning interest in a twin tub washer.

Pedro's Mum brought in a crisp cold Marguerita red onion pizza that was cut in half for their lunch. They sat out on the washing machines dangling their legs inches from passing traffic. Neither with a shirt on and both in white shorts. One or two drivers almost came a cropper gawping at the lotharios. Together they went out back to peg out Mama's sheets and then had a pee together to save the cistern. They were just boys when they had first done that together. The pizza and the small beer slowed them down for the second half of the day and productivity was halved. But by five they met at the final corner and then the job of moving the stuff back in.

Pedro's Dad, freshly shorn, had no customers during the day and had spent his time hand drawing a plan of what was to go where. It was effectively a very heavy jigsaw to get each piece in the right place. The drawing wasn't to scale so most appliances wouldn't fit where expected, resulting in shuffling stuff for a second and third time. It was nine when they were done, exhausted.

"Can I stay the night?"

"I was hoping you would," said Pedro.

"I need a wash, look at me I'm covered in white spots."

"So am I. Let's have a bath eh? That should be relaxing."

Giuseppe raised an eyebrow. *Is this going where I think it's going?* he thought.

"Can we get Mum's washing in first and fold that and put it in my panniers. Then we can go and get that bath."

They did the sheet folding routine and bumped hips a few times. Giuseppe thought *I wonder what Joan and Frederick are doing at this minute.* Pedro and he had known each other since primary school. It was only this past ten years that his Dad had moved them all from the village and bought the big corner shop becoming more prosperous as a result, making them into a busy family. Candys were flying out of the door.

Pedro's Mum had prepared them a hot evening meal and brought it over to the cottage away from the main house. Afterwards they bathed in the huge iron bath, then virtually fell into Pedro's big double bed, asleep until the early hours. Pedro was first in spooning Giuseppe and cuddled him from behind but his flesh got the better of him and soon he was pressing himself against his friend's hairy buttocks. One movement led to another until they finally and wholesomely cemented their friendship of twenty five years for the first and last time.

24. FREDERICK

"Who will teach me how to do ironing Joan? I've never had to do it. I've had quite a sheltered life haven't I?" appealed Frederick

"I suppose you have Frederick and most men would say it's women's work, but the world is changing and over in London, bras are being burned to protest about women being treated as home objects. My book that went missing on the plane was basically all about that. It was awfully written, but Betty Friedman maintained that women would no longer put up with being subservient to men, that sex was to be enjoyed by women and that men can do their fair share of housework. It's your turn to join in."

"Well that told me. So will you teach me to iron? I could buy one this week when we go to Verona if we leave a bit earlier. I will use the table to iron on."

"That will be awkward, you will have to make sure you scrub it first to draw out the oil or stain on it, otherwise everything you iron will turn brown" Joan said as she poured them more coffee. This was turning into a lazy breakfast with not much on the agenda for the day ahead.

"Do you think we should go to the village today Joan? I saw Francesca on her doorstep this morning when I went in for the loaf. They are having the service later and apparently going to put the Nonna in a niche in the cemetery on the other side of the village. Father Leo says she is a wonderous benefactor and must be given due recognition and not a pauper's grave. There were dozens of chrysanthemums on the steps of the church as I passed."

"I didn't know her Frederick, so my attendance would be peculiar. You go by all means, but you didn't really know her, apart from dropping off your washing occasionally."

"It's still a mystery to me about the whole episode. How did she have that much money?"

"Do you suspect there was something in the communion wine?" asked Joan.

"It makes you wonder doesn't it. But what would the motive be?"

"A million Lira is quite enough motive isn't it?"

"But why polish her off sooner to get at it if she had pledged it already."

"Was there something else going on in that laundry?"

"Francesca alluded to it being a brothel but she was a bit old for that wasn't she? She was our age at least Joan. You can hear it now - 'just hang about there deary, while I peg out these sheets and then I will see to you'. No that doesn't stack up. I've never heard any of the lads at the Trattoria or the bar saying they are just popping over the laundry for a quick scrub."

Joan was grinning. *Once upon a time I would never have engaged in listening to this smut and now I'm sitting here revelling in it.*

"It's human behaviour, the world over Frederick. The oldest profession. But I do agree it is implausible in this case." she said

"So if it wasn't prostitution, what is the next biggest crime on earth?"

They both came up with the same answer.

They put out and engaged their little fingers ... "Snap."

Joan went off to clank and hiss and Frederick cleared the breakfast table to the kitchen sink. Joan gathered a tea towel and dried up alongside Frederick who was gazing into space pushing the dishmop over the same plate time and again.

"Shall we just walk into the village and watch from a respectable distance. As if we are paying respects as outsiders, that way we won't be criticised for not attending and not intruding either. And we can observe who is there."

"That's an idea Frederick. I will take along my sketch book and pencils because I've wanted to draw the little street, it's very pretty, but I will save that activity until after the actual ceremony. I expect the village will have a lot of people out. I have a black shawl that I can wear above some black slacks. I didn't know that I would be attending a cortege but seem to have come well prepared for all eventualities."

"Yes you have Joan, preparedness is your middle name. I will go change my trousers and perhaps wear that nice new white shirt you gave me. Should I wear a tie or not? A black tie perhaps? Yes I will wear that. Give me twenty minutes and we will set off," having a conversation with himself.

The village street was already lined, everyone dressed in black. They found a space and nodded to their neighbours. Frederick exchanged a few greetings whilst Joan nodded in feigned recognition. A few women exchanged words like 'Who are they?' and 'That is the foreigner at the Canonica and some English woman who has turned up lately, not his wife though' followed by a disapproving look of the tittle tattle variety.

Suddenly Joan was taken aback and felt a bolt hit her system. There, over the road, was Giuseppe standing with an older woman. He was looking the other way as he spoke with the woman. She was holding his arm and clearly upset and putting a handkerchief to her eyes. Clearly Giuseppe knew her well, but it distressed Joan. *How have I become proprietorial over a holiday romance? Oh Lord this is upsetting my equilibrium. Another older woman. Has he been through this entire village of elderly women? Am I just another conquest? Oh no.*

Frederick had finished chatting to the man on his side and turned to Joan.

"That fellow on my side Joan went to school with the Nonna. He said she will only be allowed to stay in the niche in the cemetery for thirty years. The church gathers rent on tombs and you can rent for thirty or sixty years and then they are cleared out of bones and rented to the next dead person." He then actually looked at her. "Are you alright Joan? Is this event distressing you or my macabre story?"

"I'm alright thank you" she sounded brittle and he detected the change of tone. "I think Giuseppe is over there unless my eyesight is failing" she pointed at a couple in black.

"Oh so he is, doesn't he look smart. Shall we cross and join them?"

Joan couldn't move her legs in that direction despite Frederick pulling at her arm.

"You can meet his mother with him. She is a nice woman, but I've only really met her in passing a couple of times. Widowed you know, this past couple of years."

Oh God, you silly cow Joan, his mother! She looks younger than me. How difficult is this going to be? At least my legs are moving. Oh Frederick stop pulling me toward this roasting pit. Joan's mind was awash *I am so feeble for these situations, I've no experience about how people hide their immoral goings on in front of others in plain sight. This is going to be strange. What would the Queen Mother say? Think Joan think.* Her black shawl fell from her shoulders into the road and she disengaged from Frederick and bent over to pick it up. As she stood up she saw different shiny black shoes and tighter black trousers and her eyes passing over the now *familiar* areas she looked up and there was Giuseppe grinning with those lovely teeth. The simple act of re-dressing herself gave her a chance to re-compose herself and just *Melt*.

25. GIUSEPPE

Formal introductions were made by Giuseppe to his Mama and they squeezed in to the side of them. Joan stood next to Giuseppe and his presence was oozing comfort. She thought of the present she had bought him on her shopping trip. She would give that to him privately some time soon. Meanwhile the cortege was approaching from the undertakers premises at the far end of the village toward the church before a blessing and then turning to return to the small graveyard. People lowered their heads one by one as the cortege passed. A single white stallion covered in a brilliant white bed sheet and a polished black leather saddle mounted by the Caballero from Catalonia who now lived here with his Italian wife, recognised as one of the best horsemen for some distance, pulled a simple open glass sided carriage containing the coffin on which were a pile of finely laundered towels and on top of these a beautiful bouquet of red and white Chrysanthemums.

Unknown to Joan, it was customary to follow the cortege to the church and they fell into step following the line of couples. Giuseppe was in front of Joan, his arm linked with his mother who was tearful for reasons of her own. Frederick walked alongside her. She was looking at Giuseppe's firm buttocks in the black trousers. *I think my purchases will fit. I hope they do.* Father Leo came down the flower strewn steps and anointed the coffin and the flowers on top and then the coffin was replaced. That was the end of the public ceremony and people started to disperse.

"Shall we try to get a coffee at Pepe's?" suggested Giuseppe.

"We will have to be quick. A lot of people will have that in mind" said Frederick.

Joan followed on with Mama but they didn't converse as neither spoke the other's language adequately. But they exchanged glances and smiles. Joan held a hand out to the distressed woman at her side still using her handkerchief. She held Joan's hand briefly and disengaged as they went up the steps to the cafe that was about to be overwhelmed. Pepe greeted them and pointed to a table and then immediately had to greet the next party of four, then six, then two.

"Mama, why don't you help Pepe with the coffees. He is going to be overwhelmed with customers. You could be a waitress for an hour. It would take your mind off your troubles for a while."

"Hey Pepe," he called as Pepe passed with another table full, "Mama here will be your waitress for a while."

"That would be really very helpful. Come with me I will get you an apron" and she was gone and they were a table for three and thus sure to be served first.

"There's a method in your madness Giuseppe" said Frederick and Joan placed an approving hand on the young man's knee which was enough to kick off a natural reaction in his already tight trousers.

"Your mother seems very distressed Giuseppe. Did she know the Nonna well?" asked Joan.

"I know, it's a bit peculiar really, she is a strong woman and not normally distressed like this. She didn't know her very well but Mama did take on her excess work through the church. Apparently she would go to the church, while I was out working at yours Frederick, and she would do washing at the back of the church when required. Maybe the memory of my father's funeral just before you moved here Frederick or something like that has upset her so much."

Mama brought their three coffees without getting an order, so they got what she thought right for them and then busied herself taking orders from the adjacent tables trying to get to them in the order they arrived. She would be occupied for at least a couple of hours at this rate and given she didn't speak English was quite happy to meet the locals, many of whom she knew.

"Why would the Nonna subcontract her workload out through the church Giuseppe? That sounds very odd. If she needed another laundress then surely they would work together in the actual laundry that had the big sinks with soapy hot water and long washing lines?" asked Frederick who was thinking to himself *this is getting murkier by the day.*

"Yes I feel the same Frederick but I only found this out yesterday morning and I was helping Pedro yesterday repaint and reorganise his father's shop and I had to leave there early this morning to be back and change to be here with Mama. She was insistent I should be with her, so I haven't really spoken to her about it. And she has been all tearful this morning so that's part of the reason to get her serving here to take her mind off it." explained Giuseppe

"Had you organised this with Pepe beforehand?" asked Joan enjoying this delicious milky coffee.

"Oh no, it was just a spur of the moment thought. She seems busy enough. She is only happy when she is busy" as he looked over to see his mother smiling and joking with a table at the far end. "She seems a natural at this doesn't she?" They followed his gaze and agreed.

"Giuseppe, I have a gift for you and it's a surprise. I do hope you will like it" Joan said as she opened her purse. She handed over a ticket.

Giuseppe read aloud "Antonietta Stella; Carlo Bergonzi; Ettore Bastianini; Fiorenza Cossotto; "IL TROVATORE"; G. Verdi and it's the day after tomorrow." He stared at the sky and his eyes filled with tears.

"Oh dear Giuseppe. What is the matter? Do you not want to go with Frederick and I? It should be quite a lovely evening although you would have to go on your motorbike because Frederick only has two seats." She handed Giuseppe a small cloth napkin that she kept in her purse. He wiped his eyes.

"It's not that Joan. Thank you so much. I would love to go with you both and it is very kind of you. These tickets must have been so much money for you … they are in the Arena and excellent seats in front of the stage."

"Oh you know the layout, so you have been to the Arena before?"

"Yes, I have been many times because my father was a stagehand and worked at the Arena for much of his life. He was passionate about it and sometimes he would take me along to see what they were doing when erecting some scaffold or scenery at the back of the stage. Sometimes Pedro would come along too with his father. His father was an electrician there before he opened his shop. He fell off a rig and hurt his hip and had to stop being at the Arena. They paid him off which is how he bought the shop where I was painting yesterday. To go back there with you will be an emotional time because I haven't been since he died. He knew many operas and would sing arias badly in the bathroom." He smiled at his reminiscences.

"I wonder if I could get one more ticket and your Mother could come too if she would like to?" asked Joan.

"No, no, don't do that Joan, thank you for the thought but Mama has had enough upset just now with this laundry funeral business without seeing yet again where her husband died."

So his father must have died in a work accident as well thought Joan *I won't press the subject.*

"Well I would like to go into town before the performance because I would like to pop into Pedro's shop for an Iron" interjected Frederick. "So how about we arrange a place to meet at about 6 where we can have pre-performance drinks. Joan and I will go by car and you come on your motorbike. Is that OK?"

"Do you want me to suggest somewhere? What about we meet at Pedro's shop at 5.30 when you buy your iron and go on from there."

"Bravo. Good idea Giuseppe" piped Joan and grabbed his knee again. It was like an electric charge straight up to his crotch.

"Oh Mama, how are you getting along? Everyone has their order after the rush?" She was by their table and had noticed Joan's hand on her son's knee.

"Pepe has asked me if I would consider working here full time. They need help and he said he is impressed with how we got through this lot just now. I haven't made one mistake. How's that then?" she said.

The three of them all stood to give her a hug of congratulations.

"If that is what you want Mama then I think you would have great fun, but don't undersell yourself, negotiate hard for a good wage" said Giuseppe grinning with those lovely teeth which Joan was casting her eye over, after eyeing up his tight black trousers filled to capacity.

"He says I can have lunch or dinner here before my shift too."

"So what about my dinner Mama?"

"We will have to discuss that. I might have to give you some cooking lessons. I must go now. There are customers waiting to pay. I'm

125

staying here for the lunch trade and see how I get on today before deciding. I wouldn't normally work in my funeral clothes but needs must today. See you later on. Nice meeting you again Frederick and Jane." And she was off to another table.

"It's Joan Mama" but he was wasting his breath and Joan just shrugged as if it didn't matter.

"Well Giuseppe, I would like you to come to the house where we might discuss building this little extension to incorporate the lavatory into the house. I went to the bank the other day and will soon have enough funds to do that, having been on a spree lately with Candy."

"Why don't you two go there and I stay in the village with my little sketch book and do some drawings starting here at the cafe and I can pay a visit to the Ladies."

"It's just through there, at the back of the cafe Joan, we will see you later then." He handed back the ticket to Joan for safekeeping as they left.

26. JOAN

Whilst passing the bar she ordered another coffee. The cups were cleared and a complimentary pastry came with it. She gathered her sketchbook, a 3B pencil and sharpener that she had remembered to pack. The midday light was intense but the awning gave some shade to most of the tables, a few of which were now empty and being cleared. Giuseppe's mother was a good subject if she could catch her still enough for a moment, a busy bee woman, non stop between clearing and serving but as she leaned forward to wipe off grubby marks from the rexene table covers, some of which had obviously been there some weeks, the light accentuated her features perfectly.

Joan caught a cragginess in the skin as she leaned forward and the muscles relaxed allowing the flesh to sag under the chin and eyes. *I guess my face looks like this when I am leaning forward* she thought and because her subject had moved on, Joan found her compact mirror and instead of looking at her mascara, *how peculiar, no mascara and I didn't even think about it*, she instead studied the lines that formed under her own eyes and the way fat in her cheeks fell down and forward slightly. It was this that she encapsulated with her pencil drawing of the Mama's face.

She had been formally introduced by Giuseppe earlier on but was in such a fluster about the older woman and dropping her shawl that she couldn't remember her name. Fortunately a customer on another table wanting to pay called out "Lily, Lily" and now Joan could put a name to the face she was drawing. She wrote Lily and the year 1963 along the bottom of the page under her image. She turned to a fresh sheet thinking *this coffee is really superb, creamy and tasty and such a lovely aroma* wondering *what was it that made me hate certain things for so long.*

She started a new drawing. She chose a circular table with the same sort of rexene gingham cover, that in itself was technically difficult to achieve the straight lines in proper perspective on a circular object and to get the folds and shading right. She had intended to draw Lily into the picture but had to spend quite a while smudging lines to get the image technically right. In the event this took longer than the portrait and an hour went by. She was so absorbed in her own zone that it wasn't until she wrote Table 1963 along the bottom that she realised she was the only customer remaining and soon people would start arriving for lunch. She called Lily for the bill and then doubled it for her attentive tip much to her astonishment. It was still worth every Lira to have such surroundings.

As she walked back through the village a woman in black was gathering the small bunches of Chrysanthemums from the church steps. Everyone else was at home by now, the day was at its hottest and yet this was a perfect subject for another sketch. She seated herself on the iron bench opposite and sharpened her pencil. She would need to be quick to get this moment and ensured she took long looks to create a photographic memory shot so that she could complete it when the woman had finished the task and taken the flowers inside. Later the best of these flowers would be taken to the niche at the other end of the village where they would fade away and rot as the memory of the Nonna would follow the same trajectory. Meanwhile she sketched and then filled in the steps after she had captured her subject. Within twenty minutes she was writing Chrysanthemums 1963 on the sheet and was pleased with her day's renditions. She could show the men when she was back at the house.

As she was passing the butchers which was about to close she noticed the delicious Prosciutto de Parma in the window, went in and ordered some for later. The handsome young butcher carefully cut the thinnest slices before her. He spoke no English but he had a perfect set of top teeth which she liked to see. As she was about to pay, he smiled and the teeth slipped and she realised they were a denture. *Oh, a complete fake set of perfect teeth in such a young handsome man.* She paid and was quite unsettled by that experience. *All that glitters Joan.* She thought of her Aunt's wise words.

"Hello" she called "Anyone at home?" The door was open and the Mistle thrush was singing, probably from the lemon tree. She placed her sketchbook and the smartly wrapped ham on the table and went to her bedroom to change out of the black outfit which had become unbearably hot on the walk back.

Deciding to take a late shower, there were lashings of hot water available she thought *this lavender soap does smell divine* and her hair had become used to the cheap shampoo but it was going very pale and colourless in perpetual sunshine but was less frizzy and much more manageable in a simple parting. She was getting dried when she heard the boards creak up above and Frederick's footsteps padding around. *He has probably has a nap.* She heard the shower on the half landing and the by now familiar clank and hiss. She took another half hour to change into some shorts and blouse and to brush her

128

unkempt hair into some respectability so that she was ready to prepare a little salad lunch for herself and Frederick.

She heard Frederick and Giuseppe talking at the patio table outside her pinned curtains so she took out the safety pins and set them aside. She drew back the curtains and opened the french doors noticing that the pane of glass had been replaced. The fresh air to the room was perfumed.

"Hello chaps. How have you got along?"

"We've prepared a plan of work for the extension and made some rough estimates. Giuseppe might start it later next week" said Frederick. Giuseppe was grinning at her.

Those are real teeth she thought to herself, somewhat reassured to see him again.

"When did you replace this glass Giuseppe?"

"I did it on the day you were in Verona getting the tickets. So that cat shouldn't upset you again."

"Oh that's good, I'd forgotten about the cat. It hasn't been back."

"I haven't" said Frederick as he held up his healing hand. "And I made sure he pinned back your curtains perfectly."

"Frederick always taught me here it is about attention to detail." He placed his hand on Frederick's and that unsettled her somewhat like the false teeth earlier.

"That reminds me" and she turned back into her bedroom and gathered a bag.

"I bought you a little present Giuseppe. I hope you like them."

"Oh Joan, you didn't need to buy me another present. We are all going to the Opera."

"She bought me one as well" piped up Frederick. "She bought me two lovely shirts, the white one I had on earlier with a collar and a lovely pink one that I will wear to the Opera."

Giuseppe reached into the bag and unravelled the tissue paper and there were three individual packs inside.

"Jockey Y front underpants! The latest fashion. Oh goodness Joan. How did you know I have been wanting some of these. I saw them on a dummy in a window in town near Pedro's and they looked so comfortable. Pedro will be very envious now."

"Good Lord Joan" said Frederick "I'm astonished at you. I never imagined you would ever buy such a ... how do I say this ... such an intimate item. I think they are a wonderful idea for a modern man. But Joan, that's not the Joan I know, or rather knew."

Joan coloured up a little at that remark but responded.

"We can all be more than we seem Frederick. You alluded to that only the other day. Windows of the soul and all that. Showing the world you are one person, when in fact you are entirely something else" and she looked at him squarely in the eye. It suddenly dawned on her ... *he and Giuseppe had been in bed together above my room when I came back.* Her inner instincts told her *my optician friend here is full of allusion. He showed himself to the world as one person but was, in private, someone else altogether. I don't mind that. I don't mind it at all. Giuseppe is handsome and virile and can sow his oats wherever he finds companionship, whether that's on me or on Frederick.* She became settled and lost all embarrassment that had been piled on to her. "There's more things in the bag Giuseppe if you look" she called.

He delved into the bag to find a second pair of the same underpants nicely wrapped and the final item was an expensive new leather belt with a wide strop and a double pronged frame and metal tip.

"Oh Joan, that is beautiful. I will wear it always" he leaned over and kissed her delicate hand.

"Why don't you try them on and model them for us Giuseppe" she asked.

"What now? In front of both of you?" he grinned.

"Yes now. Change here, behind us, in my room and I will stay sitting next to Frederick and we can give you marks out of ten on your modelling skills, like they do on the catwalk. I hope they are the right size. They are marked large on the label. You are large aren't you?" *If you want allusion Frederick you've come to the right person.*

Frederick was still absorbing her earlier remark. *She has twigged about Giuseppe and me* he was thinking. Unable to restart the conversation and not often stuck for words but knew he was due to face some embarrassment himself when the young man came out and paraded himself and his more than adequate manhood, albeit in new underpants, before them both. *What dare I say?*

Giuseppe removed his funeral clothes for a second time. His old fashioned underpants should be discarded anyway and made into cleaning rags, they were so tatty, but his Mum had not brought him any new underwear since father died and he was even given some of his Dad's old underwear which was very uncomfortable. Most often, when in his shorts, he was going commando as they now called it. *How naughty of Joan and yet so kind and caring* he thought as he was slipping them on. They were so snug and held him in all the right places and the upside down Y made him look so big, punching everything forward, and there was more than enough to fill them. There wasn't a full length mirror and he wanted to see if his bum looked good too. Pedro liked his bum, a lot, especially through the shop window when they were painting. He strapped the new belt around his waist loosely. He pumped up his biceps and stiffened his thighs and walked around to perform a modelling routine with them 'his audience of two' behind the table. *I can be naughty. I am naughty. Oh well, here goes.*

27. FREDERICK

Giuseppe had obviously seen too many of those tiresome seedy game shows on Italian TV with the assistant presenters, always female, pouting, prancing, pushing their boobs forward. In Italy men were men and women were either scantily clad voluptuous creatures or dressed entirely in barren black. But that was what was presented to the world. Dig a little deeper and you found a sex mad population who now in the swinging sixties, were up for it and any hole was a goal.

He jumped out from the kitchen door and swirled across the patio. He had his black shirt on that was long enough to hide the lower regions. He placed his feet four feet apart, posed lowering his bottom to the floor as a squat and rose again, then repeated the squat half a dozen times so that his audience had just a glimpse of the white under gusset. He wanted some music but his audience started clapping at pace with his movements. He faced them upright and slowly to the clap he unbuttoned from the top down and twirled away for the last button, pulling the shirt over his muscular shoulders slowly and revealingly until his full biceps were shown from behind and the shirt was around his waist. His strong back defined his torso. The buckle of the belt rested on and accentuated his bulge.

Then using the shirt as a muleta like a matador with a bull before him, he still hid the best of his new garment. Swishing the shirt to right and left and twirling away from the imaginary bull, they could get full view of his peachy buttocks contained snug within the white fabric. The waistband read Jockey ... Y front ... Jockey Y front ... Jockey Y Front. They were beautifully crafted, brought from Manchester or Chicago. Giuseppe was in his element. He loved people to pay attention to his manhood and these pants thrust him forward to create a harness of pure sex. He camped his finale, breathed deeply to create the hirsute chest with the small patch of hair, now dripping with sweat running down the six pack. He flung the black shirt over toward the door where he had made his entrance. It was time for the full frontal. Four eyes like saucers were transfixed on his masculine bulge that was pulling the garment away from his legs. He pulled in the belt tight around his toned waist. He turned sideways, first to make a Charles Atlas dynamic tension pose and finally grabbing a plate from the table he became the spectacular Diskopolus of Myron.

"Bravo. Bravo" called Frederick clapping loudly, visibly taken aback at the bravado of this young man.

"Encore. Encore." Joan was ecstatic at this personal show of masculinity before her. She clapped and waved her arms and stood in admiration.

Giuseppe broke his closing pose and took a bow. His back was running with sweat and his pants were soaking his gluteal cleft and sticking to his buttocks. He felt sorry that Pedro wasn't here too. He took another bow and gathered his shirt and headed into the lavatory. He was busting.

"Well Joan, that was quite a private show for us wasn't it?"

"I should say. That lad should be on the catwalk. He would be a sensation."

They were both a bit wobbly and feeling their age against the display of youth they had witnessed.

"On a more mundane note Frederick, I bought some prosciutto in town. Shall I make us all some poached eggs on ham toast for lunch?"

"Lunch in fifteen minutes Giuseppe" she called to him as he passed to go change yet again.

"Do you have some shorts I can borrow Frederick to save me putting on funeral clothes again please?"

"Sure."

The two men laid the table and brought out the water jug and glasses. They sat.

"She knows you know" Frederick launched.

"Knows what?"

"That we are lovers as well as colleagues and friends."

"Did you tell her?"

"No, but I know she has put two and two together, from the other night, from this morning, various things."

"Will she be alright about it?"

"I think so, there's not much she can do about it is there?"

"Well I ought to tell you about me and Joan" said Giuseppe.

Joan arrived at that point with two of the three appetising plates. As she went back to fetch her own plate Frederick said

"Tell me what about you and Joan?" he whispered.

But she was back.

"Buon appetito as they say."

"This looks delicious Joan. Thank you and I haven't yet said thank you for my gift, a pair of which I have on now." And he leaned over and kissed her on the lips.

So that's what he was going to tell me thought Frederick. *He's made love to her as well. Oh that boy and his amazing penis. His brain is in that thing."*

"Giuseppe was just telling me how fond he is of you Joan. How he finds you alluring and mystical."

"Well I don't know about mystical. Alluring maybe. I find him very alluring Frederick, especially in those new undergarments" said Joan very matter of factly.

Giuseppe ate his egg thinking *this is going somewhere and I'm not sure I want to be amongst it.*

"When did you know Frederick."

"Know what Joan?"

"That you were attracted to the male form and liked the company of other gentlemen."

Well well, that is a very discreet way of putting it. Very clever. Not when did you know you were a hommersexual as you usually call it. He thought a while and finished masticating the ham.

"When I was fourteen. Harry Belcombe. He sat next to me in school. The desks were in twos. We all wore short trousers in those days for school. He rubbed his leg up and down mine often and one day we both became so excited that we went into the woods at lunchtime and stayed there over an hour fiddling with each other I suppose you would say. We both knew then what we felt but we didn't actually know what to do about it. We were in trouble when we got back. They thought we had been smoking and made us breathe at the teacher. They moved us apart a week later and I had to sit next to Chapple. He was horrid."

"Funny what we remember from school days isn't it?" said Joan pouring another glass of water.

"Didn't you have any experience like that?" he asked.

"You mean Lesbianism? Yes I did as a matter of fact. I went to a convent school. There are different levels of nunnery and we had what were called aspirants who were the lowest level who worked in the kitchen as assistants or did the cleaning and other menial things and then we had novices who we took for junior teachers, but in retrospect they knew very little except the bible and they had a go at keeping us girls in order and then the Junior sisters who did the teaching ... mainly dull bible studies and the boss of them all was called Sister. Sister Maria, a hardened sharp featured nasty woman who constantly complained about everything. Nothing was right for Sister Maria. Everything was wrong. Back then, all of us thought all of them were lesbians, but only a few of my fellow classmates were that way inclined, but they all tried it on with us all over the years."

Giuseppe kept quiet. He had done his show for the day and ate slowly having not thought before that these two who he had bedded had had any life before he met them. He had never asked Frederick about his past when he had his head on Fredericks hairy chest and neither did he put Joan into any inquisition about her previous sex life. This was changing his view of them and making him realise that they were twice his age. *Not that age is anything to do with it. It's about attraction and companionship and scent.*

"Is it inappropriate for me to ask you Frederick" and she paused a moment before choosing her words "who is the man?"

"Oh Joan, that is a highly improper question. It would be like me asking you when you made love with Giuseppe whether you gave him

French or Greek?" Frederick was quite astonished that *this person who less than a week ago was grumbling about smut she encountered on TV was now asking who did what to whom in which position and all over ham and eggs on toast.*

"I feel like I am the subject here Joan" said Giuseppe "and so I think I can help with your understanding. When two men find each other attractive, it is perhaps a thing of pheromones, of attraction by the smell of sweat or of our glands that we cannot necessarily know that we smell. There is physical attraction like there is between a man and a woman but in this case it is not a basic instinct of procreation. It is something different about admiration, about submissiveness, about sharing. You see if I meet a man and am attracted I don't know from looking at them that they will perform as the man or as the woman as you put it, it is not a predefined role. The individuals may have preferences but they are not cast in stone. And when men do play with each other it doesn't necessarily have to be penetrative."

Frederick coughed, almost spluttered, when Giuseppe decided to carry on with educating Joan.

"As an example only. I stayed with my friend Pedro the other night, last night actually, I've lost track of time today, after we painted his shop. After supper we had a bath together. His father bought an old farmhouse with a little cottage and it has a huge bath. We shared the bath and laughed and drank a couple of beers. Pedro has a girlfriend in the village here and she is very sweet to him but she has not been well lately and he is very highly sexed. He became excited in the bath and that made me hard so we pleasured each other but not to fulfilment. It was just men playing naughtily. Anyway, we settled down and relaxed in the hot water and were very sleepy after a hard day's work and went to bed.

In the early hours Pedro woke me and he was very excited again, if you get my meaning, and I was still quite tired so I turned so that he could take me and he did so very passionately and vigorously. I have known Pedro for twenty five years since being schoolboys together and we have always just larked about but never done that before. It was very thrilling and we both enjoyed it and slept soundly until I had to rush back to be with Mama for this morning's funeral."

"That is a very frank and honest story and it shows your kind and loving character. Would you thus describe yourself as bisexual Giuseppe?" asked Joan.

"I am attracted to either sex and in any role that feels right for both of us at the time. So in that sense I guess the answer is Yes."

"Well" said Joan putting her cutlery together, "I should put on record that I found your lovemaking earlier this week one of the most healing and satisfying experiences of my life. My only regret is that I did not manage such an event earlier. It has altered me in ways I cannot express."

"It's altered you in ways that we can appreciate Joan" said Frederick reaching out to hold her hand. She acquiesced and they sat like that for some moments before both holding out a hand to Giuseppe who made the tripartite."

"Gentlemen, there is something I still don't understand. Two things really. Why is hommersexuality regarded as a crime and, and this is a bit of a delicate subject, but isn't sex up the anus really painful and damaging. I ask that because my boyfriend twenty five years ago wanted me to try it and I recall screaming with the pain and made him stop straight away. But don't answer me if it is embarrassing."

Giuseppe then broke off from them by standing.

"I will let you explain that to Joan. My English isn't good enough and I need to go now and check that Mama is OK after her day's work. She thought she was going to have a day's grieving and it all changed to a day of serving. I hope she is all right."

"I hope she takes the job Giuseppe, she seemed to be enjoying herself and with purpose."

"Bye Giuseppe. See you at Pedro's shop as arranged." And he was gone, walking back to the village.

"Have you heard of the Huntley and Palmer report Joan?"

"You mean the biscuit makers?"

"No, I mean the Woolfenden report published I think about five or six years ago. It was chaired by Lord Woolfenden and he suggested that, for the ladies on the committee, to spare their blushes that Homosexuals would be referred to as Huntleys and that female

137

Prostitutes would be referred to as Palmers. So it became called the Huntley and Palmer report. Anyway, it was quite enlightened."

"Sounds intriguing. I hope they had tea and biscuits when they met" she added.

"Very droll. Well back in 1954 I think it was, Lord Montague of Beaulieu in Hampshire was arrested and tried for the buggery of two airmen somewhere on his country estate. Homosexuality was a crime punishable by imprisonment then in the UK. In Italy, surprisingly given the Catholic Church prevalence for choirboys and dressing up and the like, same sex sex has been legal for men and women since 1890. Anyway, as we speak I think there are still over a thousand men in prison in England having been convicted of homosexual behaviour. The Huntley and Palmer report recommends that between consenting adults over twenty one it should be decriminalised and since then the persecution and prosecutions have largely stopped although some Chief Constables still send out their prettier police officers to entrap men looking for sex in known places where cottaging and cruising takes place."

"Cottaging and Cruising?" asked Joan.

"Loitering about a public convenience in the hope of importuning is Cottaging, the toilets being built like little cottages. And Cruising meaning strolling along embankments of canals and around graveyards and the like, with again, the intention of finding casual sex."

"Goodness me Frederick, this is a lesson of a world which is completely unknown to me. I had no idea about any of it. I do recall a family moving away from the village after their son was arrested in some difficult circumstances as it was put to the committee. I suppose he had been doing one or other, thinking back to it. He was a handsome boy too. And my second question."

"Well, since you ask I suppose you want to know. Being a nurse you would know men and women are different, anatomically speaking. And a man has a gland called a prostate that basically sorts out the coming from the going, as it were. Well that is just a couple of inches inside the rectum and a doctor will put his finger up inside to see if there is a swelling of the gland causing urinary problems."

"Yes I know all that from my training."

"Well if this gland is stimulated by an object rubbing against it inside the rectum it can cause a very enhanced orgasm and ejaculation in some men and any pain that you mention is set aside for the pleasure and can be mitigated by applying vaseline to the affected area beforehand."

"Well Frederick, Thank you for that explanation. After this I shall never look at a Huntley and Palmer's Rich Tea Finger the same way."

She is quite a wag on the quiet thought Frederick.

"Let's change the topic shall we. May I show you my sketches that I did at the cafe this morning?" She gathered her sketchbook.

"Lily 1963." he said as he held it in a better light. "Well, I must say Joan. What a likeness you have drawn there. I would recognise her anywhere. You are jolly good at this aren't you. For an amateur."

The afternoon drifted into evening with a lengthy chat about art.

28. JOAN

"What would you like to do today Joan?" asked Frederick as she was buttering a large slice of toast.

"I would like to go back to the cafe Frederick and get a table on the pavement where I can see down the street. I do hope Lily will be there. She makes the most delicious coffee and she gave me a lovely pastry. I haven't had a sweet pastry in twenty years. I will be putting on the pounds here, all this toast, marmalade and a pastry." She smiled widely.

"OK, I will do a little housework and sorting out here. And some thinking too. I feel we have moved over a threshold with our friendship Joan since yesterday's very personal discussions."

"I think the modern expression is that we both Came Out of the Closet."

"And it is a bright world outside that closet and I am unaccustomed to it. If I wore a bra I suppose I should be burning it just now" he said.

"And I would join you Frederick burning my old corsets that kept me in strictures of properness. We have both been showing the world a human being that is not the true soul."

"It seems that that young Giuseppe is the only one of the three of us who is truly content. He doesn't seem to have a worry in the world that young man. And he has a fine body with all his bits in all the right places and is prepared to try any challenge and what do they say now 'Go with the flow.' I do envy his new generation if they are all like him. Such freedom of expression."

"I'm going to have a lemon tea Frederick, I might as well use them as I brought them all this way. More than half the stuff I have in my bag I haven't touched. By the way, while you are buying your iron tomorrow I need to go into the travel agency I found in town to book a different flight. I will give Dan Air a miss on the return and have a bit of a journey back but I think it will be worth it. I'm looking forward to seeing an opera. I've never seen one before."

"Yes, I will try one of your teas Joan. It might get me going. I'm feeling a bit lethargic today. A secret weight I've carried for a long time is off my shoulders I feel."

He sat and listened to the periodic call of the Mistle Thrush. *Such a sweet call - I wonder what they are saying?* Minutes passed where he stared into the avenue of Cypress thinking of some of his former tennis holiday buddies. *There wasn't much tennis played.* Most of them were married professional men like accountants and lawyers and respectable members of the community with wives in comfortable detached homes and they were all leading a double life, desperate to be in the arms of another man for a week or two a year. *The racquet and hairy balls brigade.* He had lost touch with them now he was here. In those memories he recalled one or two who had laid on the bed after intense manliness and discussed the idea of running away together, they felt so much more compatible. Of course it was pure fantasy and they moved on back to their daily commute and their bowler hat and brolly. And that one younger fellow who was in the clinic for some new spectacles was so mixed up, his family having pushed him into marrying an awful frump of a nagging woman who he thought was a lesbian, so that he had never had any sex. He went into a terrible tizz after a week of being properly bedded down. Such a shame he flung himself off a bridge in Macclesfield in front of a fast train. *How desperate was that ... poor soul ... I really did look into those windows. Such a lovely boy but driven mad as a march hare.*

"Here we go Frederick, a nice cup of Lemon tea brewed to perfection." She sat alongside him to take in the view. "You seem deep in thought?" she asked.

"Just thinking about the ships that pass in the night" he replied. "No use dwelling in the past is there Joan. If we knew then what we know now, we would have lived our lives very differently."

"I subscribe to that Frederick, I am going through a sea change of thoughts and emotions. My past life would have been far less proper. It doesn't bear thinking about the time I've wasted without Joy."

" Joy. Yes Joy, that's the word. Where is the Joy?"

They sipped their tea in silence a while. The Thrush had flown off and was now a distant chirp.

"I have this little portable watercolour set. Do you suppose they will mind if I set up on a table at the cafe. I will perhaps take yesterday's sketches too."

"Knowing them Joan I think they will be delighted to have you as a celebrity artist there but expect some interruptions from admirers" he suggested. "If you are ready in five minutes I will take you in the Sunbeam, I need to get some groceries and more bread. What shall we have for supper? Fish or Meat?"

Joan was pleased to find Lily on duty with her white pinnie over a cotton dress today. She looked more comfortable and obviously had taken up the offer of the job. Joan showed her her sketches from yesterday but Lily didn't think they were a true likeness . Surely she didn't have so many lines in her skin and so much sagging on her real face. She turned to look in one of the advertisement mirrors, one showing a bottle of chianti and dodged about to get a complete reflection. She pulled at the sags and thought to herself *I suppose that's what people see in me. Where did my beauty go?*

Joan set herself up to face the street this time. She saw Frederick wearing his white tennis shorts further down the road. He came out of one shop and was outside another with a somewhat feminine basket on his elbow. She gathered new meaning from that glimpse. *He usually used a bag* she thought as she saw him lingering outside the butchers. The boy with the false teeth was no doubt rearranging his meat. *Is it better to have brown tombstones or white plastic removable ones?* She shuddered at her thoughts. Lily brought her coffee and she asked for a bowl of cold water for her brushes. She should have brought one of the many empty jam jars in the pantry but had forgotten.

There was a good vista up and down the street. Her first subject she thought ought to be the laundry with Francesca in her vestibule opposite sitting inside, just out of the direct sunlight, legs clad in black. The yellow stone buildings and the lovely pots of pelargoniums hanging from some upper windows and outside front doors created the sort of scene that would make a good rendition on her paper. She would get the doors of the old laundry to the right of her sketch including a couple of pretty Judas trees with a few blue flowers into the scene as well. She started, lightly in pencil, so as to get the perspective right for the part-cobbled road and the edge of the footpaths. Her coffee was just right. She felt the presence of Lily behind her watching how she went about this relaxing hobby. There were no other customers to attend to just yet.

She was looking up and down between subject and image. An elderly man was walking a seemingly older dog with a thick string lead. It was sniffing and peeing up one of the Judas trees minding its own business. It was then that she saw movement behind the glass doors of the laundry. There were two men. They didn't open the doors but were going about somewhere inside. At first she imagined it to be the reflection of the dog walker, but it wasn't. He had moved on and there were definitely figures inside. What were they doing and how did they get in? *Around the back presumably.*

Lily had seen them too and thought she knew who they were.

29. FREDERICK

The butcher's apron was spotless and a traditional blue chalkstripe. He was polite with a lovely smile. He looked a bit younger than Giuseppe, twenty eight Frederick guessed. There was another man out in the back of the shop shifting carcasses and making intermittent commotion. Being on the south side of the street meant their window was not troubled by the sunlight that would otherwise turn the fresh meat grey.

"I'd like some of that sausage" said Frederick.

The lad grinned from ear to ear.

"The times I hear that" came the reply.

I'm on to a winner thought Frederick, *quick witted and a camp response generally is a good indicator.*

"You are the Englishman who bought the Canonica aren't you. A friend of Giuseppe I think" he forwarded.

"Yes that's right. Do you know Giuseppe?"

"He was in the class two above me at school and was known to be naughty. Which sausage would you like Sir" and Frederick was sure that the eyelids fluttered a little with the question.

"The soppressa vicentina salami I think would be best." *Oh if this fella only knew how much I love being called 'Sir'.*

"A good choice if I might say so" and he took it to the slicing machine.

They concluded their transaction with an amiable parting.

"I hope to see more of you from time to time" said Frederick.

The lad pretty much understood and waved him on beyond the window.

Some reasonable Eye Candy in the village this morning thought Frederick which took him back to thinking about his wandering washing machine. *I must remind Giuseppe to level the base for that*

144

Candy machine when he makes the floor for the lavatory extension next week.

The shopping basket was getting heavier so he took it from the crook of his elbow and carried it in a more manly manner into the greengrocers. *Have I found a new freedom that I don't care what people think? This is the new me? Is that it?* He noticed Joan on the porch of the cafe with Lily standing a respectable distance behind her admiring the artist at work. He waved but they didn't see him. He finished his rounds with a visit to the baker for a fresh loaf and then walked on the shady side back to the car.

As he was passing the glass doors of the laundry he caught Joan's eye and waved over the road. She pointed and held her hands either side of her eyes indicating he should look into the laundry. He placed his basket and did that and at the back of the room could see light coming from an open door somewhere out the back. After dropping his shopping at the Sunbeam he wandered down the side path around the back of the shop, trying his best to appear nonchalant as if he were going on the meadow walk again.

At the meadow gate he turned and saw Father Leo and another man in and out of the back of the laundry taking something into one of the stores. It looked as if they were tidying. Boxes of washing powder and the like were being taken out of back of the laundry into the outhouse. *Perhaps the place is going to be sold and the proceeds will go to the church? But why would the village priest be doing this sort of task, albeit with some help? Perhaps he is the only keyholder. None of my business really.* On his way back up to the car he had to pass the ivy clad walls and he hadn't noticed before that the ivy had been moved even though it grew from the ground over the top of the two metre high stone walls. There was a huge section that was not attached to the wall but just hung there. He gently pulled at the Ivy and it came away to reveal an old door behind it that nobody would know was there. *So this is the way anyone could go in and out.* He pushed the ivy back and the door was invisible. It just looked like the continuation of the wall.

He drove back home pondering his new knowledge and pondering his new found butchery friend. The motorbike was at the top of the lane.

"Oh, Giuseppe, you are a mindreader" said Frederick addressing his remark to the builder's butt crack looking up to him.

145

"I thought I would get this machine floor level now to stop it wandering around before I come back next week to start the extension." He didn't look up whilst he was busy swiping a rectangular trowel across the wet cement to get the material level inside the wooden frame which he could remove in a few days once the cement had gone off. "You won't be able to use Candy for a couple of days Frederick. I shifted her over there as you see. She weighs a tonne."

"I will put the coffee on" said Frederick as he took his grocery basket in. Giuseppe turned to look at Frederick's legs topped by clean shorts. *For an older man he really does have nice pert buttocks.*

Fifteen minutes later the coffee tray was out on the terrace. Giuseppe hosed down his cement mixing board and then washed his hands with a further clank and hiss.

"How do you feel after yesterday's discussion between us with Joan?"

"I haven't thought about it much, but she has certainly changed dramatically since she arrived. She was very starchy and brittle and then once we had, you know, she altered to a much softer character. It's been a complete transformation."

"Yes I noticed it after I had committed to buy Candy here." He pointed to the machine that was adjacent at the end of the table for a couple of days. "So putting two and two together I suppose you two were at it while I was at Pedro's shop?"

"That's right. I'm sorry I didn't tell you Frederick but I thought Joan was leaving before today and it would just be a little fling for us. I didn't want you to be jealous or anything and to tell the truth I didn't know we would go the whole way as we did. It started very innocently as she was eating a banana."

"Well you can spare me the detail of that but as long as you enjoyed yourselves. I would never be jealous. It has certainly done her the world of good. It does me the world of good when we have fun too" said Frederick putting his hand on Giuseppe's arm.

"Perhaps after coffee Frederick" he said with a cheeky grin and winked.

"Mama had a good time working with Pepe you know. She didn't mention the Nonna or the church as if she had wiped it from her memory. She's back there today and will do four or five days a week full time, split shifts. She says she needs the money, but I think it gives her self respect and the ability to get to know some of the villagers a little better. Much better for her than being stuck out the back of the church washing other people's grubby smalls."

"I know she is back at the cafe this morning. Joan is there doing some watercolours, I took her in earlier and then I met the butcher boy who knows you when I was buying this salami."

"You need to be careful of him Frederick. Word has it that he took to bribing the last Father at the church for a regular weekly stipend just for giving him a one-time hand job. He seems to like to get men into compromising positions with their work or with their wives and take regular income from it. A blackmailer. Try not to get mixed up with him Frederick."

"Oh really, he is very handsome, pretty almost and knows the score doesn't he."

"He doesn't look so pretty without his false teeth. They were knocked out by a hefty baritone of the cast in Verona some years ago after he attempted to bribe him. My Dad told me about that. You would have thought that would have warned him off, but old habits die hard I guess. Odd thing is he goes out with that girl in the bakers down the road. Likes his bread buttered on both sides does that one."

"I get the message Giuseppe. Some more coffee?" Frederick poured for them both while waiting for a response. He continued …

"This business at the laundry still doesn't stack up Giuseppe. I just had a walk around the back toward the meadow whilst I was in the village and found a back gate hidden in the thick ivy over the walls. Why would the Nonna want to hide the back way in. Nobody was going to come and steal the sheets pegged on the line surely?"

"That's odd isn't it. Was there anything else going on? What made you walk around there?"

"Joan was over the road in the cafe under the awning and she nodded over that I should look in as I passed. The back door was open because I could see the daylight beyond, so I went down toward the meadow at the back."

"And?"

"And there were two men in and out between the back door and one of the outhouses taking boxes of washing powders or something out of the laundry and storing it I suppose. But one of the men was definitely Father Leo."

"Mama knows something, I'm sure or suspects it anyway. She hasn't spoken to me about it but I suspect she will. She was just too upset about a woman she didn't really know. And why was the washing brought to her to do in the church when there was all that facility along the road. Something changed when Father Leo arrived here. And I suspect that butcher boy had something to do with the changeover when it took place. There's something been going on. I've finished my coffee Frederick." he said grinning.

"So have I."

They went upstairs for a while.

30. GIUSEPPE

"I'm famished Mama."

"You will have to get yourself some lunch and dinner today. I'm working at the cafe." said Lily

"I'm going out tonight and will eat out but it's like Old Mamma Hubbard's in here, the pantry is bare."

"That's because you eat us out of house and home. I suggest you go shopping once in a while. The bakers sells bread, the butchers sells meat and the greengrocers sells vegetables."

"I'll do that Mama now you are busy with a new job. Come, please sit down with me and have a coffee before you go waitressing again?" asked Giuseppe.

"That lady Joan came to the cafe yesterday and she did some painting at a table for several hours. She is very good Giuseppe. I wish I could paint and draw like that. She did a sketch of me which I didn't think a very good likeness, it made me look so old." She sipped the coffee which was bitter compared to that she now had at the cafe. *You get what you pay for I guess, I can't buy this cheap stuff again.*

"I know, I went over to Frederick's and laid a floor for his washing machine yesterday," Giuseppe responded thinking to himself as he said it *Laid Frederick as well.*

"We saw some people in the old Laundry yesterday Giuseppe. I think one of them was Father Leo. I don't know why they are there really. I would like to find out what is going to happen to the place. I haven't spoken to him since the day after she died."

"You know him well enough Mama, you worked in the vestibule washing the village smalls for a couple of years and saw him often enough then. Didn't you become friendly during that time?"

"That's the oddity about it Seppe, thinking back. Why didn't I just work with Nonna over in the laundry? What was going on over there while I was doing her work? Father Leo would bring a big blue bag of clothes, never sheets or towels, they would have been too heavy for me. Sometimes two bags and I would manage to get through them. I was paid well. Always in cash and he always paid me, not her. And when it was dry, I folded it and put it carefully back in the blue bag and it was taken back over to the Laundry by Father Leo. Something was being hidden from me by both of them and it's still being hidden."

"Do you think the Nonna died of natural causes Mama? "

"Are you suggesting she was murdered?"

"Poisoned possibly?"

"That's murder. Oh Lord Seppe, I don't know what to think. There is something strange going on now and been going on this past couple of years and I am wracking my brains to figure out what it is. If she was murdered then the prime suspect is Father Leo. How can we find out more about him? He's a man of the cloth"

"Well you have fortunately landed the prime job to be able to keep a watchful eye on the old Laundry and to hear any tittle-tattle going

149

about. Something might crop up. And who is that old lady always in her porch? She is the eyes and ears of the village."

"That's Francesca, plays her cards very close to her chest does that old crone."

"Invite her along to the cafe for a coffee somehow. She could do with getting out more."

"Did you know that she is the butcher boy's grandmother, the lad with the false teeth?"

"I never knew that." He stared into the dregs in his cup.

"I need to get off for work, I can't start being late. Enjoy your grocery shopping." she kissed his forehead.

"I will be out tonight Mama, see you later tomorrow. Enjoy the waitressing."

"I will" and she banged the door behind her.

30. FREDERICK

"I think we will need to leave at about two Joan, especially if you want to go to the travel agency."

"Shall I wear my lemon frock with a black jacket and take the black shawl in case it gets a bit chilly because we are sitting outdoors albeit inside the Forum aren't we?"

"Yes, under the stars Joan. That sounds a nice ensemble, yellow and black go well together. I'm sure we will see some snazzy Italian fashions tonight. I'm going to wear the lovely new pink shirt."

"We should look quite the couple Frederick."

"Have you thought of phoning the travel agent Joan. You can use the phone. It's treated as a local call so it costs no more, amazingly. Do you know their phone number?"

"Yes, I do, I have a card. Let me get it and I will try. That would save a lot of aggravation and loitering before the show."

They finished lunch and Frederick cleared the things while Joan found the card.

"Do I have to dial any special code or anything or just this number?" She showed him the card.

"I'll get you through." He took the card over to the telephone which was covered in pollen as it was seldom used nor rang. The last call was when she had been cut off from Manchester Airport which seemed like a lifetime ago but was only about a week. The call connected and he passed her the receiver. She asked her questions and set her new itinerary.

"Thank you Frederick. I hadn't thought about how I could pay them before Monday night but they have reserved me a new flight and have given me details of the trains, as best they knew them from their Cooks Rail Timetable, that will get me back home from London airport."

"As long as you are sure of what you are doing Joan, it does sound quite a bother by missing that Dan Air flight" he said.

"I will be fine, I can always get into a hotel if I get stuck. I think I might take the bus again on Monday. I enjoyed that ride out last week. But let me ring them back and see what to do." She paused and then exclaimed "No. Come to think of it, I have some Cook's Travellers Cheques in my purse that I keep for emergencies like this and I've had them for years and never spent them. I could pay the fare with those, that would make sense and save a lot of palaver. They are accepted worldwide."

Joan felt pleased with herself that she would finally rid herself of something. She was burdened by being perpetually prepared.

"That's jolly good, we can leave a bit later after lunch and still meet Giuseppe at Pedro's shop at five thirty."

"You will be a domestic Goddess with your new Iron."

"God Joan. Domestic God. If you don't mind ! Despite the predilection." He grinned, so did she.

They felt a bit overdressed to buy an iron but nevertheless were able to park only a short distance from the shop. There was a breeze so no smog. They were dismayed to find the shop shut. There was a handwritten card on the door that read. Due to family bereavement, we will be closed until Tuesday.

"Oh dear I expect young Pedro's elderly grandma has died. These things always require a lot of effort to make arrangements." said Frederick. "We had better wait in the car until Giuseppe turns up and then we will go get something to eat together before the performance. You do have all three tickets don't you Joan?"

"It's a lot of good asking me that now isn't it, we would never get back in time if I hadn't." *We are bickering like an old married couple.* "I will get you an iron while I'm in town next week seeing the travel agent" offered Joan.

They sat back in the car and fifteen minutes later Giuseppe arrived on his motorbike. Frederick walked over.

"Hello Giuseppe" as they hugged. "They've had a family bereavement so I can't buy an iron. I expect Pedro's grandma died. She was quite an age I believe. Let's go on into town and get some early supper so that we can all head home straight after the performance. Is that OK?"

"Oh no, I do hope Pedro is alright because he was very fond of Grandma. She was a lovely old soul. She used to walk us two to school sometimes. That's really upsetting."

"Do you want to go see him and miss the Opera?" said Frederick holding Giuseppe's shoulders.

"No, I will go see Pedro tomorrow. I'm OK thanks, I'll follow the Sunbeam now. So you two get going and we will eat somewhere near the Arena - it will be my treat."

The meal was mediocre and served too fast to have any flavour so as to get them out of the door with the proprietors having the idea of pushing another party through before the performance.

Joan held Giuseppe's hand and reassured him. "Thank you for a nice meal out Giuseppe" she said and kissed his hand. He tingled. They had discussed his childhood with Pedro and his grandmother's role in their upbringing.

Giuseppe hadn't revisited those memories in one sitting ever before. *Peculiar how a bereavement acts as the consolidator of a lifetime of events and wraps them in a binder* he thought

Frederick was still smarting from seeing his young friend ripped off by the restaurant on the only occasion he has bought them all a meal.

"It's always the way near venues of any sort, the restaurants can get away with poor service or bland food because the people won't be coming back and they know there will be a steady stream of new faces tomorrow gullible enough to see the menu or listen to the spiel of the maitre d' out front and get away with sub standard fare" said Frederick.

They settled by joining the queue for the auditorium and soon an usher was escorting them to their allocated row. Giuseppe was between them, Joan had a woman to her left and Frederick a gentleman to his right. Both exchanged civil pleasantries with their new neighbours.

"To tell the truth, I have never before been to an opera so I have no idea what to expect" Joan said to the neighbouring woman who, despite being Italian, spoke cut-glass English.

"May I explain a few of the rules of Opera to you. Do you have your programme and I will take you through it" she said.

I've made a mistake revealing that Joan thought to herself and prepared herself for what became a fifteen minute intensive introduction to the world of Opera. She was literally saved by the bell and the woman turned away to her husband who had tapped her on the arm.

Frederick meanwhile was asking the man on his right about smoking etiquette. His pipe was ready in his pocket and wanted the whereabouts he might get a drink and a smoke at the Intermission.

Giuseppe put out both hands palms up on the seat arms and his two older lovers each took one hand. Other members of the audience behind them simply thought it enchanting that mother, son and father were so devoted that they took to holding hands. Giuseppe looked out to see if there were any familiar faces from when he last came here with his father but three years had passed and there seemed to be several changes. He was pleased that Mama wasn't here, she would only be tearful about the life she used to enjoy when father worked here.

-o-

At the end, the three of them were standing and shouting "More" for the standing ovation. The whole city must have heard the calls for Stella to sing again.

"Truly exhilarating" said Joan. "Utterly Fantastic" said Fredrick "Meravigliosa" said Giuseppe.

Giuseppe rode in front of them all the way to his home where he waved them goodnight. Joan was full of wonder at what she had missed for a lifetime. *I have some catching up to do when it comes to music.* Frederick had a brain full of earworms from the orchestra and cast and only made the last mile before collapsing into bed exhausted.

31. GIUSEPPE

Lily was still awake well after midnight and had been listening for his motorbike. He had crept in the front door thinking she was asleep and he went straight up to his bed so she left him until the morning.

He was still asleep when Mama came into his room. He stirred and woke as she opened the outer shutters letting in the bright sunlight. Seeing him wince she pulled the shutters enough to shade his eyes and sat on his bed. She hadn't done that since his father died and before that was when he was in trouble at senior school. At least they had some fresh air to rid the manly fug. She had a cup of coffee for him and he sat up in bed.

"Is everything alright Mama? What day is it? It's Sunday isn't it. You are up early. Have you had trouble at the cafe with the new job? What is it?" he took a hot sip and she looked on fondly.

"I heard some very bad news Seppe at work last evening." she said.

"Do you mean about Pedro's grandma?"

"What's happened to Pedro's grandma?" she asked.

"We called at the shop yesterday for Frederick to buy an iron and we saw a note on the door saying about the bereavement."

"Well that's just it Seppe dear, that's what I wanted to speak about as soon as you were awake." She took the cup from him and put it on the bedside cabinet in the expectation of what was to come.

"It's not Grandma who has died, Giuseppe, my love, It's Pedro. Pedro was killed in the little truck."

"Oh no, that can't be true, I was only with him a couple of days ago and we had such fun painting the shop." *And later on he made love to me, I never knew anything like it* he thought.

"It's a mistake surely Mama. Who told you this? They must be wrong."

She shook her head.

155

His face folded and his eyes filled with tears and he started to breath intermittently and his nose ran and the sobbing began. Lily moved up the bed and comforted him and she herself allowed her tears to fall onto his lovely hair at the thought of his sweet childhood friend snatched away at only thirty two.

"Oh Mama, Mama, Mama no. Please say it isn't true. Not Pedro, Please dear God." He sobbed into his mothers arms, the sobs only a grown man can make. He hit the bedclothes with his arm. Lily held him at arm's length and let him sit up.

"I know Seppe my love. I know. It is so very very sad. Your lovely hard working friend. I've known him since he was a baby. He was born a few months before you and I was just pregnant when he was born. I helped her that day."

She then sobbed at the memory and her maternal instinct took her to her knees, on the floor, at his bedside and she laid her head on his knees and she cried and cried and cried. The bedsheets were wet with her tears so much so that Giuseppe blew his nose onto the sheet. They would need to be washed yet again.

"What happened Mama? Do you know?"

"He was apparently out delivering fridges and washing machines, like he does. Like he did. He was on one of the tracks on Monte Valdo up to a village house there in the campo. A car came the other way and he presumably had to move over for them to get through. They assume the appliances shifted to the side and the truck went over the edge and rolled a few times over before coming to a stop some way down. The people in the car presumably couldn't save him, there was a fire."

"Oh dear God no." He sobbed again. He just couldn't help himself. He held the wet snotty sheet to his face and Mama got up and leaned over to hug him. "Poor Pedro, lovely Pedro. My lovely friend Pedro." His tears were salty and flowing down his fine features and into the sides of his mouth. "I really loved that man Mama, he loved me too. His parents will be in such a state, and so will Grandma. Oh no, no, no."

They held hands, it's all they had. The loss. Unfathomable loss.

"Shall we go out and see them do you think?" he asked.

156

"I'm not working today" she replied, they have a girl who's done Sundays for some time and it gives me an extra day off so we could go there if you feel up to it Seppe."

"I think we should go. Pass me the coffee please Mama and I will get washed and dressed. Black for a second time in a week." He wiped his nose on the sheet. "I will strip my bed and ask Frederick if I can use his machine when I go up there again and move it. I will do that tomorrow."

Lily left him and went to the bathroom to refresh her eyes. *There have been a lot of tears this week. It goes like that. Laughter and Tears of life and death. Goes in threes they say* she thought.

They arrived on the motorbike just after midday. There was a car outside but not the usual truck. The door was open. Calling out they found Grandma in her chair appearing very frail. She had been shedding a lot of tears for her grandson. When she saw Lily, who was like a second daughter, the second mother to Pedro before they moved out here, she started to cry again. Giuseppe left them together and went on through and found Pedro's parents sitting at a table in the back garden going through a few faded old photographs.

"You've heard?" is all they said as Giuseppe walked over and embraced them as they sobbed together.

"Giuseppe, my boy, I want you to take me to the site of the accident please. I want to go see for myself what is left. I have only heard from the Police but I have to go to see. I don't want Isabella or her mother to go, so they can stay with your Mama here a while and console one another. Will you take me please Giuseppe? We can go in my car, but it would be best on your bike in case we need to pass any road block that might have been put up. Please. May we?"

"Of course we will. I'll just have a glass of water and let's tell the women what we are doing and we will go now. Get a sensible jacket on, it might be chilly on the mountainside."

"Sorry Giuseppe, very remiss of me. I haven't offered you a drink. I'm sorry dear boy. Help yourself to anything. The ladies are making coffee I smell."

The ride was about forty five minutes, Pedro's father shouted directions into Giuseppe's ear from time to time. The fridge was destined for good customers who had bought several appliances since he ran the business and they were still waiting. But that was not the purpose of this visit. From an adjacent hillside it looked like the accident spot was over the valley that they would climb around circuitously. There appeared to be what looked like a fridge over the edge some distance away, the door of it had come off on the way down the hill. People here tended their olives and fruit trees and vines and didn't litter the countryside with old fridges.

As they neared the spot where the truck had gone over the edge they could see how the edge had broken away. Giuseppe parked the bike in a little overtaking spot a few metres ahead and walked back. Looking over the edge he could see the battered fridge and then further down the two brand new washing machines completely battered and ruined laying twenty metres apart as they had rolled like boulders. There was no sign of the truck.

"You stay here. It's too dangerous and steep for you to go clambering down here. I will go down slowly and see if I can see the truck" said Giuseppe.

"Please be careful. Call out to me every minute or so to let me know you are OK."

He got to the fridge and its broken door easily enough. *They were obviously the first things to get flung off the flatbed* and made his way down the slope toward one of the washing machines, the bakelite front and controls had shattered and the circular door was gone, the rest of the machine was almost triangular shaped. And from this point down, the terrain was even steeper and it was unlikely he could get much further. The other machine, a rectangular twin tub was in pieces with the electric mangle attachment halfway up the steep bank. It had been stopped from going further by a sturdy ancient olive tree and alongside it there was a freshly broken large stump of a smaller olive that might have been damaged by the truck. He called out "I'm OK" and scrambled across toward the stump. The shale was loose and a large boulder went over the edge causing him to lose his footing for a moment. There followed an audible clang as the boulder hit metal below. From the secure vantage point of the torn stump he was able to stand upright behind it and look over the steep edge. There it was. Four metal wheels facing the sky. A rear axle. A broken shaft and the bottom of the oil sump and big gearbox. No tyres, just a rust coloured burned out pile of metal. An upside down former truck. A complete belly flop.

"Oh dear God." He was overcome with emotion. "Pedro dear friend. God rest your soul." *He must have been pierced to death by the steering column and then cremated there and then. What is left of you is heaven sent.* "Oh Pedro, Pedro, Pedro." He fell back toward the hill and sat for a moment trying to gather composure after witnessing the finality of this scene. The shards of olive tree bore witness to the force of four or five tonnes of truck smashing it to pieces. He called up again "I'm OK." *But I'm not OK at all. There is nothing, absolutely nothing I can do. That truck will stay there until it rots into the ground.*

It was easier to scramble up than it had been down. His best black shoes were getting spoiled. He had expected to pay condolences, not to see a scene of devastation and a cremation. He hauled himself back up onto the road. The older man was waiting for him, waiting for news, almost waiting in hope.

"What did the Police tell you?" Giuseppe asked gathering his breath.

"Not very much, except they had found the truck and that Pedro was, that Pedro was, was ..." he couldn't say the word.

Giuseppe took hold of his shoulders, pulled him close and whispered "perished" with which he hugged the sobbing man who had been a surrogate uncle, a surrogate father, a friend and a hero for him for so much of his life and now he felt the frailty of a man beaten by the circumstance of his son's untimely death. His plans were shattered. His life was suddenly without meaning. He would have nobody to pass the business on to. And then straightening his form and gathering his breath he called out over Giuseppe's shoulder. Called to the heavens as loud as you could ever hear a man shout for all the Gods and all the valleys below to hear with echoes travelling far and wide

"P E D R O."

And he sobbed and whispered into Giuseppe's ear, "I loved my boy, for all my life."

The breeze took the name to the Universe. They took a slow ride back to the women.

159

32. FREDERICK

"I found the whole experience quite extraordinary Frederick. The atmosphere of the audience. The way people hung on every word. Not that I understood most of it, but I could feel it" said Joan.

"Someone said to me once that Opera is just controlled shouting."advised Frederick

"Very well controlled shouting and beautifully articulated. I had no idea the human voice could be so mesmerising. I think I sat there with my jaw dropping open for so much of the performance."

"That is age Joan, the mandible becomes weak." He emulated a goldfish.

"I thought I would regret telling the woman next to me that it was my first time at the Opera. She did go on a bit. But as the performance went on, her interpretation of the programme was actually invaluable and I understood most of the plot and the way the cast, those playing the hiding gypsies, were able to sing so loudly. But the voice of Stella mesmerised me the most playing Leonora. How can one person hold an audience of thousands so enthralled. You could hear a pin drop."

"I know, it was spectacular. Thank you so much Joan for getting those tickets. It was a lovely thought. What inspired you to do it?"

"Oddly there was a sheet of paper down inside my holdall bag. It must have belonged to the woman with smelly feet who sat next to me on the plane. It was their programme of events that their group was going to see. It must have fallen off her lap into my bag. Or maybe the interfering hostess who kept moving my things probably put my book in her bag and her programme in mine. Whatever. Anyway, they were finishing their Opera tour with Il Trovatore. Their performance was the night before last. I went along to the box office and asked to look inside the Arena and the lady said she had three or four tickets returned just then so I nabbed them. Spontaneous synchronicity."

"Well I think young Giuseppe enjoyed the evening. I could feel his pulse race sometimes as he held my hand throughout."

"And mine. He is a very sensitive young chap for someone so strong and good looking isn't he?"

"Lovely company. Been very good to me while I've been here. My right hand man you could say."

She leaned forward looking up toward him knowingly.

"What are you alluding to Frederick?"

"I will be glad when he puts Candy in her rightful place, hopefully he will do it tomorrow so that we can get some of this laundry washed. I have two shirts and lots of smalls to get done."

"I have some laundry too Frederick. I spilled pasta sauce on my yellow frock yesterday at supper. It needs a rinse."

"The meal wasn't very inspiring was it? Sorry about that but sweet of Giuseppe to treat us. I guess he is helping his mother with chores today now that she has a full time job."

"Well, she had a full time job before didn't she? Washing smalls in the back of the church? That was a very odd set up Frederick. It still puzzles me. Have you made any sense of it?"

"In a word. No. Shall I make us a cup of coffee and get a sheet of paper and write down what we do know and maybe that will tell us what we don't know?"

"Yes let's do that. Let's become sleuths for the day. I'll just nip to the ladies."

They sat side by side and looked down the Cypresses. It didn't take too long to make the list of what they did know.

"You have nice handwriting Joan. Very flowing."

"It's a good fountain pen Frederick with a broad gold plated nib. It's a Conway Stuart. One of the best. But I might run out of Ink. Do you have a pot?"

"I do have some somewhere in one of the drawers. Let me write the other list of what we don't know. I have a Biro which is quite reliable."

They started their list each throwing ideas into the melting pot which Frederick swiftly noted.

- Did Nonna die of natural causes ?
- How did she accumulate over a million Lira ?
- Who is in the laundry now ?
- Why was the washing swiftly taken off the lines ?
- Why did Lily have to do the extra washing in the church ?
- What has Father Leo got to do with laundry work ?
- Why have they shifted all the washing powder again ?
- Why did they hide the rear entrance behind the ivy ?
- Who were the gentleman callers ?
- What are the signs of hidden crime ?

They both stared into space and were quiet. And then simultaneously spoke with the same idea.

"How about a nice Sunday walk before we come back and have some lunch. I have some nice salami sausage."

"Shall we go to the meadow behind the laundry again."

"Yes let's."

33. JOAN

"I would like to lay here Frederick, on the ground, surrounded by the cornflowers and the ox eye daisies. Absorb some of this lovely sunshine that we so seldom see in the north of England."

She folded her legs so lowering herself and then lay on her back into the thick grass and picked one of the cornflowers and twirled it.

"The blue is the same colour as the pattern on your frock" commented Fredrick as he lay on the gentle slope next to her.

"This really is a lovely part of the world you have decided to settle in for your retirement. The air is clean and fresh and it is so quiet. Just the birds chirping. Even the sound of horseshoes on the cobbles in the village from time to time. A lot of people still don't have motorised transport do they?"

"Indeed they don't, they prefer the simple pleasures I suppose. Uncomplicated. Good food and a warm home is all they basically need and strive for in the countryside here. But you have seen how different it is in the towns and cities. Commerce, cars, vans and trucks moving people and stuff around all the time, keeping everyone busy."

"And polluted Frederick. Why would they do it when this is on the doorstep?"

"The young find this boring, or most of them do. Giuseppe is an exception, but even he has a motorbike to get to see his pal Pedro."

"When I was a schoolgirl, between the wars, we would occasionally get the odd warm sunny day and get a chance to do this. A bunch of us girls, all dressed in the same convent school uniform, would take ourselves across the playing fields to the grassy bank and lay and look at the sky. We used to look at the clouds and make shapes of them and call out to the others ... I see a dragon in that one there and another would say I see a Zeppelin in that one ... or one girl always used to shout out I can see Charlie Chaplin's face in that one and we would all groan because she was besotted with him and his silent movies. Isn't it funny what we remember from all those years ago."reminisced Joan

"On sunny days we would be playing tennis, or waiting for a court. It was so popular back then and so few places to play. Gable end walls

163

often had a line at net height or a set of goal posts painted onto them. It was OK on a corner shop where there was nobody living downstairs but when it was the end of a terrace it must have driven the people inside nutty with the sound of the ball. We never saw an aeroplane, yet in some parts now you see them all the time." said Frederick

"Yes I hadn't thought about that. It all changed in the war didn't it Frederick."

"We were, in parts of the UK, in many respects, somewhat shielded from the worst of it. This country, Italy, is long and thin and not that many miles North of this meadow is Germany and they had great control with the aid of Mussolini and his Fascist party. And after he was done, there was the civil war which split this long thin country into three or four segments. It was a mess and it's only just recovering from it and I reckon it might take another fifty years to sort it out. It's a basket case country where every man has an opinion, will shout about it, make a feathery fuss, go womanise all evening and then go to sleep until the next day to start all over again."

"Well this bit of it is very beautiful Frederick."

"We aren't far from the lakes and I think you might like a day out there in the coming week. Shall we do that?" he asked

"That would be rather fun. Yes please. But first, I've had enough of laying here. My back is getting a bit damp. I wonder what you think about trying that back gate behind the Ivy and going to have a look about the laundry if there's nobody about?"

"You are a bit of a daredevil on the quiet Joan. But whilst we are within spitting distance, why not? Just a neighbourly check up, as it were."

The gate was unlocked and a simple latch opened it, but they were covered in dust and bits of ivy that fell from above. They were in the rough patch of ground down from the washing lines that criss-crossed the old stone paving toward the house. A simple iron bench was itself getting encapsulated by the ivy that was the main greenery in this garden. Occasional wild flowers and weeds grew in cracks between the pavements and even though it was only a week since she had died, already her patch of earth was starting the process of dereliction that was so prevalent all over Italy. The Napoleonic laws did not deal sensibly with property matters and there was always a tussle between the state and the beneficiaries after a death. The state came off best and the properties inevitably came off worst. It was an endemic issue across the continent. Britain's freehold laws seldom got in the way of succession to title.

They called out 'Hello' a few times but there was no sign of life today. It was coming up to lunchtime and much of the country would either be at Mass or just be getting up. Sunday was a day of rest and everything was shut. They ducked under the drooping laundry lines and avoided the hundreds of clothes pegs dangling like sparrows on a phone wire. Close up, the white distemper was flaking off the walls and a few straggly pelargoniums in hefty pots were crying out for water.

Frederick tried the main back door and it was locked. They looked around over toward the meadow and there was no sight nor sound of any life. Joan tried the door of one of the outhouses and it was open. Inside were a dozen woven laundry baskets that looked as if they hadn't moved for years each covered in cobwebs and dust. Beyond, a few enamel bowls covered with dirt and grit so again unused for two or three years at least.

"What's in there Joan?"

"Just a few old baskets and bowls that haven't been touched in a couple of years. Try that door Frederick."

"This one is locked but you can see someone has been in recently because there is a torn piece of material down there caught on the door."

"So there is, that is a little bit of black cassock I reckon. Father Leo might be the confirmed visitor" said Joan.

Frederick tried a couple of other doors, one locked and another open so he poked his head in.

"Outside lavatory."

Walking down out of the Ivy gate Joan's frizz filled with more bits and likewise down Frederick's neck.

"I wonder if anyone else has the keys. I would like to know what's in those locked outhouses."

They had a leisurely walk back to the canonica for a light lunch and a glass or two of white wine.

34. GIUSEPPE

"Hello Frederick. Hello Joan. I thought I would call by and say that I'll start the extension work tomorrow if that's alright. I had a busy day yesterday with Mama and needed a day to just rest if that's OK? Mama has asked a favour of you. May we wash these sheets in Candy, just this once?"

"Of course it's alright Giuseppe, you know we are flexible and accommodating here" said Frederick. "But we need to move Candy back onto her new flat base and connect her again. And would you mind showing me what to do to get the cable back onto the wireless so we can hear the radio during the day. I'll just fetch the cable that Pedro gave me last week and perhaps we need a screwdriver and pliers."

As Frederick headed into the kitchen he called back "and how is that crafty young boyfriend of yours, the little rascal?"

"He's dead" said Giuseppe flatly.

Frederick bounced back with the tools and cables and said "what did you say? I didn't hear you correctly."

"I said Pedro is dead. He died on the morning we went to the Opera. The little truck was driven off the road up in the foothills and tumbled over the edge with his deliveries on the back."

"Oh dear God Giuseppe. So that explains the note on the shop door. Oh my Lord."

Joan emerged from her bedroom onto the patio, observed the men staring at each other and she detected Giuseppe was about to break down.

"What's the matter here? Have you two had a tiff? I hope it's not about the meal before the performance. We all so enjoyed the opera Giuseppe" she rambled, completely unaware of the situation.

"Ahem. Joan, It's Pedro, Joan. He's been killed in a road accident in the little truck" Frederick informed after clearing his throat.

"Oh dear God. No. No. Not Pedro surely" she said. *How clumsy of me, I didn't know* she thought.

Giuseppe could contain himself no longer. Tears streamed down his face as his lips quivered and his face creased into an expression of the deepest hurt and sadness. Joan pulled a small hanky from her sleeve and handed it over and he filled it in one blow. "Come come" she said and hugged him and put his head on her shoulder where he could sob against her frizzy hair. It was hurting his back bending so low but her hair smelled familiar and comforting. After a while he straightened up and threw the hanky onto the pile of sheets waiting on the table.

"Let's shift Candy and get these sheets in. Pedro would want her earning her keep" said Giuseppe as more tears filled his eyes and nose.

The men shifted the machine and Joan tidied the wire and pliers on the table and brought the pile of sheets off the table and placed them on Candy.

"You go now Giuseppe and rest a while and come back soon, either tomorrow or the next day. When you are ready, you've a few things to do" Frederick held him squarely in a *be brave* manner.
And as Giuseppe was leaving Frederick called after him ...

"Please ask your mother if she has a set of keys to the old Nonna's laundry for me to borrow?"

Giuseppe was perplexed by this last request and a bit annoyed. *What business has Frederick poking about the old Laundry. And Mama cannot be put into a position where she is in trouble with Father Leo. Couldn't he see I'm upset about Pedro?*

Frederick meanwhile checked the pipes on Candy as she was pumping to make sure she didn't leak on the nice new floor. *Hopefully she won't go walkabout again.*

Joan felt punched by the news. Although she didn't know Pedro and had only exchanged words with him the other morning, she empathised the deeper meaning for Giuseppe. He had revealed that he and his friend had been intimate after a quarter century of knowing each other and that had formed a sort of male bond between them and now that bond was gone. *That is an exceptionally sad loss to bear. I wish I hadn't rattled on about the evening out.* She set Candy to do his sheets.

"Mama, don't you have to be in work today?" he asked her as he arrived back on the bike.

"Not until the lunch serving and again this evening for dinner." Lily was catching up on chores that should have been done yesterday. The kitchen was untidy after Giuseppe had attempted to make a meal for himself. *I must teach him again how to crack an egg on the side of a pan and not over the stove.*

"Do you have a set of keys to the old Nonna's laundry Mama? Frederick would like to borrow them. I think he and Joan are coming up with some theories about what has been going on in there."

"Sit down Giuseppe. I'll make us a coffee. I need to talk with you because I don't know what to do about what I know."

He sat at the table and waited for the coffee. He could see she was thinking about how to tell him something important. *What now? This is all too much.*

"Let's have sugar in this coffee, it's bitter compared to the stuff at the cafe."

"Spill the beans Mama."

"I don't know where to begin Seppe because there is a lot I don't know. So there are facts and there is supposition or guesswork."

"Before that Mama, do you have a set of keys?"

"No I don't, but I know where there should be some. We'll deal with that later."

She started her story from a time before Father Leo arrived and she finished it at the point that she went to the church after finding out from Pedro that the Nonna had left a million Lira to the church.

"And that is all I know Giuseppe and I am frightened about what might happen next. I think you are the only person who can be between your friend Frederick and his theories and what I've told you.

I cannot speak English well enough to convey any of this and I think he shouldn't be told all of it. Not yet anyway."

"OK Mama, I understand. How complicated this all is and all going on in our little village too. How have we become mixed up in this?"

"If we can lay blame anywhere Seppe then I think I know where" she said.

"Do you think it is anything to do with Pedro's accident?"

"It is quite possible Giuseppe. We might all be in their sights."

"I think I will go to church and sit quietly." Giuseppe felt exhausted by all this information. *I'm good with my hands but not so with my brain*, he thought. *Oh, and my loins.*

"If that is where you are going, let me tell you where there are some keys. But be very careful."

Lily resumed her housework feeling better for sharing her burden and Giuseppe walked to church.
It was sultry. His mind was in a funk. He knew he wouldn't cry again about Pedro, but he did need to join forces with Frederick to solve what had been going on in the village, especially if it implicated Pedro and his grisly death. And Mama knew something was adrift with Father Leo, but what did he have over the Nonna? She was a sturdy woman and years of laundry made her strong as an ox, so why was she so devoted so as to leave a fortune to a village church and where would the money go?

The heavy church door was closed and coincidentally the bell went clank for the half hour just as he turned the handle. That too went with a clunk. There was no quiet when visiting this church. He closed the door behind him and walked a little way up the aisle, stopped and performed his Signum Crucis which his mother had taught him and Pedro together a quarter century ago. He moved into a pew to the left and knelt on a thin velvet pad. After his rituals he just sat in the silence looking forward to the Altar and the images of the Virgin painted over the stone columns. There was nobody else there. It was cool, quiet and solemn. It occurred to him he should say a prayer for Pedro. So he merely repeated over and over what he had learned as a child at his own Grandpa's demise.

"Hail Mary, full of grace. The Lord is with thee.
Blessed art thou amongst women, and blessed is the fruit of thy
womb, Jesus.
Holy Mary, Mother of God, pray for us sinners, now and at the hour of
our death,
Riposa in Pace. Amen."

Thirty two such devotions for each year of Pedro's life.

He felt connected and content. To conclude his personal mourning he
then asked out loud ...

"Spirit. Lord. Universe or God. Please guide me to a solution of the
misdeeds in this village and within this church, I pray. Amen."

He stood in the aisle and performed a second Signum Crucis to give
thanks for guidance, turned and left. The door latch clicked loudly.

Along the road he disappeared down the side path and found his way
through the Ivy door up to the third outhouse. He reached up and felt
inside a brick under the broken gutter and as Mama had indicated
and found a set of skeleton keys on a large metal ring. The Nonna had
only shown Lily this once when they first met and they were never
mentioned again, but Lily had remembered, as if a dream.

35. FREDERICK

"Joan dear, I know you want to catch the bus to Verona today but how about I take you in tomorrow morning instead? I would like to meet Pedro's father and also get an iron because that will be a heavy thing for you to carry about all day" asked Frederick.

"I really don't mind, I'm sure the travel agent can wait a day for the travellers cheque payment and there is a market on Tuesdays which I would like to see in operation with the fresh fruit and vegetables and fish and so on" she responded and added "but if it doesn't work out for any reason then I can still get the bus tomorrow and get your iron because the bus stops just a short walk from their shop and I could get on the bus there on the way back and not carry it all day long."

"OK let's see what transpires today."

Candy had finished Lily's sheets and subsequently a load of his smalls and he gathered them in the basket ... Joan sorted her coloured things while Frederick opened the new pack of powder especially for those and helped her choose a gentle program. *The last thing I want is to boil her yellow crimplene frock* he thought. They went down to the washing lines together to peg out the loads.

"What are all those coloured granules in the powder Frederick?"

"Well funnily enough Joan, young Pedro, God rest his soul waa a rather clever fellow, not just a delivery driver, and he told me about this the other day when demonstrating his machines. Did you know detergent was a scientific discovery in Germany about the time of World War One. It's partially a petrochemical deriving from oil and that the name Persil is derived from Perborate and Silica that are two main ingredients in it. But the coloured bits are just added colour to the same white detergent. They make the coloured batches into granules and add a few of them to the same stuff that is white so you have mainly white powder with blue, orange and red grains in it and people pay more for it because they think the coloured bits contain some special ingredient to make it wash better, whereas it's just a marketing ploy to be able to charge more."

"So why is that called colour powder?" she continued.

"Because it has less chlorine bleach in it, unlike the stuff for white sheets and towels."

"So it has less and they charge more?"

"Clever isn't it? That's modern Marketing."

"It's the same with Beechams Powders Frederick. Did you know that a Beechams Powder contains only Aspirin. You can buy a hundred aspirins for two and sixpence or you can buy ten Beechams Powders in a box for two shillings which are basically ten bashed up aspirins wrapped in ten bits of paper. Clever isn't it? Marketing."

They finished pegging out.

"Well given Giuseppe isn't coming here to work today why don't we have that drive out to the lakes this afternoon and see where it leads us. It's set to be another sunny day so we could have the top down."

"That's a nice idea Frederick. I think my dress will be washed shortly so why don't we have a cuppa before we go. I will get changed into some walking slacks and prepare a scarf."
"And I will make up a quick picnic and we will find a nice spot to admire the views" suggested Frederick.

Frederick prepared the Sunbeam and wiped the windscreen of all the petals and debris. Joan packed her bag and the picnic basket into the boot. She made one last check of Candy which had completed its cycle.

"Frederick look, I see Candy knows this load is man-made fibre and drip dry. How clever. I will just peg these out and be in the car in a jiffy" said Joan.

After pegging, a clank and hiss they were ready and made headway.

"Stop a moment will you Frederick" said Joan when they were only just past the church. He pulled up across from the laundry.

"What's the matter? Forgotten something?" asked Frederick.

"No, not at all. Let me out a moment." she was aware she was in the road but there wa no other traffic

Joan hoisted herself out of the Sunbeam and walked back to a car parked on the roadside between the church and the laundry. It was unoccupied. Frederick was watching in his rear view mirror. *What is she up to? Joan isn't a car fanatic but that looks like a lovely Lancia.* He watched as she walked around it and then came back to seat herself beside him.

"OK we can go on now Frederick."

"Not until I know what that was all about?" he said

"That pale blue sports car parked up behind us."

"Yes I can see it in the mirror" he pointed at it between them stuck to the windscreen with one of those suction caps.

"I've seen it before, because it is very noticeable and quite unique. I remember it now and am surprised to see it here."

"So where did you see it? Do you want to buy one? Worth a fortune I shouldn't wonder. It's a Lancia I think Joan." he explained

"It's a Lancia Flamina GT and looks almost new actually."

"You know your stuff Joan." he was impressed

"Don't be silly, I just read the label on it."

"Badge dear." he corrected

"Anyway, I saw it when I was waiting for you at the airport. Waiting in the wrong place."

"And?"

"And it was driven by a very chi chi woman with blond hair and big sunglasses. She came whizzing in and then picked up a Pilot fellow in a uniform."

"Well, I suppose they have to live somewhere."

"Hmmm. Can we stay sitting here for five or ten minutes and see if anyone comes back to it Frederick. We are in the shade so we will be alright just for a while".

174

"Well, I tell you what. You just sit here and look in the mirror to see what happens. I'm going to walk along and just have a chat with the butcher boy."

He adjusted the mirror a little as he got out and Joan took over to get it right for the left seat. She was quite short so could go unnoticed. Frederick pushed the door to quietly and walked away.

"Hello my dear young fellow. How is the good looking butcher today?" Frederick flirted.

"Good morning Sir. Did you enjoy my sausage from last week?"

"I did indeed." *Here we go with the camp banter* he thought.

"And would you like some more of it? Perhaps I can interest you in this one?" he pointed into the counter.

"And what are the attributes of that particular one?"

"Well for a start it's longer and thicker and very tasty for an older gentleman like yourself."

He's trying to hook me in thought Frederick. "Where's the boss today? Is he out the back cutting meat?"

"No he goes to market on Mondays so I am always here by myself on Mondays and it's always quiet about this time."

He is giving me all the cues to come back or get involved.

The blue car shot past the window.

"Oh goodness" said Frederick. "Did you see that sports car. That's a Lancia if I'm not mistaken."

"It's a 1962 Lancia Flamina GT in duck egg blue with triple carburetors and would have cost what I will earn in the next ten years working here" said butcher boy.

"Have you seen it before then? Do they live here?"

"No she doesn't live here. She comes to church here every week. Same time dressed in her fancy sunglasses. Never spends anything in the village."

"I wonder who she is and why she comes here to pray?"

"I don't know, but Pedro knows her, ask him."

So he doesn't know about Pedro. Shall I tell him or not? "Sorry, I need to go. I suddenly need the lavatory. I will pop back and see you in the week. So sorry. Must go now."

"The boss isn't here Thursday afternoons, he has the afternoon off so I'm alone on Thursday afternoons."

I know your game sunshine, keep trying. "I will try to come back then then. Bye for now" finished Frederick feigning urgency as a customer came into the shop.

"What did you see Joan?" as he hopped back in. "Shall we scoot after it?" he adjusted the mirror and was away. Passing the butchers he waved but the boy was busy serving.

"It was her Frederick. The same woman I saw at the airport. I'm pretty certain I saw her come from the path at the side of the laundry although I am not sure about that because the old woman in black had emerged from her porch and walked up the road opposite the butchers, she saw you go in and was watching you inside the shop, I am surprised you didn't see her over the road when you were dealing with the boy with the false teeth. Anyway, the blonde then disappeared into the church. I kept an eye on the church and no more than two minutes later she came barging out of the church and seemed very cross. Not what you would expect of someone who has just received a blessing. She was carrying a similar briefcase to the pilot she picked up. All pilots seem to use them because the Dan Air pilot had one as well I noticed, or maybe the second officer but it must be standard issue. But I'm not certain if she had that with her when she went into the church, I was distracted."

"I think those bags are called Alassio Pilot cases Joan. Alassio is a lovely town that could be mistaken for Torquay in its heyday. The English used to come in droves to Alassio in the eighteen eighties. A new railway connected Genoa to London and it was the fashionable

Edwardian resort for those that could afford it. Those that could only aspire to Alassio went to Torquay instead."

"Could we go there now instead of the lakes?"

"Ha ha. Not likely. Alassio is much too far old girl. We need to get the Atlas out later on and I will show you where it is. It must be about two or three hundred miles from here. It's halfway between Nice and Genoa."

"So getting back to the woman in the Lancia Fredrick. What was she doing in the village visiting the church or the laundry?"

"And how come Pedro knew her?" he said.

"Pedro? The late Pedro?"

"Yes, the butcher boy told me he saw that car turn up more or less the same time every week and the same woman driving it. He knew what model Lancia it was. It's the sort of car that would turn a boy's head. You know, I reckon she will turn right for the airport whereas we go left for the lakes, but just up along here we might get to see her heading East."

Having a right hand drive car was handy because he pulled into the layby before the junction on the right and could see for miles over the hillside and down toward the valley where the tail end of the duck egg blue convertible was heading East as he expected.

36. GIUSEPPE

There were three old keys on the blackened copper hoop, black from at least a hundred years of fingers secreting sweat into them over the age.

One of them fitted an outhouse door which had a torn piece of black cloth on the bottom. He entered. This was a big room used for drying and storage. There on the wooden racking were some recently folded sheets and towels. *Probably the lot that Mama took from the line a week ago. Very neat and precise but meant for nobody presumably, nobody claimed them?* Further along the same rack was another set folded some time earlier as the spiders had woven a few little webs on the creases. These were almost identical. *Like a changeover set just for the laundry line?* On the other side of the room was identical racking made with softened edges of a good carpenter who had planed them well and hidden the screws so they didn't catch the linens. On these shelves were small cardboard boxes labelled Washing Soda and a dozen or so, again empty, labelled Roberts Talcum Powder. On the back wall there were about twenty tins with lids like those for Tate and Lyle golden syrup but with an Italian brand Borotalco Talc. On the lower shelves were old packets of foreign soap powder, opened and empty like Skip, Tide and Sunil printed in French and a few German Echwan Pulver. Other odds and sods laid about including an old set of weighing scales with a pyramid of gramme weights but a few of them seemed to be missing from the pile and various sized spoons.

An odd range of stuff to be in the room Giuseppe thought. *Nothing to do with laundry except the sheets and old laundry powders but they almost look like stage props that Dad used to show me at the Opera.* He emerged and locked up behind him squinting in the bright sunlight.

He needed to pee and opened another door with a small room full of bowls and baskets which had laid dormant for some time and next to this he found the outside lavatory. He was being polite for some unknown reason and wondered to himself *why didn't I just pee in the outside gulley? I usually do, at Frederick's and at home.*

The second key opened the remaining outhouse that he tried and was locked. The key was awkward to turn and needed jiggling about. *Perhaps someone has tried the wrong key or forced this one recently.* This was a smaller room similarly racked out like the one with the sheets. He could tell the Nonna had not left this outhouse in this state. This had boxes again which were full or part opened and they were stacked on their sides as if moved in here in a hurry in piles of half a dozen. As much as someone could carry at a time without spilling any contents and they were not in order like the tins and empty packets. These were a jumble. There were packs of Chalk powder, Talcum powder but it had no scent, Starch. *Useful for old fashioned collars and cuffs and formal wear* Giuseppe considered, plus a few packs of Soda crystals, *water softening I suppose to make suds* and Caustic soda, *presumably to get out greasy marks?* There was another set of scales with two little tin trays either side like a jeweller might use to weigh the gold ring you were going to sell or pawn when times were tough. That had imperial weights in ounces with eight tiny little weights. He played with them putting an ounce one side and counted eight into the other tray to see these delicate little scales come to balance.

The final key must get me into the house he thought as he locked up behind him. He was coming to understand what was going on here in the middle of this little village. *How amazing. And how was Pedro wrapped up in this?* He closed his eyes and rested with his back against the wall. *Mama was unwittingly party to all this too. She is all I have left and I must, must, must protect her. Oh Pedro, you silly man bless your heart.* He was getting emotional again. *I must go straight up to see Frederick when I've looked in here* he thought as he turned the third key.

There were a few flies circling in this scullery so he left the door open in the expectation they would make for the door and leave. They didn't, they just aimlessly flew in circles as though it was the only route to avoid the two spiders waiting on the ceiling and wall. This room led into a sort of old kitchen which then went through to the front of the shop where if anyone passed he would be seen so he closed the inner door to see what was to be seen in here. There was a big Kenwood electric planetary food mixer like the one they had at the bakers and then alongside a smaller hand held mixer called a Sunbeam. *The same maker as Frederick's car. I must tell him later.* He went back down to the scullery.

In the corners were wooden countertops made of planks between a huge white porcelain sink that had a big tap above one corner. The window above was whitewashed with distemper so there was light but you could neither see out nor in. *This must be where the main wash was done.* He lifted the lid to see a big pot, the sort in which cannibals

179

would cook the other tribe. It was copper and the corner chimney behind it would allow Nonna to light a fire below to keep it hot. A lone spider jumped at the sudden light landing further down the pot, maybe hoping that a few of the pesky flies hovering above Giuseppe's head would commit hari kari and dive into the pot. He quietly replaced the lid carefully covering his tracks when he accidentally kicked the metal bucket under the sink making a racket as it fell over and rolled side to side.

In the corner opposite the back door was another wooden cover and maybe another boiling copper. This had four wide loose planks so he had to remove one at a time and set it aside over the sink. He had just placed the final rear plank on the sink to find he had opened the Well. There was a shrivelled bar of soap behind the sink. *Ideal to see how deep it is. Certainly deep and a long way down* he thought as he held the soap ready to drop and conscious that he must count to see how deep it is. He would have to listen carefully to hear the splosh. He leaned as far as he dare and let the soap go and started counting. A split second later he thought it was suddenly darker in the scullery, a shadow perhaps from the door, the air changed, faintly scented and in haste he dropped the keys. As he heard them clank and then splosh below him he felt his trousers shift around his ankles as he was tipped forward over the edge. His last recollection was a woman's voice

"Want to know how deep it is do you?" is all she said

It went blackest black. Pain and then a still nothingness.

The planks were carefully replaced for him.

37. JOAN

"This is a lovely spontaneous idea Frederick. What gorgeous scenery and there's nobody about. Where is that place, over there, in the distance?"

"That's Garda and this is Lake Garda."

"It's wonderful and with that mountain backdrop. Simply perfect. Shall I get the rug from the boot and we set up here?"

"I thought that might be a good idea Joan. I've been just here before."

They laid out the blanket together. Frederick placed stones on the four corners whilst Joan gathered and presented the picnic.

"Good idea to use those lemon tea bags in the Thermos Joan."

"Yes, it's quite refreshing and doesn't over-brew like ordinary tea or coffee would. I brought exactly enough for my seven days but after, ahem." She paused to choose her words carefully and with a momentary flashback, she took a sip of tea. "After I spent a little time with Giuseppe I seem to have gone off the slightly bitter flavour a little. I put a spoon of sugar in the flask with them and it has worked well. We might as well use them, I don't want to haul them back to England. I brought far too much stuff as it is" said Joan.

They took in the landscape with the brew. A cool breeze came up wafting the long grass creating ripples of yellow and green. A few butterflies and bees emerged to see their new temporary neighbours on the hillside. She continued

"I thought tomorrow Frederick when Giuseppe comes to start the extension work that I might ask him if he would like to come to England and stay with me a little while. How long will it take him to do the work on the Canonica?"

"I would think about three weeks Joan, but inevitably things go a little awry and jobs take longer so say about a month. I don't know yet how to finish the roof. If we have tiles it will make the area a bit dark inside. I will talk with him tomorrow and see if he thinks some of that new clear plastic stuff will be any good. But about a month I guess providing we don't get any more interruptions."

181

"Do you know if he has ever been to England Frederick?"

"I don't think he has ever been out of Italy Joan. You would need to help him with his fare and I guess you will pay him to do work for you if that is what you have in mind."

"Oh, of course I would send him a ticket, or he could go to that travel agent and I will somehow pay them and yes I would make sure he is paid for his working time. I need my plumbing seeing to."

Frederick raised an eyebrow over his flask cup as he finished the tea. He unwrapped the sandwiches and brought the vine of tomatoes from the basket whilst trying not to imagine how thoroughly Giuseppe would attend to her plumbing needs over the course of two or three weeks in rainy England.

"Goodness knows we have had some interruptions from the normal quiet life this past week or so haven't we Joan?" he continued.

"Yes I never imagined that your village life would be so interesting. It just goes to show that life is the same all over the world. We all think we are in control but as Harold Macmillan said when he was Prime Minister what gets in the way of our plans are 'Events dear boy, Events'."

They nodded agreement and gnawed at the delicious but slightly dry bread. Joan would not gnaw at the crusts but was happy to eat from the middle outwards.

"Delicious soft cheese with the salami Frederick. What is it? Delicate flavour and I don't usually eat much cheese" Joan asked.

"I think it's Burrata Joan. It's local and the butchers sell it. Which reminds me that I think I ought to do two things tomorrow once Giuseppe is all set up and once I've waved my arms around explaining what I think we should build."

Joan laughed at his actions with his arms because she had witnessed him illustrating his vision for his projects by waving his hands in thin air in the hope that his workforce could see the same mind manifestation that he could see. Of course, they couldn't, and in the end to make sure they were all heading in the same direction would resort to a drawing on paper, often on the back of a cigarette packet. He continued

"I think I should go to see Francesca, the lady in black who is the butcher boy's Grandmother because as you witnessed she walked the street to see who was talking to the boy when it was me. She sees and knows a lot in our little investigation and then we should go to see Pedro's father at his shop because I think Pedro was somehow involved in whatever was going on. He knew the blonde in the Lancia. We wrote a list but I can't remember it and I can't even remember where I put the list. I'm going dotty."

"Well you are in luck" said Joan rising and going over to the car, "because as luck would have it I have the said list in my handbag here" and she unfolded the paper which had a pen already attached to it.

"Oh you are a champion Joan. Just like Miss Prentice, she was administratively efficient. Shall we go through it and see if we can answer any of the questions?"

Frederick lay on his back facing the sun which was interrupted by fluffy clouds going over giving half shade and respite with intermittent warmth and cool. He thought he saw some shapes in the clouds.

"Shall I read them one by one Frederick?"

"Go ahead. Let's see whether we can make sense of it."

- "Did Nonna die of natural causes?"

"She may or may not have done would be how I sum that one up. Whichever it was, we will never find out. She is well and truly sealed up in a niche in the graveyard. What do you think Joan?"

"I agree with you Frederick. We have nothing to gain by pursuing that line. We don't have the forensic ability to determine whether or not she was poisoned. That is an open verdict that can go one way or the other."

- "How did she accumulate over a million Lira?"

"That is the Million Lira question eh? Let's think. She could have inherited it recently, I say recently because she wouldn't do laundry if she didn't have to. From what we have seen in the outhouses it looked as though not much laundry has been going on in there anyway. It looks to be a cover for some other activity."

"I agree and the other activity as you call it is presumably an illegal one that pays very well. And presumably Nonna had her hand in the till and got found out by whoever is in charge of the proceeds of crime" said Joan.

"So let's come back to that question at the end. Is there any more tea in that Thermos Joan?"

- "Who is in the laundry now?"

Joan poured as Frederick contemplated.

"This relates to who we saw and has been seen in the Laundry or the yard and we suspect it is Father Leo and A N Other unknown person or persons who may or may not be alive now."

"Here's your tea Frederick. Are you suggesting that Pedro might have been one of the people meeting Father Leo?"

"It's not out of the question that he may have been. Let's move on to the next question."

- "Why was the washing swiftly taken off the lines?"

"I think we need to ask Lily a bit more about that day."

"Or maybe Giuseppe will tell us more tomorrow if his Mama has spoken to him."

"I agree with you Joan. I think Lily hides behind the language barrier because she is fearful of what she thinks she knows."

- "Why did Lily have to do the extra washing in the church?"

"So we know that since the accident at the Opera Forum Lily has been short of money so she needed the work."

"And she is now earning at the cafe instead, which is a blessing that came along" added Joan.

"And we know that father Leo was the instigator and often the mule between the laundry and the church bringing over all the smalls."

"So what happened to the bigger stuff, the sheets and towels and heavy things?" asked Joan.

"Well if they weren't done in the laundry, they must have gone off in a van to another commercial laundry or to someone with washing machines."

"Pedro?" they said his name at the same time.

"We mustn't jump to false conclusions Joan but let's keep on with the puzzle."
- "What has Father Leo got to do with laundry work?"

"I think we can sum that up in one word Joan. Nothing. Moving on."

- "Why have they shifted all the washing powder again?"

"We need the laundry keys to look around the place to see what other evidence we find. I do hope Lily has some keys or knows how to *borrow* Father Leo's set - assuming he has a set. Hopefully Giuseppe will bring us some keys in the morning, or maybe even tonight when we get back. You know how he is, he just turns up all unexpectedly looking for a bed for the night."

"With a man or woman in it, ready to receive him" added Joan very matter of factly. *I continue to surprise myself at my new candour* she thought.

- "Why did they hide the rear entrance behind the ivy?"

"Is that the last question yet? I need a pee Joan. I didn't realise we had listed so many questions."

"There's only two more questions. Just have a pee over there behind the car, there's nobody about but me."

He dragged himself up off the blanket and hid behind the open boot lid peeing out toward the lane and the gate they had opened to get into the field. The breeze was getting stronger and cooler.

"What was the question again?" he asked as he stayed standing and looking out over the lake.

- "Why did they hide the rear entrance behind the ivy?"

"Another one word answer I think Joan. Some criminal activity."

"That's three words."

"Ok Smart Alec. Crime."

"I agree."

- "Who were the gentleman callers?"

"Men fetching and taking away supplies and possibly Pedro fetching and carrying sheets and towels" said Frederick picking up the corner stones. The blanket folded over itself along the leading edge.

"Finally then Frederick, last question ..."

- What are the signs of hidden crime?"

"I think this is a three word answer Joan. All of them."

"Yes, it reeks of it, doesn't it. I need a pee now. It's all that lemon tea. I haven't peed in a field since I was a girl. You can look the other way while I go behind the car."

"Don't worry Joan. I'm hardly likely to try to sneak a peek am I?"

Frederick gathered and folded the blanket and thought of Giuseppe. *I hope he does call by tonight. I wonder which bed he will choose. Maybe he will do a split shift like they do in the Candy factory to catch up with demand.* He sniggered to himself.

An hour later they were back indoors where they agreed who would be first and second with the showers so as to not scald and freeze the other.

Frederick prepared them a simple omelette supper and they each retired to bed without Giuseppe and thus slept well.

38. GIUSEPPE

My God, the pain.
And the stench.
Where am I?
Am I alive?
Am I awake?
I can't move.
Can I move?

All these thoughts rather like he had in the past shortly after his father had died when he suffered awful nightmares that would wake him in a cold sweat at two in the morning when it was pitch dark. With the shutters closed in winter his bedroom was a dungeon and he had to feel out with one hand to touch the wall and with the other to touch the side of the bed.

That's it, I'm having a nightmare, go back to sleep.

Black for a few hours.

He put his left hand out and it touched something.
Cold damp bricks or stones.
He put out just one finger and traced a groove.
Bricks definitely bricks.
He put his left hand up above his head.
But that's not up, that's down.
He let his arm muscles relax and they fell above his head.
I'm hanging upside down.
He brought his hands towards his hips and he felt a little rocking motion.
It's so dark.
I'm hanging upside down in the dark.
It stinks of shit.
I stink of shit.
I've shit myself.

Black for more hours.

His hands reached his hips.
That's Up.
A bar.
A metal bar.

I have a metal bar across my stomach.
My head is pounding.
I'm hanging upside down over a metal bar in the dark.
What's happened to me?
Has there been an accident?
Where am I?
Shall I call out?
Can I call out?
What do people call out when they are upside down reeking of their own shit?
Is this still the same nightmare

Black for several more hours.

I feel warm.
Lovely wet warm on my belly, on my chest, on my neck, itchy warm on my neck and round my ears and stinging in the corner of my eyes.
And I smell a smell, a smell of piss.
It's me.
I'm pissing my Y fronts.
Joan.
Y fronts.
Where am I?
Frederick.
Joan.
Mama.

Black . more hours.

Want to know how deep it is, do you?
Want to know how deep it is, do you?
Want to know how deep it is, do you?
Italian but with a New York twang.
Who said that?
Who am I?
Where am I?
Am I conscious?
Am I dreaming?
Am I dying?
Is this what dying is like?

Black more time

Do I have legs?
I can't feel any legs.
Do I have toes?
I feel dried piss.
I smell of piss
I feel wet pants, wet Y fronts.
I feel crusty stinking shitty Y fronts.
I smell of shit.
I'm cold and dark and my head, oh my head.
Can I call out.
I'm going to be sick

Black.

39. FREDERICK

"It's not like Giuseppe not to turn up when he says he will. Maybe he is at Pedro's shop helping his father. Or maybe with his mother."

"It's ten o'clock Frederick. Perhaps we should get on with the day as we mentioned yesterday and Giuseppe will turn up a little later. I'm sure he can get along a little with the extension."

"That's true. That boy doesn't have idle hands. He will get on with something."

They both thought of Giuseppe's hands and what he can usually get on with, but neither said anything to the other preferring to bring their minds back to the subject of the day being their investigations.

"I'm almost ready to go Frederick and can just get my purse and the travellers cheques and so on that I need after a quick trip to the heartland."

"The heartland? What do you mean?"

"The outside lavatory. At the moment it is the heartland. When I go in there of a morning there is a heart shape on my nightie from the sun rising and shining through the heart in the door. That won't be there when the extension is built and incorporates the lavvy will it?"

"I hadn't thought about that. Probably because I stand up and it's shining on my back and you sit down. But it's a good reason to have the clear plastic roof, at least in part of it." I will talk to Giuseppe about that when we find him. I will just get some sensible shoes on and we need to get some petrol in the Sunbeam, it's running on fumes."

By 10.30 having clanked and hissed they were ready and by the car.

"I think I will ask Giuseppe to get a new cistern for the lavatory or perhaps an entire new lavatory pan. Did you notice that the toilets in the Opera were silent and the cistern is low and attached to the toilet so there is no chain? I've never seen those before and thought they were rather posh. What do you think Joan?"

They were heading toward the village.

"Well, it will change the character of the house a bit. At the moment you might say it has rustic charm whereas with an inside lavatory and a lowl cistern with no chain it becomes more modern. In some ways that is more agreeable, but it is also a loss of character. But it is the way of the world, or what they call the Western world isn't it? Steady progress, much of it coming from America."

"That old pan is very difficult to clean as well Joan. I think I will have the lot replaced while I am at it and maybe a little hand basin too that could drain into where Candy drains away."

"Oh look Frederick, there's Lily in the cafe. Let's stop and ask her where Giuseppe is? You go over and ask, my Italian is too poor and she looks at me a little skeptical since I drew an over-craggy face. That didn't please her, no more than my cracked compact that makes my face look crooked pleases me."

"Good morning Lily. Nice to see you here. Are you enjoying the job?"

"Ah Frederick" as she waved to Joan down in the car, "I love it. I can't tell you the difference it has made to me. Just a moment though because I am here by myself this morning to serve and make the coffees. Let me attend to that table and I will come talk to you briefly." Lily was gone five minutes and Frederick held up his palm to Joan to indicate the delay. On the wall by the mirrors Pepe had hung Joan's drawings in glass covered frames so he went over and admired the good amateur work. Lily returned.

"So is Giuseppe at yours getting on with your extension? He told me what he was going to do."

"When was that Lily?"

"Yesterday morning. We had a long chat about you and the church and the Nonna. I feel much better for it. Did he tell you last evening after he went to Church?"

"No he didn't come over to us last evening and he is not at mine now. Joan and I had a ride out to the Lakes yesterday afternoon and had a picnic."

"Oh how lovely. Good for you. Perhaps he went over to you and found you were out and then decided to go elsewhere. He wasn't home last night. His bed hasn't been slept in."

"Ah, right. Well Joan and I are just going over to see Pedro's father at the shop which he said would reopen today. I need to buy an iron and Joan needs to go to the travel agency."

"Oh poor Pedro, it still makes me weep when I think of him. I looked after that boy from a baby you know. We were very close while they lived in the village, that's before his father bought the shop. But don't get me started on that, otherwise my mascara will run and I'll look a right mess for the customers."

"I expect to find Giuseppe at the shop, probably trying to help sort out the outstanding orders. They lost two or three appliances in the accident, so those will need to be delivered."

"I'm sure customers will have heard of the tragedy and will be understanding for a few days until they sort themselves out. Tell Seppe to come back tonight for supper please because Pepe here is making a big Risottto and he says I can take two or three portions and Giuseppe loves Risotto. Tell him about nine thirty please, tonight, with his Mama."

"Ok Lily, you have a good day and don't work too hard. You don't get the profits, Pepe does."

She laughed as she waved them off "I don't mind, I am happy again."

"Well Joan, Giuseppe wasn't home last night so he must be at the shop, helping sort out the mess they are in. That's probably more important than the extension. She said he came up to the house while we were at the lake, after going to Church. I suppose he said a prayer for Pedro."

After getting fuel, the journey into town was clear virtually all the way. It was only the last ten minutes that they were behind the bus that Joan would have been on. The so called express that was going at snail's pace.

"The fumes from that bus are utterly appalling Frederick. When I was on it last week I had no idea I was polluting the lungs of all the traffic behind us. It's disgusting."

"I have to agree with you Joan, it's pure diesel soot coming out of there and blowing directly in our face. It's an Esatau and probably ten years old. Part of the Lancia group I believe."

"It should be banned" was Joan's riposte.

Frederick parked around the corner from the shop.

"I can walk to the travel agent from here Frederick. It's not that far, so why don't I see you back here in about an hour or so."

"Ok, I will catch up with the chaps here and get an iron. Are you sure you don't want to advise what sort of iron I should have?"

"They might have the latest one that makes steam and irons out the creases but it will be expensive no doubt. See you in an hour or two."

Pedro's father was at the back of the shop staring blankly at his desk covered in paper as he had left it four or five days ago before the Police turned up. He looked up, but didn't recognise Frederick. His memory was fixated on his son. His dead cremated son. He stood, as he always did for a customer.

"Good day Sir, how may I help you?"

"Hello, I'm Frederick. I met your son Pedro last week and he sold me a Candy and delivered it. I am a very good friend of his friend Giuseppe. I know about the incident and wondered if I could sit with you a moment and talk about a few things."

"Oh yes, I'm sorry I didn't recognise you. I'm Ferrando, Pedro's father. Pleased to meet you properly. Come sit at my desk. Forgive me, but my mind is elsewhere and wondering how I will manage things now. Pedro did so much here."

"Yes I see it is all nice fresh paint and orderly. It was all a bit of a jumble when I last came."

"It's less than a week ago that the two boys did the repainting. Playing about they were, like they do at that age. You know, we have all been there. They sent me out for a haircut and when I came back they were teasing some girls at the shop window, exposing themselves virtually. I'm sure you'd have been the same, in your day."

Ferrando's eyes were full of tears and he found his handkerchief and dabbed the corner of each eye.

"Is Giuseppe here today to help you? I was expecting him at mine today to build a little extension that has resulted from acquiring Candy as we call it. She is certainly earning her keep."

"No, I haven't seen Giuseppe since he came over with Lily at the weekend. She was best friends with my wife when we lived in the village. Present at the birth and all that, like women do."

"Oh, that's peculiar. He didn't go home last night and he wasn't with Joan and I last evening so we assumed he would be here."

"Joan is your lady wife?" asked Ferrando

"Oh, no no, just a good friend. A girlfriend."

Ferrando was satisfied with that explanation.

"Oh well, I'm sure he will turn up. He is a young fellow and if he sees a field to sow his oats he will spread them. Give him until this evening. They always come home for dinner when they get hungry."

"So what brings you here today?"

"Two things. Firstly I need to buy a smoothing iron for my clothes. We no longer have a laundry in the village. I expect you heard all about that."

"Yes, Lily told my wife all about it. All sounds a bit odd to me" Ferrando interjected.

"So I will need to iron all the stuff that comes out of Candy after it's been dried. Joan said I should get a steaming iron. Do you have such a thing?" enquired Frederick.

"Well as luck would have it there is a brand new one made in Italy that is much cheaper than those American specialised things. I only have a few and you would be the first customer to own one. It's called a Pony Senior. It's in the box up there on the shelf behind my desk." He stretched up but was unable to reach it.

"Let me do it, I'm just a bit taller. This one is it?"

"Yes, young Pedro put that up there. The next generation are always taller than us oldies."

Just saying that started him off. He was determined not to break down again, particularly when at the shop, but everywhere he looked Pedro had laid a hand and he was aware that he was now alone in his business.

"I'm sorry Mr Frederick, it's just that I planned to retire in a year or two and spend more time with the wife whilst just keeping an eye from a distance while Pedro took over the shop and got a lad in to do deliveries, like he has done this past few years. We had a nice new truck you know. Giuseppe took me to see it. It's on the mountainside. I couldn't see it. It was a wreck hidden in a ravine. Overturned and burned out with PEDRO IN IT" Ferrando shouted and sobbed those last three words and hit his desk in anger at the unfairness of it.

Frederick was still holding the iron in the box. He set it on the desk and went around and put his arm across Ferrando's shoulder. Ferrando in turn turned to him and put his head on his shoulder and wept for a little longer.

"Thank you for listening to me. Silly old man that I am. I'm sorry and we have only just met. Take the iron home in the box and give it a try and if your girlfriend likes it then you can pay me next week. If she doesn't then keep the box and bring it back when it suits you. It's not every day someone walks in and wants an electric steam iron. I will do you a favourable price as you are a good customer and a good listener."

"There is a second reason for me being here Ferrando. Can we sit and I explain. It relates to the Nonna in the village."

"This sounds like it will take a while. Shall I make us a coffee in my little kitchenette? I have a machine you know. Perks of the shop."

He disappeared to the back and there was grinding, whirring and hissing and he emerged with a cafe quality pair of macchiato. Frederick then told his tale of what he did and didn't know which kept Ferrando encapsulated.

"And you are saying this could have a bearing on my son's death?" he enquired at the end.

"Well I am not a private detective, nor a policeman, but you can see where I am heading with this can't you. Would you agree to me looking in your son's room. "

"Certainly. Although I will stay here at the shop if you don't mind and will ring my wife now to arrange that for you. You can look with her. She might be upset though, so it might be best if you take your lady friend here with you" he pointed to the doorway where Joan was back from her walk to the travel agency.

"Mad dogs and Englishmen go out in the mid-day sun. I forgot my hat so had to buy another one." she posed

"Water with ice I suggest for you. Ferrando Madam, pleased to make your acquaintance" as he shook her hand before going to get a glass for her. Then he phoned Isabella leaving Joan and Frederick to look around the shop.

"I'll draw you a map. It's not far. My wife Isabella will be expecting you. She will look out for you in say twenty minutes. I've told her you are in a car with the wheel on the wrong side."

Joan fanned her face with the soft cotton cloth that Ferrando had given her around the glass.

40. JOAN

"Has Ferrando explained what's going on to his wife?" asked Joan

"He said he would ring Isabella again now while we are driving there and give her more information."

"That's a relief Frederick because I won't be able to do that. We have lots of questions, but not many answers and it won't bring Pedro back to her, in fact, it might make her feel embittered. What do you want me to do?"

"If you can catch her tears if we find anything that upsets her. I understand from Giuseppe that Pedro basically lived in a little cottage they have at the family home and that's where his bedroom is. Isabella would sometimes bring him dinner of an evening. I think we need to search there to see if we find anything. I hope she doesn't mind too much."

Isabella was waiting in the doorway dead-heading a few roses. The two women could not converse directly. Frederick became their makeshift interpreter. Smiles and gestures made up more than half of their conversation. Isabella explained to Frederick that since the accident the cottage had been sacrosanct. Neither Ferrando nor she could bear the thought of going into Pedro's private space. He was a grown man after all and did whatever he needed to do in that space.

"Would you mind if we look around Isabella?" Joan asked and Frederick interpreted.

She deliberately tilted her head in a pondering pose to illustrate they were not a threat but moreover keen on settling unsolved questions.

"I hope you are not suggesting Pedro was involved in any crime?" asked Isabella.

"Oh no, not at all, at least not wittingly. But may we see if there are any clues?"

"You two go in and see. I could make you some coffee if you would like or maybe something stronger? A glass of wine possibly?"

"Yes perfect, refreshing for us both I think?" Frederick suggested and Joan nodded approval as they turned toward the cottage.

It was unlocked and left as Pedro had left it a few mornings ago. His cold coffee cup remained. There were paint speckled trousers over the back of the settee with underpants hanging out of them. The place looked comfortable and masculine without ornament, simply functional space. An old television with two dials encased in a bakelite and cardboard body on splayed narrow metal legs was alongside the firestove. On top a V shape aerial probably tuned into the busty game shows.

The door to the bedroom was open and this was untidier. The bed was unmade and flung open by a man in a hurry to get to work and on his rounds. He had a mahogany Gentleman's Press for storage of clothes which were few. The mahogany top doors did not close properly given the uneven floor threw them out of parallel and the drawers were stiff to pull out. The bottom drawer had obviously been pulled a few many times as one of the wooden knobs was loose. One of those jobs to fix, Frederick assumed that Pedro never quite got around to despite it annoying him every day. Frederick persevered with this one to open it fully and found it to be a short drawer, only half the depth of the cabinet. Perhaps it had broken or been subject to woodworm or termites at some earlier time and been badly fixed by taking off the back half of the drawer. *Probably been through multiple owners* thought Frederick during the struggle. It had little wooden pegs in either side of the drawer to stop it falling out or coming too far forward. Frederick removed these pegs and the drawer came out. He passed it to Joan who put it on the bed. Frederick went down on his knees.

"Goodness me Joan, the first place we look and it's just as I thought. Come and look down here in the back of this."

Joan pulled the front of her frock above her knees and knelt beside him. She steadied herself on the lower frame which made the cabinet topple slightly. Frederick held it to the wall.

"A bit top heavy Joan. Isabella wouldn't go messing about with this. Can you reach in there?. I have hold of the furniture?"

Joan stretched in to the back of the cabinet with her left arm and grasped a tin and brought it forward so that Fredrick could take it from her while she regained composure and stood brushing herself down.

"There are six or seven of those in there Frederick, they are all the same."

"Borotalco Talcum Powder" said Frederick as he read the branding to her.

"Why would he hide talcum powder from his mother. Was he a hommersexual?" *Where did that come from* she thought of herself disparagingly. "I'm sorry Frederick, that was uncalled for, I don't know why I said that. Anyone can use talcum powder whatever their sexual preference."

"He goes out with a girl in the village, but he was also intimate with Giuseppe, we know that, but as far as I'm aware Joan talcum powder doesn't feature in the necessities of being a homosexual" he crisply reprimanded as he prised open the lid with his penknife with the pipe smokers attachment.

"What does it smell like?"

"This lid has been opened before. These are not new cans of talc. I will let you sniff it Joan." He held the tin forward.

Joan sniffed at the contents, gradually getting closer until Frederick took it away.

"It doesn't have much smell, it's gone off I think because it's been opened or if anything now I do detect a slight ammonia or cornstarch oddly" said Joan looking intently at Frederick as he was staring into her eyes.

"As I expected Joan your pupils have dilated. I kept it a decent inch or two away from your nose but even a few specs of the dust will have an effect on you, albeit minimal, but I can see in your eyes you have had exposure to a drug which I suspect is cut cocaine."

Joan was shocked and felt violated. She was on the verge of protesting innocence and disbelief but nothing emerged from her lips.

"The first natural reaction is dilation of the pupil. I've seen it in the past when in practice. It's called The Optician's Allusion because cocaine causes, amongst other things, Optical Illusions. It's our professional code."

"Is that worth much Frederick?" said Joan, slightly lightheaded and pointing toward the wardrobe.

"At a guess Joan that half dozen tins, if good quality might have a street value of a hundred thousand Lira."

"Have we now found out why the Nonna died and maybe why Pedro has died as well?" she asked feeling a sudden rush through her brain as she did so.

"I am not sure we know why but we do know what was the basis of the activity in the laundry that is behind all this."

She laughed loudly and flung herself face up onto the bed almost hitting her head on the loose drawer. The room went in circles and she laughed uncontrollably. "Wheeeee" she called.

"You are just going on a little trip Joan. It won't last long."

"A trip, hooray, the first trip of my life. I've been fucked senseless this past week and now having a senseless trip ... fuck fuck fuck ... I'm swearing out loud, Frederick, can you hear me. I've never sworn, never and now I can shout out fuck fuck fuck as much as I like ... it's lovely to be so liberated. Fuck fuck fuck. Fuck you Aunty. Fuck, fuck, fuck. Mummy."

She passed out and started snoring with her mouth wide open.

41. FREDERICK

While Joan was asleep Frederick moved the remaining canisters from the back of the mahogany wardrobe and, after taking Joan's limp and wandering arm out of it, replaced the drawer and re-inserted the pegs. *Amazing how all the time she was on ceremony as such an upright doyen of the village community, being all proper whilst she really wanted to say 'fuck it'. Inhibitions and the human suffering they cause* thought Frederick as he left her asleep and went back over to see Isabella.

"Well that was very kind of you Isabella to allow us to see the cottage."

She was in the kitchen and it had all mod-cons as might be expected of an electrical retailer.

"I've made you both coffee because you didn't come for your water. Where is your lady friend Joan?"

"She suddenly felt sleepy Isabella and has dozed off on the bed over there. I hope you don't mind. I thought I would leave her for five minutes. She did say she will stay and help you tidy up and clean if you would like some assistance. She said you might find it difficult to do it alone."

"Oh, no. Ferrando and I spoke about it yesterday and we agreed we will do it this coming weekend. But that is very kind of her to offer. Did you find anything of interest?"

"Not of immediate interest. I thought I would go back to the shop later this week and see Ferrando and discuss it with him" said Frederick thinking *best not upset Isabella further this week and what will we do with this new information anyway.*

"Shall I take this coffee over to Joan and see if I can wake her? She only needed a little nap. I think she is overcome with the heat. She keeps forgetting her hat."

"A hat is essential during the mid-day. Yes take that one over and bring her back here."

He made a call to the car to open the boot and gathered a small wooden vegetable box that he had noticed propped against the wall.

"Wakey wakey Joan. Here's a nice cup of coffee that Isabella has made for you" called Frederick. *She only had a small sniff and it's her first ever, the effects should not be too deep.*

Joan stirred. "Oh, I went out like a light. Did I swear just then? I profusely apologise if I did."

"You did Joan, just the effects of the drug. Lowers your inhibitions, like excessive alcohol, that's all."

She sat up and looked vaguely about her surroundings and then took the cup into both hands unaware of the heat. Frederick gathered the tins into the vegetable box and took them to the door, checking Isabella's whereabouts. She was in the kitchen clanking a few dishes. He hastened to the car and closed the box of talcum powders into the boot. Joan emerged after him and he indicated they should go see Isabella.

"Joan said she is happy to stay a while and help if you need it Isabella" he winked at Joan as he made this offer about which she had no idea.

"No, no, I will be fine thank you. I'm pleased you haven't found anything about Pedro. He was such a wonderful boy and a good young man to his mother. He often passed me the occasional thousand Lira to go buy something new for myself. Such a good boy. I can't believe he is …" she looked tearful as she stood next to her open dishwasher. Joan felt she should steer the conversation

"Is that one of those new washing-up machines Isabella?" Joan asked and Frederick interpreted.

"It is, Ferrando brought it home last month. The shop is doing very well and this was a bonus gift to him from the manufacturers as a sort of thank you. Once you have one you never go back to washing the dishes in the sink."

"May I see it to understand" said Joan, pleased that she had averted the tears that were welling up in Isabella.

Isabella illustrated how the water sprayed up from the bottom.

"So the dishes don't go around and around?" asked Joan.

Isabella laughed. *First time I've laughed in a week* she thought.

"Can you imagine all the broken china if they did, all mangled around with cutlery? How funny Joan. No, it all sprays up from below and down from above and gets filtered clean."

"What happens if you open the door? Won't all the water pour out?" asked Joan quite naively.

"It only needs five litres of water to wash and the same to rinse twice so it's much more efficient than dish washing by hand with a tap running" said Isabella repeating the sales blurb from the shop like Ferrando would explain to his customers.

Joan didn't know how much a litre was until she thought of her consumption of wine. *A bottle of wine is three quarters of a litre which is about twenty five fluid ounces and there are twenty fluid ounces in a pint so about eight pints. Hmmm a gallon a fill* she thought. Mental arithmetic was useful.

"I think we better get going" interjected Frederick as the two women still had their bottoms in the air staring into the dishwasher. "I need to see Giuseppe this afternoon." he added.

"Are you going to see Ferrando on your way back at the shop?" asked Isabella straightening up.

"I don't think we should trouble him today Isabella. He is trying to sort out his deliveries and the missing goods and has to phone the insurance companies which will probably be enough for one day. Will you tell him we will come see him later in the week. I owe him for an iron he sold me so have to come back."

Joan and Isabella kissed cheeks and Joan hugged the bereaved woman attempting to convey female affection and empathy by holding her shoulders. Isabella's eyes were watery. Frederick held her hand in two, one above and one below, conveying his condolences.

"Shall we have the roof down Joan?"

"Yes, let's get back and see Gusieppe. He must have had a late start. We need to get that key and get to see the laundry if we can. We need to piece this all together."

"And when we have done so Joan, what exactly are we going to do with the information?"

"Good question Frederick and may I ask what you are going to do with a hundred thousand Lira worth of Cocaine that is in the boot?"

"Both you and I will be in Jail pronto if we are stopped by the Polizia for any reason" reasoned Frederick.

"Better go a bit slower then" she said as her frizzy greying hair was on end all over her head and face like barley wafting and ripening in the sun.

"I'm still a bit squiffy Frederick after the sniff of the talcum."

"Snort Joan. You had a small snort of cocaine" he shouted as the wind carried his voice away.

They remained silent until back at the Canonica.

"No motorbike?" said Joan.

"That's strange" said Frederick opening the boot and removing the Pony Senior Iron in its box.

"My, my Frederick. You will be able to set up a laundry for the village with all these appliances. Generate a bit of income. I'll go and put the kettle on, while you find a place for the tins of talc."

Frederick chose the shelf above the lavatory cistern where he kept a stock of Izal. He replaced the toilet rolls in front of the tins noticing a large spider had set up home inside one roll.

As they had a cup of tea, Joan suggested

"Shall we go back into the village and see Lily, she will still be on the late lunchtime shift and find out if Giuseppe appeared?"

"Yes, let's get a sandwich at the cafe while we are there. Let's have this cuppa and go."

42. GIUSEPPE

That's blood. I taste blood.

He licked his lips as he awoke.

Oh God, my head, the pain. I can't get up.

And my guts. The pain. The shit.

My arse is in the air and it's covered in stinking shit.

Where is the blood coming from?

It's my blood, must be, unless there is someone else hanging above me.

"Hello. Hello."

I can speak.

'Hello hello' echoed back up from the well.

That's a long way down.

Can I move my legs?

Did the toes just move a bit?

He kicked himself in the face with a leather shoe.

My legs are asleep - paralysed almost.

I'm folded in half over a bar and destined to die here.

Fading away. Exhausted.

BLACK

43. JOAN

"Hello Lily. Lovely to see you here." Lily and Joan kissed cheeks, "are you enjoying yourself?"

She was in a smart black and white apron and was clearly still very busy. Lunch went on until four by the time people had finished.

"I love it, I am so happy, I can't tell you what dignity this job gives me and I think they are very pleased because I have had a pay rise already and I've only been here a week."

"It seems like the week has flown by. You are a fixture now Lily" said Joan encouragingly.

"What can I get you both?" She brought out a little ticket book and licked the end of a pencil that she had in her top pocket.

"Well firstly, you could get that son of yours around to the Canonica. And secondly we would both like a sandwich and a chilled glass of wine I think. What say you Joan?"

Lily's face dropped.

"Oh, I thought Seppe was with you already, you were heading to see Ferrando and expecting him there. As I said earlier he wasn't at home last night. The last I saw of him was he was going to the Church to pray for poor Pedro. Let me go and get you both something to eat and drink. I will be back in a moment."

She hurried to the kitchen, stopping to gather a few finished plates en route. Her efficiency was becoming noted and bringing more custom of people who didn't have all day to wait for food. There was a table of four workmen enjoying a meaty secondo, one of whom had caught Frederick's eye whilst his colleague was admiring Lily's calves.

"Where can he be Frederick? He said he would be doing the extension today" asked Joan as she adjusted her scarf and followed Frederick's gaze. Lily returned with the snack of the day and two small glasses of Rose.

"Was there anything else Giuseppe said he was going to do Lily, besides go to church?"

207

"No I cannot think of anything. I thought he was going on to see you to update you on a few things. He and I had a nice chat yesterday about the circumstances at the laundry and the church."

"Did he ask you if you had a set of keys for the laundry? I had asked him to ask you."

"Oh yes, I forgot that. I don't have the keys but I told him where he might find a set, so he may have gone to look for them before coming on to you. Yes that's what he probably did."

Joan was cutting into her sandwich. Toasted parma ham, cheese and mustard. She interjected

"Where are these keys Lily? I think Frederick and I should just go see for ourselves in a few minutes" Joan said and took a bite. "Very tasty" she added approvingly. Frederick interpreted.

"OK, I can tell you but I had better draw a little diagram possibly. Let me serve the men over there and I will come back in a minute. Eat your sandwich while it's warm Frederick, I made it with our best prosciutto for you."

"It's delicious Lily" added Joan before she was gone.

Frederick noticed the wandering hand of the workman as Lily looked after the table. Whilst he seemed entertained with Lily the other winked at Frederick which gave him a stirring. Lily took it in her stride knowing she would get a good tip from the table. Joan followed Frederick's gaze again and the winker grinned. *Lovely teeth* she thought.

"Do you think we have more trouble about to turn up Frederick? Do you think Giuseppe will be alright?"

"I really hope he is OK Joan but I wouldn't like to predict. I think we should eat up as soon as we can and get to finding these keys."

"Shall we go to the church first Frederick? It will soon be three o clock and time for the villagers to wander in won't it?"

"I think they ring the bell at three but the vespers actually start about three thirty, that's earlier than elsewhere in Italy. I've never been to such a service so I don't really know."

Lily returned with a small slip and she explained where the keys were, when she last saw them, years ago.

"Can I settle this now Lily and we'll go as soon as we are finished eating" said Joan, handing over a couple of the rolled smaller notes from her purse, that she had hardly touched apart from her trips to town..

Frederick gave his new found workman a friendly wave as they left and he thought the fellow looked a little disappointed. *Another one for the future* Frederick thought.

Joan spotted a black shoe poking from a vestibule as they walked the street.

"Frederick, have you spoken to the lady in black in her vestibule lately? She is sitting there now watching out as usual. She sees everything. Ask her if she has seen Giuseppe lately."

"Ah, Francesca, how good to see you. Are you keeping well?" Frederick asked.

"I see you still have your lady friend here with you" she replied. "I thought she was going home after a week?" She turned toward Joan, "I saw you in the car when he went to the butchers to talk to my grandson" pointing her wizened finger at Frederick.

Frederick reddened a little. *She's been around the block hasn't she? Doesn't miss a trick and knows her grandson's antics too,* he thought to himself.

"Yes, yes. Joan was having such a good time she decided to stay another week" he got back on track.

"Wanted a little more company of our resident gigolo Giuseppe I shouldn't wonder?" said Francesca as ever to the point.

The smile wiped from Joan's flushed face. *The temerity of the woman. But I suppose she is right and she doesn't gossip, she just drops it straight on your face. What a Cow* thought Joan.

"We were expecting to see Giuseppe today as a matter of fact but he hasn't turned up" said Joan.

"I haven't seen him today. I saw him yesterday twice. He walked past me to go to church, then half hour or so later he went down the side path to the meadow."

"Oh really" said Frederick.

"I see a lot of men go down the meadow. I don't know what they get up to. I can't get there with my stick these days, otherwise I would know. I've seen it all at my age. Doesn't bother an old crone like me."

Crone. Yes Crone. Good self description. Both Joan and Frederick were thinking the same thought.

"The woman in the fancy car followed him there a few minutes later so I expect they got up to some hanky panky in the long grass. I expect the daisies are quite tall just now."

"Do you mean the blue convertible Lancia?" asked Frederick.

"I don't know what type of car it is, but yes, the pale blue open top one."

"Have you seen her before?" asked Joan.

"Yes, She usually comes just once a week and goes to church but I've seen her three times this past week."

"Did you know there's a back gate to the laundry down that way?"

"Oh that's all hidden and overgrown. You haven't been able to get in through that for years" said Francesca.

"When were you last able to walk there? To the meadow I mean" asked Frederick.

"I followed my grandson down there a few years ago. He went with that last priest we had here, I saw him praying on his knees."

"He was giving him Holy Communion I expect" said Frederick.

"Something like that" Francesca said raising her eye enough to indicate she knew what's what.

"Well, we better head off Francesca, nice chatting to you."

"Where are you going now?"

"Church" replied Joan.

"You will have a job. They haven't rung the bell and its quarter past" Francesca tapped her tiny old wristwatch. "The old women are waiting on the steps."

44. FREDERICK

"Is the door locked Ladies?"

"It is. Never known it. Must be some trouble. No notice either" said a woman who was counting her five sorrowful mysteries on her Rosary beads.

"Let's go down the path Joan. I'm getting worried by all this information and peculiar goings on." said Frederick

"I do hope he is alright? Do you suppose he is in the meadow or in the laundry or been taken away by the mystery woman?" Joan felt quite edgy about Giuseppe.

"First things first Joan. Let's check for the keys, then the laundry if we can get in and then the meadow."

"We didn't ask the old crone Francesca if she saw him in the blue car as it left yesterday." said Joan

"If we don't find him here, then goodness only knows where she will have taken him. We will have to go back to Francesca and ask."

"The Ivy has been pulled off the gate Joan. Look."

"Try it. Is it still open? Has it been locked?" she asked.

"That's a relief, it's open."

They hurried up over the broken concrete.

"Where's the little diagram of where the keys are?" asked Frederick.

"Here, here, it's in my bag."

She unravelled it.

"They are under the gutter in the dip of a brick about there Frederick. Can you reach?"

He felt along through the debris, dead spiders and dust.

"There's nothing here. Are you sure it's the right place?" he was getting panicky as he demanded to know.

"Yes, yes. Feel along again. You might have missed them. There must be a ladder or a box to stand on," she was also becoming distressed.

"I was going to ask Giuseppe to come to England Frederick. Just for a while. He has become quite important to me this past week" she was getting tearful.

"He is important to me as well Joan. I love that man." He was frantically feeling along the bricks and scuffed his hand where the cat had injured it.

"So do I Frederick, I think, so do I, especially amongst all this sordid business."

"Go see if you can find a ladder or a box to stand on please Joan."

She turned and tried the various doors to sheds and in her mystified mental state she tried the back door of the laundry as well.

"It's already open Frederick, It's open. Stop searching. The laundry is open" she called excitedly.

"After all that and I've opened up my wound a little." He felt annoyed. "Go quietly Joan. This is all too mysterious."

"Stop" Joan said as she became rigid. "Stop, stop, go back Frederick. Back out."

"What on earth's the matter Joan" he asked stepping back out to the courtyard.

"My perception is altered. What did I just see?"

"Where, what are you on about?" he asked wondering if she was still tripping and her imagination was going wild.

"There, back there in one of the outhouses. Look again in each of those doors Frederick. I was looking for a box or a ladder and didn't see one" she exclaimed.

"Yes, I know and then you opened the back door."

213

"But Frederick, look in the outhouses. Look at what's in there. Please now look."

He turned and calmly looked in each of the open doors and then realised her fervour. The talcum powder tins, empty ones on a shelf. She stood beside him. She then pointed out the sets of scales.

"So this is where the Nonna cut the Cocaine."

"What does that mean Frederick? Cutting the cocaine. What does it mean?" Joan needed to know.

"When Coke is sold to those who snort it, it is not pure. It is mixed with other substances to make it go further, to reduce its potency. They might mix it with cornflour, baking soda, washing powder, talcum powder, chalk. Anything white and powdery."

"Oh really. It all now makes sense. She weighed it out on those little scales."

Frederick stood outside in the courtyard and took out his pipe. It had a little tobacco in the bowl packed tight and he had a few tobacco crumbs in his pocket which he rifled out. He lit up and stood with his back to the scullery wall. The breeze took the smoke which was as sweet as a briar.

"This is a professional set up here Joan. They've pretty much cleared the place. Certainly of the valuable stuff. I reckon the woman in the blue car has been supplying the pilot or maybe pilots at the aerodrome who presumably enhance their already considerable salaries with supplementary income by selling the gear in their home marketplace. I suspect poor Pedro was also a mule dragged into it somehow. His father's reliable truck handy for local deliveries hidden in the machines and fridges and maybe he squirrelled away some canisters in his wardrobe so that losses to the supply chain were noted and mounting up."

Frederick took another long puff and savoured the taste and smell. He added another layer of nicotine to his already brown teeth.

"How would Pedro become involved in such an enterprise?" she asked.

"His father used to work in the Opera company before the accident that killed Lily's husband. Those theatrical types earn good money, but need to calm their nerves before the performance. Cocaine enhances performance Joan. Sexual performance, singing performance, theatrical performance. There was bound to be some demand for the gear in Verona."

"Is this the trade of the Mafia Frederick?"

"Most probably Joan. Either them or the church or both."

"And what of Giuseppe Frederick? Poor Giuseppe. He was here yesterday, he must have the keys but he forgot to lock up behind him. Had we better continue our search for him in the meadow perhaps."

"I don't think we will find him here or in the meadow Joan. I reckon he went off with the woman in the blue car. Why don't I go over the road and ask Francesca whether she saw the blue car leave and if Giuseppe was in it yesterday. Just while you have a little look around here."

"OK but please don't be long. I don't want to get caught trespassing here and particularly not by the Mafia who would probably kill me."

"As comfortably retired old folk Joan, we don't want to mess with them do we," he responded as he walked down toward the back wall gate.

Retired Old Folks? Give me a break, it's been non stop here this past week she thought.

45. JOAN

Joan carefully looked again into each outhouse making a mental note of the important contents then closed each door behind her. Then back into the main laundry house and again closed the door behind her. She detected a faintly unpleasant smell. *The drains?* She looked around at the sparse surroundings. A huge stone sink under the whitewashed window. A dusty spider had wrapped its long legs under itself to fold away ready for death. The huge cold tap, a later addition. The corner copper wash pot with chimneystack behind it but no ash or sign of use in the grate below. Wooden boards over it and a similar wooden plank covered unit in the other corner. Frederick's pipe smoke lingered in the air occasionally improving the odour. She turned.

Making her way into the kitchen she noted the food mixer with a glass top with a cut out to accommodate the gyrator *probably used to mix cocaine with other ingredients.* She looked in the cupboards. Cutlery in a wooden compartment box, mainly EPNS and tarnished. A few chipped or cracked plates of various sizes and colours. Small linens. Cups, small and large. *But where's the food? What did she eat?* Joan looked opposite in the other dresser and cabinet which had glasses and a few cooking pots and pans below. *But no pasta. This is Italy. Every kitchen has pasta, even if they don't eat it. This place has not been lived in for some time.* Her thoughts were racing but trying to piece together the absurdity. *Nonna has only been dead a week. Left everything to the Church. But nothing here to live with. Virtually empty. Abandoned.*

Joan stepped through to the front room, what was formerly a shop at some time with half glazed double doors on to the street. Over the road she saw Frederick talking to Francesca in the vestibule and then they both went inside her front room. *Unusual to be allowed in to someone's home here.* Up the street through the trees she could just see the cafe and spotted Lily buzzing about. She felt as if she were in a fish bowl looking out from a silent world of water to a place of air and light and movement. She didn't like it. Felt uneasy. Not right.

The staircase to the Nonna's rooms and her bedroom went up against the wall to one side. She climbed them. The stairs became enclosed by panelling halfway up and the top three stairs made a turn through ninety degrees where she now faced a door with a low handle so as to open it whilst still on the stairs. An awkward arrangement but presumably gave a former shopkeeper some privacy in their living accommodation. It was locked. She had never seen this arrangement before. In England, the small labourers cottages in the village that she had been in had a door at the bottom of the stairs.

So Giuseppe didn't get this far? Or is he locked in behind there? Joan made her way back down. She took another look from her fish bowl out to the quiet street. A man with a dog on a string passed but he didn't notice her. He praised his little dog for peeing up the tree. She walked back into the scullery and took her bag from her shoulder and put it on the planks in the corner. The smell came in waves so she opened the back door and looked out to the courtyard. A couple of sparrows were perched on the gutter preening. In the distance was a rumble of thunder. She looked over the courtyard toward the meadow, dark anvil shaped clouds were approaching from the distance.

She then heard something. Like someone being sick. Retching. She turned and the hairs on her neck stood on end. It was as though there was someone where she had just been, being sick. A man being sick. She stood still and quiet. A distant flash gave the clouds a sudden whiteness. She started counting as she did as a child *One jeckelly jones, Two jeckelly jones, Three jeckelly jones, Four jeckelly jones, Five jeckelly jones.* The thunder rumbled again. *It's five miles away.* She detected the faint smell of vomit. Her senses were heightened, presumably from the morning's snorting event. *Was that only this morning?* All sense of time was distorted. Fast one minute, dead slow the next. She turned and lifted her handbag and looked at the bottom of it to see if she had placed it in some vomit or other unmentionable shit. She lifted one of the planks covering the second corner copper and the smell *Oh dear God, the smell.* She turned and was violently sick onto the stone floor. Gagging and retching. *I haven't been involuntarily sick like that for thirty years. A soldier wounded on his steering wheel brought into casualty.* Joan's memory was photographic for the instant. The smell took her back to nursing. A runaway uncontrollable truck had smashed face on into a brick wall at the end of a terrace. A child playing ball games had been flattened and the driver was impaled on the steering wheel. A terrible accident from a faulty vehicle. His guts were hanging out when she had cut his shirt and trousers off him with surgical scissors. *I can see it now and the stench, unlike any other stench on earth.*

Another distant flash and then the room darkened. There was someone in the door looking at her in this state. She was doubled over looking at the mess she had made of her Hush Puppies. All yellow and littered with red bits of prosciutto from Lily's toasted sandwich.

Frederick was in the doorway.

"Oh Joan. Let me help. What's happened? Something didn't agree with you?"

She was pointing behind her into the corner still doubled over. *My lovely Hush Puppies splattered.*

"The smell Frederick. The smell. In there. In the corner" she cried out.

"It's the drain's old girl. Come, let me get you outside. Come get some fresh air. Stand up now and lean against the wall.

Another distant flash and she instinctively started her mental counting.

"Four miles" she said when the rumble came through.

Frederick then stood observing her blanched features, spoiled frock and shoes.

"Did I hear someone being sick? Just then. Did you hear it?" he asked.

He held his breath as he went back into the scullery and skidded on the vomitty stone floor but kept his balance. He turned another plank over on top of the one behind and looked down into the dark space.

"It's a well Joan. An old water well." And peering in he saw the stained white cloth just about four feet down at floor level.

Joan had found a clean hanky in her bag and was wiping her mouth when he stood beside her.

"What on earth is the matter Frederick? You look like you have seen a ghost" she held out her other clean hand.

"I've found him Joan. I think he's dead. Giuseppe. I think he's dead Joan. Oh my God Joan. Not another one."

"Are you sure? Let me see him. I need to see him. Never dead until there is no pulse to feel. No pulse Frederick? Matron always said that!

The heart goes on beating long after we might take someone for dead. It's all in the pulse."

She avoided her vomit and put her stinking hanky over her nose.

"Help me move these planks Frederick, we can't see properly."

Another flash and the pitter patter of heavy raindrops provided percussion on the corrugated tin roof between the outhouses starting a tonic and dominant timpani. *Three miles* She thought.

"He's fallen down the well Joan. He must have been here twenty four hours."

"Oh yes Frederick. Don't be silly. He fell down the well and put the planks back on top of the well. Think on Frederick. He was pushed down the well and is hanging over the old brace bar at floor level. He probably grabbed the rope in the split second he knew he was going over."

"Sorry Joan. My mind is still processing the information Francesca gave me. I was obviously quite wrong about Giuseppe."

"Look at the state of him Frederick. His shorts and his dignity are trounced. How can we get him out of there without doing more harm?" she asked.

"I'll run to the butchers. I'll get soaked, but it's our only hope. I just hope he is open and is there" with which Frederick was gone.

"Giuseppe. Giuseppe. Don't worry darling, we are going to get you out of here. Just a few minutes."

Another violent flash. *One jeckelly jones.* Crack, bang and rumble. *A mile away. It's nearby.*

The timpani was in full force.

She repeated her line over and over again. *The hearing is the last sense to go. Another of Matron's lessons. Keep them alive by talking to them.* Joan held out her arms out over the centre of the well, palms down. *I can feel a little warmth, the body is alive.*

Time again going slow. Eternity. How much longer?

"Giuseppe sweetheart. It's all going to be OK. We are going to lift you out of here. Just a few more minutes."

A flash and crack simultaneously. The storm was right here. It must have struck somewhere nearby.

The men arrived gasping, soaked to the skin with ropes and meat hooks. Joan stepped aside.

"He's down there in the old well in the corner" said Frederick. They were making pools wherever they stood.

"And what is your name?" asked Joan.

"I'm Bartholomew, but everyone calls me Bari" said the butcher boy and he grinned with his perfect denture.

"Mind the mess on the floor. Sorry" said Joan. *I do dislike dentures* she thought.

"The floor of our slaughterhouse gets covered in blood and guts. I'm used to it. Don't worry" Bari responded.

His ropes were ready to take hooks. He moved Frederick to one side and dangled a large hook on a rope over the edge of the well.

"I'm going to drag that one up his spine and along his bum crack to catch his belt and shorts" he explained to Frederick who was peering down the well.

"If you move aside Frederick I will have more light" and as he said that the whitewashed window lit up with multiple flashes of lightning followed almost immediately by the crack and rumble.

Rain bounced on the concrete and bashed at the steel roofing but the instant flash lightning gave Bari enough to see Giuseppe's hairy crack. His hook followed the contours and it was in place.

"I've got his belt hooked. Take this rope the pair of you. Frederick you go at the end and Joan you stand behind me. We are going to pull. But slowly"

"Is it strong enough Bari?"

"This will hold a hundred and fifty kilo pig easily. Giuseppe will weigh less than that. Are you two ready? We will go slow. We don't want to hurt his chin on the bar. Just steady as we go. I pull and you take the strain so he doesn't drop. He has a strong leather belt on. That's good."

Bari reached into the well and pulled. The belt would not hold out forever. They needed to be gentle and quick. One of Giuseppe's shoes dragged off as his heel scraped the side of the well. The hook punctured the shorts and his Y front elastic appeared above his waistline. Another pull, keeping the rope away from the edge of the well.

"Take the strain, take the strain" he called.

"I'm not doing much" called Joan.

"Can you hold him Frederick?"

"I'm OK for a while" he responded and wound himself around the rope toward Joan. He would go down with Giuseppe if he fell.

"Come here Joan to help get him when he's at the top. Just another half metre, if that. Be ready."

Joan peered over the top to see the soiled shorts and the dead weight figure dragged up a little further as Bari heaved on the rope.

"Is he OK Joan?"

"Yes, just one more pull like that and we can get him."

Bari now had to pull the rope over the edge.

"We are both pulling now Frederick. Ready ... Heave ... Heave."

"I can reach him but can't manage him by myself. If I lift his arms the hook will come out of his pants. We all have to grab his pants and get our arms around his waist."

"Take the entire strain Frederick. Can you manage it?" Bari slowly released his grip slowly making sure the older man had the strength to hold on.

Frederick's injured hand was agonising. Bari moved in alongside Joan and he slid his hand down the back of Giuseppe's Y fronts. Joan did the same on the other buttock.

"Heave Joan. Heave." The lightning and thunder struck again with a burst of heavy rain playing like steel drums on the roof

They had their rag doll on the sill. Giuseppe was slumped forward, his head still looking down the shaft of the well. Joan pulled out the hook and it clanged onto the floor and she was disappointed to see his new Y fronts pierced and soiled, his shorts ripped. She would get him another pair when he came to visit. His new strong belt strop probably saved his life, certainly it enabled them to rescue him.

"We have him Frederick. Come and put your hands around his waist so we can get him off."

Frederick released the rope, it falling on the slushy vomit and puddles. He pushed between Joan and Bari and put his arms around his young friend's middle and pulled him back. The stench from Giuseppe's backside was foul. Frederick was aware he would stain his nice clean shirt and probably his vest too but Candy would sort all that out later on. Giuseppe's remaining shoe caught and fell into the well giving a delayed distant splash. Joan instinctively held his head whilst Bari and Frederick supported the torso side to side. They sat him on the cold wet floor of the scullery but he couldn't sit. Bari held his shoulders. Joan knelt and felt for a pulse. The two men looked on. She nodded.

"Weak but alive. Move him please onto the table in there. I need to clean him and prepare him for hospital and to take a look at his tummy." she said.

Frederick took his legs and Giuseppe gave out a groan as Bari lifted his shoulders. It was a sound they all found faintly reassuring.

Frederick leaned over Giuseppe's face and lifted the eyelids one by one, both bloodshot from the excessive blood pressure from being upended. He needed a bright light to see if the pupils reacted but he didn't have anything to hand in these surroundings, however both eyes were looking in the same direction and there was no sign of tache noir. He was alive, depleted and needed hydration.

Joan had already found a clean cup for drinking water and started by moistening his mouth. She then went in search of one of the enamel bowls and the linen cloths.

Maybe amongst this lot is some actual washing soap. It is a laundry after all, she was thinking.

"Is there a hosepipe around here Joan?" Frederick called out as Bari was rinsing his ropes in the big scullery sink.

"Not that I've seen, oddly, you would think a laundry would have a hose. A rectal douche would be the fastest way to rehydrate him. Hopefully the ambulance will bring one and attend to that."

"It's a bit messy down there Joan. I've undone his belt, marvellous gift that was, old Gal."

"I'm ready to clean him up. You chaps can get going and tell Lily." *Old Gal indeed* she thought.

46. FREDERICK

Frederick was already soaked so a little more rain would make it no worse, it might rinse some of the shit that had soaked into his shirt. It was stained around his tummy and he gave off an odour. The storm had moved on, thunder more distant and the rain would stop shortly. They were walking back toward the butchers shop that had been left open in the rush.

"Thank you for all that help Bari. I'm sorry it was such a horrid task, but I didn't know who else to ask" said Frederick.

"I'm happy to help any time Frederick. I'm relieved he is alive. But my questions are how did he get there and what was he doing in the old laundry in the first place?" asked Bari.

"Very astute questions Bari. I'm not sure I can answer them for you yet. For the time being you will need to refer to your grandmother who doesn't miss much. Anything I say would be a supposition."

"I'd ask her now if she were awake. See her?" Bari pointed over the road and the old woman's chin was on her chest showing the balding parting of her thin grey hair. One shoe poked from the vestibule like a Collie's nose peering around a corner.

"Yes leave her to rest just now. I saw her an hour ago, she was quite informative" said Frederick.

"Does it involve the fancy woman in the blue Lancia?"

"I think she is implicated somewhere along the line."

"I thought I saw her leave yesterday afternoon with Father Leo in the car."

"That would explain why the church is locked today. Are you sure it was him?" asked Frederick.

"No, I can't be sure, it was a man that looked like him but he wore ordinary things."

"What do you mean by Ordinary?"

"Well, no cassock nor Saturno hat."

"That hat would soon disappear in a convertible Bari" Frederick laughed. "It would doubtless end up on Saturn."

They had reached the cafe. Bari held Frederick's hand momentarily and asked

"Will you call by on Thursday afternoon Frederick for your sausages?"

"Perhaps next week Bari, when Joan has gone home. Hopefully much of this will have blown over by then. Like the storm" Frederick pointed to the sky and the receding clouds. The sun had again emerged. *How will I avoid getting ensnared by him? Or does he really fancy me?* Frederick thought.

Bari raised his hand in acknowledgement and went on with his ropes and hooks. There had been no meat custom during the storm.

Lily was in the back of the cafe twirling pasta around a fork. Her boss and his wife were in the kitchen clearing up and deciding upon the menu special for tonight after another successful lunchtime. Lily looked up with a mouthful whilst the fork was being twirled for a second helping.

"Late lunch? Spaghetti Bolognese?"asked Frederick.

"It's delicious. Do you want some? Try this fork" as she held it forward.

"No no, you eat it Lily. It looks good and I am hungry."

"The sauce has been on all day and it's so ripe and tender. They make me a fresh bowl of pasta" as she pointed to the kitchen.

Pepe looked through to see who Lily was talking to. He waved his teatowel at Frederick and continued wiping the pots.

"We have found Giuseppe Lily."

"Oh, I am relieved. Don't tell me where. I don't need to know who he has been gallivanting around with this time. That boy's brains are firmly in his loins, but he will grow out of it. Is he now working at yours, on your house?"

225

"Not yet Lily. Do you think Pepe will let me use the phone because I need to ring a doctor. There has been a slight accident."

"Accident? What sort of accident? "

"There is no need to panic Lily. Finish your meal while I use the phone and then I'll take you to see him."

"Where is he? Is he alright?"

"Joan is with him at the moment but we want him to see a doctor and get him to hospital this afternoon to be checked over."

Lily stuck the fork back into the pasta and scraped back her chair.

"He's in the laundry isn't he? He found the key. What's happened to him?. I'm going over there."

She gathered her handbag from the hook at the kitchen door and dashed off.

Frederick stuck his head through the bead curtain.

"Pepe, can I use the phone please, we need an ambulance and a doctor over at the laundry. Young Giuseppe has been injured."

"No use you ringing an ambulance from Verona, It will take over an hour. You need one from the Lakes. Let me help you. What sort of injury? We had a girl injured in the kitchen a year or so ago and this lot are very efficient. Leave it with me and they will arrive within the half hour. You go after Lily and make sure she is alright. Nobody stands in the way of her precious boy. By the way old chap you need to change that shirt, it's a bit soiled."

Pepe was glad to see the back of Frederick or rather get the smell of him out of his cafe.

Frederick didn't know how to navigate the Italian health care system, such as it was, so was grateful for Pepe's assistance. He did as he was told and with the sun on his back he pulled his shirt tails from his trousers and fanned it in the warm humid breeze. When at the back door of the scullery he was met by a heated conversation going on between the two women.

"What do you mean what I am I doing? I am rinsing the filthy pants and shorts I've removed from your son" Joan called out clearly annoyed by the mothers sudden intrusion at this, of all moments.

"But he lays there naked with only his shirt. What is going on between you all."

"I am a nurse Lily. I have done this many times in the past."

Frederick arrived just in time to interject.

"Lily, Lily, don't distress yourself. Joan is examining his wounds and cleaning him. You can tell from the stench he was in a bad way when we found him." he stepped in between them.

Joan continued at the sink wringing out the garments in order to dress him again before the ambulance.

"These are all ripped Lily. We really need clean pants and shorts for him if you could go home and get some" said Joan as they stood around the table with the semi naked man before them. His flaccid manliness looking as forlorn as his torso crested by a mound of tight curly pubic hair.

Lily calmed and bent over to kiss Giuseppe's forehead and both Joan and Fredrick had fleeting thoughts of the more intimate times they had had with him.

"Where did you find him? Where has he been? His middle is all bruised and swollen" asked Lily.

"He was part way down the well Lily, doubled over the old brace-bar that they built into the floor. He is lucky to be alive. It may be a hundred metres deep" said Frederick.

"He must have been there for twenty four hours or so? How did he get there? Was he pushed in?" enquired Lily.

"Yes, most probably pushed Lily. He has damaged his internals and his brain is presumably in a state of shock from being inverted for so long. The lungs are designed to be above the other heavy organs so it is good that he has been sick and soiled himself so much, because that has taken weight out of his system and allowed his lungs to still partially inflate. I saw there was a little blood around his mouth which I've wiped away. I think that's his tummy rupturing from being unable to digest any further." explained Joan.

"He will get a thorough check at the hospital Lily and they will put him on a saline drip to help him recover. It's good that he sleeps just now. It's the brain's natural reaction to the trauma. Pepe has called the doctor. I've checked his eyes and although bloodshot they are functioning alright" explained Frederick.

"I'll go and find some shorts for him, no need for underwear is there. We can't put those wet things back on him. I haven't seen those before, perhaps they were Pedro's."

As she saw that Joan was still holding the wrung out pants.

"I'm sorry I shouted at you Joan. I didn't mean anything by it. I'm sorry." Lily looked to the floor and then gathered her bag. She looked down the open well, shuddered and left.

Joan immediately shouted after her, "he needs some socks and soft shoes Lily."

"I better see if I can find a key to open the front door Joan. We can't expect the ambulance or doctor to traipse around the back, look at all the huge puddles. Particularly if he has to go out on a stretcher" said Frederick mainly talking to himself.

"I noticed a couple of keys near those coffee cups on the dresser Fredrick. Try those. I will peg out these shorts in the sun, Lily might be able to repair them."

"Better not do that Joan. We are still trespassing after all. No need to advertise our presence."

"I hadn't thought of that" responded Joan.

Forty five minutes later Lily was in an ambulance with her stretchered clean dressed son.

47. JOAN

"Let's get Candy to work on those clothes of yours Frederick. Make a pile of them by the machine. I need to take a shower. This afternoon has brought back memories of many of the horrors I had to deal with thirty odd years ago when a junior nurse" advised Joan.

"What a day Joan? What a day. I need a nap. I will see you at the table at seven. We will knock something up for supper then."

"OK. I'm sure we can rustle something up. My brain is awash Frederick."

She had only napped briefly on top of the bed and decided to take a look at her things in the wardrobe and those remaining in her bags, most virtually untouched.

It was like looking into a different past inside that bag. *Only a little under a fortnight ago I packed this lot deciding what scarf I needed and now all those decisions dissolve into complete triviality. My holiday which started disaster prone and starchy has become a wholesome adventure into the unknown realities of life on the bigger planet.*

She stayed on the bed in a daydream state. She was now certain that when someone in the village next approached her to say they had seen a kitkat wrapper discarded on the village green and only yards from a waste basket she would snap a response to them *"Oh, get a life and pick it up."*

She removed a bag inside the holdall that was full of hair care things; a comb, a brush, a set of rollers, metal curlers, setting lotions, colouring potions, hair slides, sponges, grips and pins. *What a load of paraphernalia for just a week and all of it entirely unnecessary.* She decided to discard all of it. The entire sub-bagful. *Maybe give Frederick the brush to look after the cat, if it ever returns.*

Her thoughts were swirling and then the phone rang. Frederick was woken by the ringing. An unusual sound, it seldom rang. Joan was there first to attend. Joan lifted the receiver and heard peeps followed by Lily speaking too quickly for her to understand.

"Frederick, come please" she called up the stairs "it's Lily on the phone from the hospital I guess. She sounds panicky."

The boards and stairs creaked. He had been in a deep sleep dreaming thoughts that vanished with the light. He took the receiver. Joan only heard one half of the conversation which comprised

"Hello Lily, I see, Yes, I see, I see, I see, Yes, Ok, Yes, in about an hour or so depending on traffic."

So whilst listening to this meaningless half she examined her hush puppies out on the doorstep which were in a ruinous state but at least now dry.

"That was Lily" he started and she looked at him as much to say *You don't say?* "She's at the hospital. They have examined Giuseppe and think he will be OK. They are keeping him in for a few days for observation and they have given him an injection and some pills and he's drowsy and has a lot of tummy pains. Anyway, Lily can come home now, but she has missed the last bus and she cannot afford a taxi, so she wants me to go and fetch her, because she doesn't know anyone else with a car."

"What about Pepe or Pedro's father?"

"He has the cafe to run and will be rushed off his feet because she is at the hospital and not there. She said if we get back by nine or ten then she will do half a shift tonight to help them. So I had better go."

"But you haven't eaten anything today Frederick except that ham toastie thing."

"I will be OK. I'll have some pasta with Lily at the cafe when we get back there. Don't wait up. We will catch up in the morning and compare notes."

"I'll make myself some poached eggs on toast and sort out my room. I have to think about the return journey and lightening the load. I can put the washing in Candy too."

"That's the gal. I'll just get myself shipshape and go. See you in the morning."

Joan returned to her room and her hairdressing bag. It gave her a feeling of despondency. She realised her life was running out and this was a moment of reality check. She returned to her thoughts.

I'm a woman in my sixties, dry, barren. I loved once, momentarily, and the loss of that companion must have hardened me and brought out the Maiden Aunt in me. Mother had never really loved me. She conceived me out of a sense of duty to Father, that's what women did. What did Betty say in Feminine Mystique? Sexual passivity and child rearing were considered by men before the war to give feminine satisfaction. Men had careers and women had babies. But I didn't have a baby and was, so briefly, sexually passive. Then my career in nursing. Where do I now fit? Where will life take me now I'm in my sixties. A passionate fling with Giuseppe, but after today, after cleaning his shitty arse and shifting his flaccid penis from side to side, the allure has worn away somewhat. He was like every other patient I dealt with once upon a time. Just another sausage in the sausage factory of life we nurses would admit when off duty. Accidents and Emergencies generally all have the same basic needs. To survive.

Her thoughts were mithering all over the show. She had been told not to mither when she was at Manchester aerodrome - perhaps this was what was meant. Aimless, pointless thinking about oneself leading to a general feeling of dissatisfaction of one's performance to date.

Two out of Ten Joan. And what about the other Betty, the neighbour who brought me the bag of Everton mints. That was a kind gesture, so why was I so horrid to her and missed her birthday when I knew when it was. That was spiteful. Why? Perhaps I was a spiteful cat at school. They say playground behaviours follow you through life. Oh these mithering thoughts and surrounded by all this stuff for such a short holiday. Where did I think I was going? To Monte Carlo to walk the promenade each evening passing lotharios in cafes and attempting to attract attention. And what would I do if I got their attention? Run a mile? Say 'how dare you' and slap them? Whereas by just peeling a banana I had the best attention a woman could get. A spontaneous wonderful fucking turned this way and that and made to fill every orifice one by one. Amazing. All this stuff in this bag and wardrobe and none of it necessary. Just appendages to looking the part rather than playing the part.

She rummaged further into the holdall and her self analysis went on.

I suppose that's what Aunty's deportment classes were all about. How to look the part. Those upstairs in the grand house actually played the part but as a servant she could only be a stagehand and look right. Placing the cutlery in the right order, making sure there was an undercloth, cloth and overcloth for dinner and no cloth at all for luncheon. Absurd. I'm not high enough to play a part, not born into the upper echelons of society. Born of lowly stock to a mine worker so could only possibly fit below stairs. So why all the high and mighty attitude at the village committee. One doesn't approve of this and that. I have a reputation of being difficult and I keep that reputation topped up at each monthly meeting.

Introspection both harmful and cathartic was creating change. But Joan was thinking *this is a bit late in life to change.* However she continued with her thoughts as she turned over the strange array of objects in her bag.

Why was I going to invite Giuseppe back to England? Was it to boost my ego? Was it to be passive and be pummelled into that ecstatic oblivion again but in my own bed or on my own kitchen table? Was it to get the plumbing seen to? Was it to show the village I'm different? Or will I become the laughing stock bringing home a toyboy from Italy? Word would soon spread and my reputation for being difficult could turn to being one of a late exult. It wouldn't work and it would put Giuseppe in an invidious position. Embarking upon a spur of the moment encounter via a banana is very different from spending three weeks peeling the same very old wrinkling peel. What other crap should I divest from this bag? To lighten my load.

She delved into the holdall and pulled out another purse containing medicines and unctions in case of need. She tipped the contents onto the bed. Doans Backache pills, a box of beechams powders, a bottle of calamine lotion, a small wartime bottle of orange juice concentrate, a little lavender oil, oil of cloves, a tin of Nivea, a small tin of vaseline, a spare pair of tweezers, a couple of pink flesh colour cloth elastoplast, some left over eczema ointment, an unopened bottle of Ambre Solaire, four cotton wool balls, a dozen Anadin and a jar of Vicks Rub liniment embrocation.

Why bring all this stuff a thousand miles from home. I haven't touched any of it and it will all go back and get put into that bloody wooden cabinet in the bathroom with the sliding mirror that is four inches too high.

Another purse tipped onto the bed contained make up, the secondary back-up stuff, different colour lipsticks, eye shadows, mascaras, foundations, more tweezers, more cotton wool, powder compacts, cold creme, a bar of soap wrapped in greaseproof paper, spare extra lemon teabags.

What for? Boredom? Loneliness? Attempting to paint my face into something I am not? I haven't touched it in ten days. Maybe loneliness is the issue. Passing that sixty pointer activates a recognition in everyone that you come onto this planet alone and you go out of it the same way. Everyone you meet, know, see on TV, hear singing, pass in the street or the shops is on a completely different journey crossing your path from time to time, but their journey is exactly the same - the movement through time from the cradle to the grave. Few people are abandoned at the very beginning or at the very end of life but in between there are periods of life of solitude. Equally there are periods of intense companionship and the physical coupling and intercourse. Loneliness creeps up on you and you feel occupied and busy but, it's when the sun goes down and you are eating a meal for one that loneliness strikes home. The average widower lives only two years after losing his wife. The average widow a little longer than that. Women have more social things, more friends at the shops, more gossip, more neighbours but some who make themselves difficult by being apart or snooty or awkward can find they spend a lot of time alone. That's me! she thought.

Now she turned to the wardrobe.

All these dresses, blouses and cardigans of different thicknesses and weight and length and colour so as to be ready for every eventuality of a one week trip, whether cold, warm, dry, wet, windy or still. And of fifteen outfits the one that was on seventy five percent of the time was the lemon crimplene easy care fling on-fling off and those hush puppies. And no bath, not even seen a bath for over ten days and don't even think about it. There's not enough hot water in the tiny roof tank for a bath anyway. A shower is perfectly alright. All those visits down to hotel receptions to complain. " When I book a room with a bath I expect a bath and not a shower." Those receptionists must have thought "Aye aye, we have Miss Difficult in room number such and such." Why?

The real Joan, the real me hasn't been so engaged in real life and so helpful and so without judgement on anyone or anything for an entire lifetime until this past ten days. I've witnessed two deaths, a near death, the drug business, brushed with Mafia and both suffering and joy of ordinary people, no different from me except I think I'm different and extraordinary. But I'm not, none of the ceremony and correctness matters. What does matter is going with the flow, helping people, engaging with people and nature and being kind. Yes kindness and unconditional love. Like those pop songs doing well by the Beatles just now - Love, love me do. She hummed it *Love Love me do, You know I love you. But how can anyone love Miss Difficult? They might love Miss Easygoing. So that's what I must become ... Joan Easygo. Take it easy. Chill. Relax and use some more modern expressions and flower power and listen to music. I'll stick a pelargonium in this frizzy grey hair when I get back. That's all it needs. I don't need a toyboy, as lovely as he is.*

Delving into the holdall she found the shoe brush set.

Perhaps I will recommend Betty Friedan to the village book club and then do a talk about a holiday in the Italian Lakes. That should keep them amused. There would be no slide show of course.
I must put this lot away and then brush my Hush Puppies and then go to bed. I forgot to make my supper. I can do without food. What a strange array of thoughts I've had but some decisions too.

She slept well thinking of a line that someone said on the wireless. She hadn't been listening but it obviously sat in her subconscious. *Ageing is a fascinating process whereby you become the person you always should have been.* It was a thought to sleep comfortably with.

48. FREDERICK

Lily was waiting outside the main hospital entrance. He pulled up right outside. She opened Frederick's car door forgetting she had to get in the other side. The evening was now cooling so Frederick got out and put the roof up.

"Good evening Lily. Have you been waiting long?"

"Hello Frederick, Only ten minutes. Thank you so much for coming to fetch me." She settled herself while he finished the roof clips. An ambulance pulled up behind him and wanted the spot.

"We will soon get you home, or to work if you prefer. So tell me, how is the main man? What do they say?" he asked as he moved out to head home, the hospital had one of those new one-way systems.

"They said he is lucky to be alive. They wanted to know how he came to be stuck down a well and I said he must have just fell in. I didn't want to open that can of worms. They didn't question me more. I explained how he was over the old bar for about a day. They said that had he been completely upturned he would be dead, but because he was folded in half he has damaged his tummy and his heart and lungs have taken a lot of strain. He has had some internal bleeding, they think from an ulcer. They did x-rays and there is nothing actually broken." Lily was very matter of fact.

"It sounds like you feel reassured that he will be OK then?"

"They say they will keep him for observation until they are happy with him."

"Is he awake?" Frederick asked.

"He was asleep again when I left him just now. They had given him an injection and said it would make him drowsy, but he was awake for about half an hour after they gave him some sort of smelling salts for the x-ray, they had needed him to stand up."

"So you spoke with him?"

"I was so relieved to do so Frederick, I can't tell you what Seppe means to me since his father died."

"And he was compos mentis?"

"Of sound mind? Oh yes, but he said he had a terrible splitting headache that made his eyes hurt. He was very sensitive to light."

"He would be Lily. Did you know I used to be an optician?"

"Oh, I didn't know that Frederick. I have such trouble with my eyes. Someone asked me to read the blackboard menu and I had to go right up to it to read it" she laughed.

"I think he was pushed down the well somehow Lily. Did Giuseppe give you any clue about how he was where we found him?"

"He can remember finding the well and he remembers someone coming into the scullery and then saying something like 'you want to know how deep it is'. But how he toppled in he can't remember."

"When you next see him can you ask him if it was a woman who said about how deep the well is?"

"Oh, it was a woman, he already said that. Sorry I didn't say."

"I think it was the woman in the blue car Lily. Have you seen her before?" asked Frederick.

"Yes, she came to the church each week to see Father Leo. Sometimes I was doing the washing out the back and she would turn up to go to confessional."

"What do you think has been going on Lily?"

"I didn't want to tell you directly Frederick because I am embarrassed by it. I am a good Catholic and I cannot speak ill of the church. I wanted Giuseppe to tell you some of what I think."

"Tell me in a moment Lily when I have filled up." Frederick pulled into a petrol station on the outskirts of town.

"OK that's done. Start at the beginning."

"Please let me pay the petrol Frederick before I tell you anything."

"Absolutely not, I needed to fill up anyway. Fire away. I am all ears."
He was in fourth gear and making headway toward a beautiful
twilight post-sunset. Venus was already glowing.

"Well Frederick. I used to do the flowers and a little cleaning at the
church for Padre Domenico and then suddenly he announced he was
retiring and going to live in a seminary for retired priests. That was
quite upsetting really because there had been some nasty rumours
circulating about him and Bari the butcher boy. Tittle tattle things.
Anyway, he told me that a new priest would be arriving from Sicily, a
younger man and that he would modernise things at our little village
church."

"And Father Leo arrived from Palermo?" said Frederick to indicate he
was keeping up.

"Yes. Well only a few months before I lost Giuseppe's father in the
accident with the opera staging so I was in a state of shock and trying
to fathom how I could make ends meet. When I first met Father Leo it
was apparent he was a very different sort of priest. Harder. Less
compassionate. Less human. I was surprised by the church choice
because he didn't seem to fit and none of us parishioners could
fathom out why he had moved from Palermo which is apparently a
much rougher city to the sleepy countryside here. Anyway, he
suggested I might do a little more work there but paid work instead of
the voluntary time I did with floral and cleaning."

"So this was the small laundry work?" asked Frederick, driving home
with darkness behind him now.

"Yes, that's right. I went and had a meeting with the Nonna and she
showed me where she kept the spare keys, the ones that Giuseppe
must have found to get in yesterday. That reminds me, did you see the
spare keys when you were there?"

"No Lily, I went looking for them after you told me where to find them
but they weren't there and then only after searching did we find the
back door and all the outside doors were open anyway" said
Frederick.

"Maybe whoever pushed him down the well has them. I must ask him
where he put them, we might need them instead of leaving the place
unlocked. Anyway, as I was saying, I met the Nonna and she
explained how she would need help with small extra items of laundry

and it was arranged I would help and I was to start the following week. Well the following week came and I was at the church doing my voluntary cleaning around the pews and floors when Father Leo said I would be doing the laundry at the back of the church and he showed me the small room and courtyard to peg out. He said he would bring over the extra bag each week and take it back for me because it was too heavy for me to bring along the road. I thought this was very strange, but when he told me what I would be paid - which was quite a lot for me each week - I didn't question it. The bag always contained a box of washing powder and some soda crystals to soften the water. We had never had hot water at the church but he had a plumber come in to install one of those small electric over the sink type of water heaters and it was very good," explained Lily.

"So what did the Nonna think of your laundry duties? Presumably she had compliments or complaints from her customers?"

"Well that's just it Frederick. I never actually saw her again. She always kept herself to herself in church, wore a heavy veil whenever she was there. Stood apart from the regulars. And weeks came and went, as they do, and the arrangement suited me and the money was good so Father Leo acted as the laundry mule and brought and took away the stuff each week and I just did my job and kept my head down. But after six months or so I wondered why it was the same stuff I was washing week in week out. Mainly mens pants and vests and and shirts and then small things. No ladies items. Just tea towels and pillowcases. Nothing big and heavy like towels or sheets. It was always whites or faded whites."

"Did you think this was strange?"

"Well yes I did and yet I had nobody to discuss it with really. Giuseppe was busy with you helping build the Canonica and Pedro's mum Isabella, who had been my friend for years, was busy with their new appliance shop business and anyhow was twenty five kilometres away. And the other ladies I knew who were married to my husband's colleagues slowly drifted away when I was widowed. And on top of this there wasn't time to think about it much. That's why I like this new job at the cafe with Pepe because I get to socialise. I forgot how to do that for two years Frederick and I am a very social person. And only yesterday I had my bottom pinched by a saucy builder fellow. That hasn't happened in a while. I gave him a friendly slap around the chops mind you." She laughed.

"I noticed that Lily. I was there. There were four of them on the table. All cheeky chappies by the look of them" said Frederick. *One, in particular, caught my eye.*

"Well anyway, about three months ago I started to get more suspicious about things because I was doing my usual smalls in the church scullery room and was running a bit late because there had been a shower and I had to bring in things off the line and then peg them out again a bit later so the drying takes longer when that happens. I could leave them out overnight because the courtyard is enclosed but I don't like doing that. I like to finish my work on the day and that's that."

"That's understandable" nodded Frederick wondering when she would get to the point of all this.

"Anyway, I was in the courtyard and I heard the woman in the blue car talking in the confessional. There is an airbrick that comes out into the courtyard and it acts like a megaphone. You know when people are on a boat offshore somewhere and you are on the beach and you can virtually hear every word they are saying. Well it was like that. I'm not a nosey person Frederick, but this woman came to church every week and always confessional. Nobody else did that to my knowledge although I am not there all the time."

"So could you hear what she was saying Lily?"

"Oh yes, very clear, but not all of it" she said.

"Why's that? he asked.

"Because a pigeon came and shat on me while I was standing there and it went over my clean laundry too, so I reacted as you would, by swearing and they must have heard me and stopped talking."

Frederick laughed picturing the scene. "So did you catch anything worth knowing?" he asked.

"They were talking about missing consignments. She was quoting numbers and talking about deals and that 'did he know the value of what was missing from the chain' and things like that. Not the sort of thing that someone discusses in confession. Others tend to be whispers like 'Oh Father I have sinned' and you hear of fornication and adultery or beatings and that sort of thing. Ordinary life between

239

the sexes. It was not that sort of discussion. It was a business discussion and it wasn't about missing laundry consignments."

"Anyway" she paused.

Frederick thought *she does say 'Anyway' a lot like some people say 'To be honest' all the time.*

"Anyway, after hearing me with the pigeon they never had confession together again, well not to my knowledge and I think she started coming to the church on a different day from my laundry day."

"Was that it then Lily?"

"Yes as far as I remember it was."

"Hmmm, she knows something else I reckon but that's enough for now" he felt.

They were arriving in the village.

"Shall I drop you at home or at the cafe?"

"I will do a couple of hours at the cafe to help Pepe."

"OK" said Frederick. "I could do with a light meal and a beer too."

"Well that treat will be on me then for coming to fetch me and listening to my diatribe."

49. JOAN

"Good morning Frederick. I must have gone out like a light. What time did you get in last night?" asked Joan

She had laid the breakfast table and had flung open her bedroom doors and was laying on the bed surrounded by bits and pieces she was planning to dispose of today. Frederick was mooching about in his dressing gown wondering where she might be and waiting to go to the lavatory.

"Ah there you are." He stood in her doorway scratching his bottom.

"I had some supper with Lily at the cafe and I suppose I was in bed before midnight. I heard you snoring."

"I don't snore Frederick." she said bluntly.

"Oh yes you do Joan. I wish I could record it. Sounds worse than my floorboards" he chuckled. "I will just go to the loo and see you here in fifteen. I see you have laid the table so will you make a pot of coffee and some toast or shall I?" he asked.

"It will all be on the table for His Majesty in fifteen minutes pronto." Another of Joan's crisp responses.

He went off and Joan came out to turn on the wireless. They were playing The Bachelor's, *Charmaine*. She hummed along and went off to prepare the breakfast tray.

"I see you have your nice Lemon frock on again. I never tire of seeing you in that" he said.

Joan didn't know if he was being sarcastic or not. "I like this yellow, it's so easy to care for and it goes well with my frizzy grey hair."

"Yes it does. It suits you. Very easy" he remarked.

"Last night I was looking at all the stuff I brought with me after you went to fetch Lily and I haven't worn eighty percent of it. A complete waste of time packing it. I would like to give some things away today if I can or dump them. All that paraphernalia on the bed for instance."

He turned to look at the array of bits and pieces. "I'm sure Lily will take it all off your hands and give bits out to various customers at the cafe if she doesn't want them herself."

"That's a good idea. I will make up a bag and perhaps walk to the village for lunchtime. So how is she and Giuseppe? Is he going to be alright?"

"They are keeping him in for observation and he will be out after the weekend probably."

"Oh, I will have gone home by then and won't see him."

"You will see him when he comes to visit you in England."

"I've decided against asking him Frederick. Various reasons, but mostly I don't want him to feel ill at ease with me or in rainy England."

"That's probably a wise decision Joan. Leave it on a high note eh?"

"Exactly." They ate their toast and drank the coffee listening to Jim Reeves *Welcome to my world.*

"Appropriate lyrics there Frederick" said Joan, "you have certainly welcomed me to your world. I had no idea that there could be so much going on in such a small place."

"This is an exception Joan, all seemingly put on for your entertainment. I would say it's been perfect timing for your visit."

"They play a lot of English and American music on this station don't they" she said.

"Yes, Italian songs are all huge ballads and very old fashioned like forties music in England. They haven't caught up yet."

"Is it the same in France Frederick, is it all English music there."

"Oh no, they have some law that eighty or ninety percent of what they are allowed to play has to be French music. When the state intervenes in anything you know it will be a disaster. That's why whenever you turn on the wireless in France you get Edith Piaf with Non, je ne regrette rien. No matter what station you tune into you can guarantee that will be playing."

"Well what happens next Fredrick? We have saved Giuseppe. We would never have found him, had he gone down the well. Perish the thought"

"I think you are right there Joan. What happens next? Good question. Do you still have that list we did? I wonder if we need to revisit it now we know what's been going on?"

"I think so. It's in my room somewhere. I'll fetch it in a mo. If we have answered all those questions then what do we do with the information?. Who do we tell?" she asked.

"Possibly nothing and tell nobody Joan. What can we do?"

"Well, shouldn't we tell someone higher up in the church or the Police?"

"And how do we go about that? What if the church is corrupt at many levels, with everyone getting a slice somehow? And what could we tell the Police Joan?"

"Well I can see it will be difficult and what would it achieve?" she said.

"We can't bring back Pedro. We have saved young Giuseppe. Lily is happy in a safe, enjoyable job. We aren't certain that the real Nonna died in the church or anyone died in the church, she hasn't actually been seen for over two years. Maybe she died then?"

"Or was killed?" added Joan.

"What for? A box of washing powder?" We could all have been mourning an empty coffin in the street. We suspect Father Leo was working with the Mafia. We know they were cutting cocaine in the laundry for the past couple of years since he arrived. We don't know where the Nonna went. We cannot know whether the hierarchy of the church knew and was party to the trade going on. We cannot know if Father Leo was even a real priest from Palermo or a stooge playing the part. We suspect that Pedro was saving a small slice of the business for himself as a saving scheme to perhaps avoid a life of selling and delivering washing machines, but maybe he was earning a second living and giving his mother occasional treats. The woman in the blue car, probably with her lover Leo will be long since on an Alitalia flight to Libya or Algeria or Somalia or some other past Italian empire country where they will be safe to lay low for a year or two and probably with a stash of a few tins of talcum powder to keep them in a life to which they have become accustomed.

"I see what you are saying Frederick. The past fortnight has just been entertainment with one sad casualty."

"Well nobody has actually turned the truck over to see if Pedro's remains are really under there have they? Giuseppe said it's inaccessible. That could also have been a set up couldn't it?"

"Oh goodness Frederick. What are you alluding to? That the entire thing was an illusion?"

"Quite possibly. An illusory allusion, wouldn't you say, Joan?"

After Word

Having finished this novel entirely from my own imagination and spontaneity I decided to ask Gemini, which is Google's Artificial Intelligence offering the following question:

"What do you think of the expression "An illusory Allusion" and here was the answer from the system verbatim:

The expression "illusory allusion" appears to be a contradiction in terms. Here's why:
* Illusory: This means something that is deceptive or misleading, not real or true.
* Allusion: This is an indirect or passing reference to something, often a literary or historical figure, event, or object.
Essentially, an allusion is a real reference, even if it's indirect.

An "illusory allusion" would be like saying a false truth or an unreal reality. It doesn't make logical sense.
It's possible that the term was used intentionally for a specific artistic or literary effect, playing on the contradiction to create a sense of unreality or deception.

However, without more context, it's difficult to say for sure.

Google Gemini December 2024

For readers' benefit I can confirm that I used the expression intentionally for the literary contradiction.

About the Author

Brian Fearn has written throughout his life yet has come to publishing now after an interesting commercial and self-employed career, granting a lifetime's experience of dealing with a wide range of property, business and personal projects and the idiosyncrasies of people involved with them. He loves the art of literary characterisation. His books show you, rather than tell you, allowing the reader to put a face to the characters that will become both familiar and embraced.

Although he started writing novels and short stories around the millennium after a number of Arvon Foundation novel writing courses, those skills obviously became embedded to emerge now as those works have been kept under wraps until now when a succession of releases over the coming months and years will illustrate the wide range of voices and styles of writing he enjoys.

Born in London into working class roots, his father a bakers chargehand in Balham and his mother a tie seamstress in Elephant and Castle, he had, what today would be described as a traumatic childhood, the upside of which provided a rich tapestry of real life events that mixed with the artistic embroidery of fiction can be retold in a fascinating patina of wordsmithery.

At sixteen he was a commercial apprentice at Vauxhall Motors where he qualified as a Management Accountant and business graduate at twenty one. Then going on to work in Travel, Banking, IT Systems and Management Consultancy before ditching all that to concentrate on his love of Historic Houses and People Healing. A fascinating mix of commercial and ethereal mindset that the reader might come to value.

He now lives in Suffolk, England and in Granada, Espana.

Printed in Great Britain
by Amazon

57291890R00139